THE WAY IT IS NOW

Garry Disher titles available from Text Publishing

THE PENINSULA MYSTERIES:

The Dragon Man

Kittyhawk Down

Snapshot

Chain of Evidence

Blood Moon

Whispering Death

Signal Loss

THE HIRSCH NOVELS:

Bitter Wash Road

Peace

Consolation

THE WYATT THRILLERS:

The Wyatt Butterfly

comprising *Port Vila Blues*

and *Fallout*

Wyatt

The Heat

Kill Shot

Under the Cold Bright Lights

The Sunken Road

The Way It Is Now

Garry Disher has published over fifty titles across multiple genres. With a growing international reputation for his bestselling crime novels, he has won four German and three Australian awards for best crime novel of the year, and been longlisted twice for a British CWA Dagger award. In 2018 he received the Ned Kelly Lifetime Achievement Award.

garrydisher.com

THE WAY
IT IS NOW

GARRY DISHER

TEXT PUBLISHING MELBOURNE AUSTRALIA

The Text Publishing Company acknowledges the Traditional Owners of the country on which we work, the Wurundjeri people of the Kulin Nation, and pays respect to their Elders past and present.

textpublishing.com.au

The Text Publishing Company
Wurundjeri Country, Level 6, Royal Bank Chambers, 287 Collins Street, Melbourne, Victoria 3000 Australia

Published by The Text Publishing Company, 2021

Cover design by Chong W.H.
Page design by Text
Typeset in Garamond 13.25/18.25 by J&M Typesetting

Printed and bound in Australia by Griffin Press, part of Ovato, an accredited ISO/NZS 14001:2004 Environmental Management System printer

ISBN: 9781922458162 (paperback)
ISBN: 9781922459510 (ebook)

A catalogue record for this book is available from the National Library of Australia

For Selma and Jonathan

JANUARY 2000

1

ON A MONDAY in January, three weeks into the new century, Charlie Deravin drove down to retrieve his surfboards. He was intending a quick in-and-out, but stopped when he saw the For Sale sign in the parched front lawn where Bass Street intersected with Tidepool. He found himself idling in the middle of the road with a strange ache in his chest. It was true. No longer an abstract notion. The sign was hand-painted, as if his old man hoped no one would take it seriously, but the offer was there for all to see.

Everything tilted for Charlie. Lost or changed

definition. He had never noticed the rusted gutters; the rotting window frames and florets of roof lichen. Not a house, no longer a home, barely a beach shack. His mother's potted geraniums absent from the veranda. And his father, watching motionless in a deckchair, also altered.

Charlie pulled his Subaru into the driveway. Got out, stretched the kinks in his spine. He could hear the sea down there where Tidepool dead-ended at the path that wound through the tea-trees and onto the sand. Smell the sea. Gulls calling. Complicated emotions calling.

He edged along the flank of his father's Holden, his T-shirt catching on the untamed driveway bushes, and stumbled into plain view.

'Dad.'

'Son.'

'Thought you'd be at work,' Charlie said.

Detective Sergeant Rhys Deravin, looking at Charlie, was shadowed by the veranda roof, by impending divorce, and by a deeply ingrained disappointment that he was being expected to swallow another lie, this time uttered by his son.

Okay, thought Charlie. He crossed the lawn, briefly blinded by a patch of sunlight, and settled into a deckchair across from his father. A mug of tea steamed on the lid of the dented army footlocker that stood between them, the repository of the family's sandshoes, flippers, thongs.

'Good drive down?'

Charlie heard the other questions: you chose a Monday

morning, hoping I'd be at work? You're dropping in on your mother, too? Did Liam come with you? And so on.

'Not bad.'

His father, alerted by a car rattling along Bass Street, raising a tiny swirl of dust, reached absently for his tea. Sipped, resettled the mug on the footlocker again and crossed his legs—thin, tanned, sinewy, beachcomber's legs; cyclist's legs in ragged shorts. Energy was always coiled in Rhys Deravin, until it uncoiled. Physical energy; mental. Renowned as a thief catcher; not so much a husband and father. Good-looking still, in his late forties.

He stood, flipping tea onto the lawn. 'I'll leave you to it.'

'Dad—'

'Didn't bring a trailer?'

'It's just the boards. I'll be fine with the roof racks.'

His father said, a little helplessly, 'Your bed? Your wardrobe?'

Charlie tensed. 'Salvos, I thought.'

It was almost a tipping point. His father flexed and gathered himself and said, 'Well, you sort that out, I'm not doing it.'

He banged through the screen door, and immediately out again. 'I need you to move your car.'

'Will do.'

In the time it took Charlie to reverse and park where he wouldn't obstruct traffic—what there was of it in Menlo Beach—his father, now wearing trousers, polished shoes, a short-sleeved shirt and a tie, was stowing a briefcase and nodding goodbye from behind the wheel of his car. Charlie nodded back. Felt the tension ease a little.

He wondered if a life—or lives—could be boiled down to a house.

His surfboards were stored on a rack in the garden shed but he opened the front door and stepped inside the house, needing to shake the sense of coming untethered from his childhood. Straight into the sitting room, a broad space with a kitchen at one end leading to a dogleg corridor and the rooms beyond: his bedroom, Liam's, his parents'; a bathroom and laundry near the back door. All pokey.

He felt rattled to see the sitting room so underpopulated, just two mismatched op-shop armchairs on either side of the coffee table, which his mother clearly hadn't wanted. Books leaning sparsely on the shelves against the back wall: encyclopaedias, Tom Clancy, sailing manuals, cricket and surfing biographies. Charlie's mother hadn't wanted those, either. A card table where the dining room table once sat, with a straight-back chair pulled up to a bowl of mostly consumed cornflakes and the dregs of orange juice in a glass.

Charlie rinsed bowl and glass at the kitchen sink as if to cling to a solid present. The way it is now, he thought. Gaps had opened in all their lives and the repairs were makeshift. No wonder his father rarely stayed down here these days, preferring to fill his time with work and his

Prahran floozy. That was Liam's word, floozy: going for alliteration. Charlie quite liked Fay. She hadn't tried to impress him—she simply regarded him as her bloke's son.

What did she think of 5 Tidepool Street? Had she ever been here? Charlie walked through to the master bedroom, then to the bathroom, looking for evidence that she stayed sometimes. He didn't find anything. Maybe she'd never been here. Maybe she didn't want to sleep with Rhys Deravin on a mattress full of history.

Charlie poked his head into Liam's room: nothing remained but four Blu Tack smudges on one wall. Finally, his own room—the smallest, as the younger son. He'd call the Salvation Army to collect his bed frame, mattress, wardrobe and bedside table, but he'd forgotten all about his tennis trophies and his Class of 1999 graduation photo, the police commissioner shaking his hand in the grounds of the academy. He took them down from the shelf, stacked them in the car and returned to check the wardrobe, the drawers, expecting maybe an old concert ticket or a five-cent coin.

Zilch.

The landline rang before he could lock up and collect the surfboards. He thought: Jess, Dad, a colleague of Dad's, Liam or Mum. The phone, a pale green relic of the seventies, was on the kitchen bench next to a basket of bills, receipts, envelopes, keys and a tube of sunblock.

'Rhys Deravin's phone, Charlie speaking.'

'It's me.'

'Hi, sweetheart.'

'Sad?'

'A bit.' Charlie paused: she deserved more. 'A bit unreal.'

'Memories?'

'Memories and absences,' Charlie said, and stopped.

His wife waited a moment. Laughed and said lightly, 'That Charlie; can't shut him up sometimes.'

Two years in, it was sometimes like that between them. Often like that. The rebukes fond rather than harsh, though. So far.

'The place looks a bit forlorn,' Charlie said.

'My lovely, I wish I could be there. Em says hello. Say hello to Daddy.'

Charlie saw his daughter in his wife's arms and heard some of her soft, gassy pops and murmurs, and, when he said, 'Hello, bubba,' silence. Maybe she'd recognised his voice and was wondering what he was doing in the hand-piece. It tickled him to think that.

Then Jess was saying something about a stinky nappy, and they said goodbye and Charlie, pulled against himself by the then and now of his life, wanted some fresh air.

On the way out an opened envelope caught his eye, 'Asbestos Audit' scrawled across it in his father's impatient hand.

The report was five pages of headings and crammed type, confirming that the fibro-cement wall sheets of 5 Tidepool Street contained asbestos. Well, they knew that.

Menlo Beach was a Peninsula beach town of unassuming shacks dating from the 1930s, side by side on a crosshatch of narrow, potholed dirt streets. Half the houses down here on the flat were fibro. Cheap housing, back when Dad and his mates started buying holiday houses and weekend getaways in the late 1970s, places that became family homes. Six cops on ten little streets. Rowdy, rampaging men who thrilled the kids and made them laugh; one or two wives, cut desperately from the same hardwood, who didn't. Booze-soaked barbecues and beach cricket, wrestling on the lawn. Sailing, catching waves, cycling up and down Arthurs Seat. Exhilarating guys who called you chicken and wore you out. Guys with big natures and a black intensity if you caught them unguarded. A fellowship pretty much disbanded now. The wives had left first, when the kids were young. Charlie's mother had been the last and she'd waited until her sons were grown—or until her husband had taken up with a floozy.

Charlie slid the report back into the envelope. It would have been his mother's idea: do the right thing, alert potential buyers. Avoid a lawsuit down the track, some home handyman drilling into the fibro and sucking in a lungful of asbestos. The well-heeled professionals were moving in on the flatland houses, now that all the adjacent clifftop blocks had fallen to suburban castles that strained for a glimpse of sea between the pines. People like that would snap up this shack, Charlie's childhood home. Tear it down, erect some cubic glass-and-timber wet dream.

Feeling distracted and out of sorts, sensing that some showy disaster was coming, Charlie locked up the house and fetched his surfboards from the garden shed. Strapped them to the roof rack while the benign sun worked powerfully on him; the brine and the tidal wash sounding upon the sand. He'd intended to drive to his mother's house in Swanage, five minutes by car. But hell, the day wasn't hot, wasn't windy: why not walk there across the familiar geography of past summers? Take him less than an hour.

2

DODGING POTHOLES, HIS runners crunching over gravel in
the windless mid-morning, Charlie set off along Tidepool
Street: six houses huddled behind gum trees and shrubs.
He crossed the bisecting clifftop path and ducked through
the tea-trees and finally down the railway-sleeper steps. At
the bottom was a little wire fence, with a child's scuffed
pink sandal on one of the pine posts. No one would ever
claim it.

He stepped out onto the sand and paused a while. The
tide was in, calm, barely lapping, and kids were splashing

or tottering with buckets as if there was no first day of school in their near futures.

'Charlie?' Mark Valente erupted from the shallows, beads of the sea clinging to his chest hair, his huge belly gleaming and his bathers pasted to his groin and massive thighs. He waded out like a man fording a torrent, jerking his head to rid his shaggy ears of water.

Valente—Rhys Deravin's partner in the old days: Major Crimes. Now a senior sergeant and head of Rosebud CIB. He stepped over the tidewrack and advanced on Charlie like an unstoppable bear, blocking the sun, one frying-pan hand outstretched.

Charlie shook. A damp hand but it gripped like a manacle briefly, affectionate challenge in it, and Charlie felt that he was a kid with a cricket bat again, Valente shouting at him from the sidelines, 'Keep your eye on the fucking ball, Charlie-boy!'

'Day off?'

Valente shook his head and water flew about them. 'No, no. Four to midnight shift. Been to see your dad?'

Charlie nodded. 'Caught him before he left for work.'

'He's on that Securicor ambush,' Valente said.

'Right.' It had been on the news, a guard shot in an armoured-car holdup, but Charlie hadn't known his father was working it. He'd never known about anything his father investigated; the old man had brought the job home with him in other ways.

Valente winked. 'And so shall the wicked wail and

weep.' Mark doing the firebrand-prophet routine they'd all found so mystifying yet amusing as kids. As far as Charlie knew, the guy had never been to church.

Valente was looking him up and down. 'Bring your togs?'

'No. Just thought I'd walk around to Mum's.'

Mark Valente had something to say about that—and thought better of it. 'Say hello for me.'

'Will do.'

They shook again, and Charlie watched Valente power upslope to the steps, parting the air and the molecules and the kids playing. Water-matted pelt, tiny backside, shrewd mind.

Charlie returned his attention to the blameless sea and let it settle him—the soft reaching of the tide and the air full of life and promise—then headed to a rocky point where the cliff line began, grasses and little trees clinging to the walls. Signs warned of rock falls. A woman on a towel spread between fallen rocks and banksias waved and called his name and he had no idea who she was. He returned the gesture and followed the sand as it curved around a tiny stretch of water bracketed by reefs and safe for swimming, his progress a series of fancy sidesteps into the kelp, avoiding sly inrushes of the tide.

Fuck it: he took off his socks and runners and waded along happily where the sea broke on the shore, his splashing a counterpoint to the susurrations of the water. He felt, curiously, both contained and expansive just then: there was a high cliff wall and pines at his left shoulder, a limitless horizon on his right. He passed a pair of sandals and a body-dented beach towel; no sign of anyone in the water. Seaweed. Dead jellyfish. Tiny plain timid shells. Driftwood. The base of a beer bottle, frosted by the abrasive motions of the sand. He pocketed it, then saw immediately a tangle of line, sinker and fishhook, which he wrapped in his handkerchief. There was a bin up ahead, at the beach path in Tulum Court. It was something you did if you grew up here, if this was home.

Around the next bend, the ridgeline and its million-dollar clifftop fortresses of tinted glass and weathered wood gave way to another huddle of holiday shacks on flat ground, set back from the beach by the foredune, a broad stretch of grasses and succulents a metre above the sand, and here a small working party was driving stakes linked by nylon rope into the sand. A sign on one of the stakes read: *Hooded Plover Nesting Area Please Keep Out.*

Mrs Ehrlich waved. Charlie nodded and carried on. Halfway along the little bay was a creek inlet and then the path up to Tulum Court and the camping reserve. He left the beach, the sand soft and heavy-going, and dumped his trove of jetsam in the rubbish bin.

Then back to the sand. Around another point, to another quarter-moon family beach. Past the Balinoe Beach yacht club and the bones of the old jetty, to the long stretch of mostly unpopulated sand where they exercised the racehorses at dawn. This was taking longer than Charlie had expected.

A short time later he encountered his third original Menlo Beach cop of the day. Noel Saltash, thin and whippet-like where Rhys Deravin was a sinuous cat and Mark Valente a bear, jogged past Charlie, running shoes flashing, breath grunting, singlet criss-crossing against his spine with each swing of his arms. Shooting a glance, a crooked grin, he said, 'Charlie', and was gone. A hundred metres ahead he swung left, up into the dunes, where a track led to a return path alongside Balinoe Creek.

Reaching the outskirts of Swanage at last, Charlie ducked through at the youth camp, onto the long front street of the strung-out town, wishing his mother's rental house wasn't at the far end. A couple of cars passed him; kids on skateboards; women friends with towels, baskets and broad hats on their way to the beach. He passed the shop and the primary school and eventually descended into a hollow, following the through road as it ascended again, then turned left near the water tower at the far end of town, into Longstaff, the last street before farmland. His mother's house, a faded weatherboard cottage, was halfway along. A white Mazda in the street: Liam was visiting. Charlie drew near, thirsty, needing the bathroom, and felt a strange jolt to see his mother's geraniums dotted along *this* veranda.

Then a sense of unease, of disarrangement, as he noticed the motorbike that claimed her carport.

3

IT WAS A GLOSSY black Ducati, hip-cocked on its side-stand, lording it over that shady space while her lustreless old Corolla baked in the street. A feeling of irritation: his mother's house; her name on the lease. She was letting the lodger take over now?

He closed the listing gate behind him, pushing at parched, untended grass. He wondered why his mother didn't borrow the Tidepool Street mower. But the answer came immediately: because it would mean negotiating with Dad.

He knocked on the screen door. It rattled in its frame, warped from the sea air. There was no answer, so he stepped into the dim hallway, into air slack with the heat of the last few days and laced with dope and aftershave. The irritation deepened. Shane Lambert's bike in the carport, his stink in the house.

The kitchen was a mess of chipboard and scorch marks, and Charlie felt the pain of it. The shack in Menlo Beach was no mansion but it was better than this. The sooner they sold it and his mother had the money to rent a nicer place—by herself—the better.

'Anyone home?'

The dingy walls took his voice and gave nothing back. He crossed to the sink, downed a glass of water and peered through the greasy window at his mother and his brother, shoulder to shoulder at one of the garden tables from Tidepool Street. Charlie watched for a moment, noting his mother's bowed head and Liam's jaw jutting as he laid things out for her, her hands clasped in his.

Alerting them with a slam of the back door, Charlie took the concrete steps onto the dying grass and crossed to the table. His mother slipped her hands out of Liam's and into her lap as if she'd not been engaged in secret business. Otherwise, her face lit up. 'Charlie!'

He dodged behind Liam, who was getting to his feet, and planted a kiss. 'Mum.'

Then the brothers faced each other, their affection landlocked. An agonising instant passed. Finally, a quick clasp and release, and Liam returned tensely to his chair. 'You've been home?'

Charlie avoided his gaze. 'Yep.'

'See Dad?'

'He was there.'

They could have entire conversations like this, fragments laden with history, tension mounting. Their mother knew that. She rested her fingers on Liam's forearm until he deflated.

Charlie said brightly, 'I walked here, like an idiot. Took forever.'

'Still,' his mother said, 'a lovely day for it. See anyone?'

Another pitfall for Charlie. He said, 'Mark. Noel,' offhandedly, feeling rather than seeing renewed tightness in Liam.

'That would have been a thrill for you,' Liam said.

The brothers shared their father's physical grace, but where Charlie had thrown himself into games as a kid—thrown himself into winning and losing—Liam, the better athlete, simply didn't care. He'd grow distracted and wander off or just not turn up. He was genuinely puzzled by the remonstrations of Mark Valente or their father, or whoever happened to be organising the beach cricket or footy that day. Vicious old homophobes, he called them now.

Charlie sighed loudly. They all looked at the table, the grass and the back wall.

He broke the impasse with a safe topic. 'Looking

forward to school going back?'

His brother taught at a private school, his mother at a state school, and they groaned in unison. The summer break had passed too quickly. Soon it would be all feral kids, lesson plans, principals, parents from hell.

There was another silence, but Liam was building up to something, shifting around in his seat. Finally he blurted, 'Charlie, Mum's been having problems with her lodger.'

She touched his wrist quickly. 'Oh, Liam, it doesn't matter. It's nothing.'

Liam swung around on her. 'It doesn't sound like nothing. It sounds like the guy's a creep.'

Charlie had never met Lambert but, watching his mother's face, saw the truth of it. 'Mum?'

'It's nothing to worry about.'

'Okay, but how come he keeps his bike in the carport and you have to park in the street?'

She tried to wave it off. 'It's nothing. The place is a rental—it's not as if I own it. Not as if I have more rights than he does.'

'You do, actually,' Liam said. 'The lease is in your name. He just rents a room from you.'

'I don't want to rock the boat.'

Charlie turned towards her. 'Why? You think he'd turn nasty?'

'It's just...' She fell silent, looking for the next word.

Charlie said, 'Where is he now?'

'He works at a timber supply in Hastings.'

19

'But his bike's here.'

'He gets a lift from a workmate.'

Liam cut in, shooting Charlie a look: *Can we get back on track, here?* 'Mum, he's a creep and you've got your head in the sand about it.'

'That's not fair, Liam,' she said, with some grit, and Charlie saw her spirit and her pain and her shame. Curiously, she shapeshifted then: she was not his mother but Rose Deravin, a woman separate from him, a woman slim and tired, who taught PE at Westernport Secondary College. Tan cargo pants, a white T-shirt and red toenails. Fine pale hair in an untidy knot. A strong, searching nose. Capable, attractive, and she saw him looking and there was defiance in her. It unsettled him.

With a warning look for Liam, he said gently, 'Tell us what bothers you about him, Mum.'

'He's just, I don't know, a bit off.'

'Has he, ah…' Charlie felt himself blush. 'Has he tried it on sexually?'

She shook her head. 'Not really.'

'Mum!' Liam cut in. 'What do you mean, not really?'

'He usually watches junk TV all evening but one night there was an SBS documentary on the female orgasm'— she shifted in her chair—'and he said he thought I might like to watch it with him. I said I was too busy. When I went out of the room, he turned the volume up.'

'Mum!'

Charlie kicked his brother under the table. 'What else?'

She shifted again, as if sorting through a list, and it came pouring out:

'He's inconsiderate. Leaves the toilet seat up—well, you boys always did that—but he's not very careful, if you know what I mean. Dumps his dishes in the sink as if I'm supposed to do them. One day I found him cleaning some engine part at the kitchen table. We agreed to buy our own food, but he never has any—he keeps taking my eggs and bread and whatnot without asking. I always shut my door at night, but I hear him in the hallway sometimes, as if he's just standing there, and one day I found him in my room, looking in my sewing box. He said he needed scissors but, you know...And he owes a month's rent. I asked him about it, and he said, "You're a teacher," as if I'm supposed to carry him whenever he's short of money.'

'Mum,' said Charlie.

'But what can I do? It was hard enough finding someone to rent the room in the first place. Now I have to start all over again, and it could take weeks.' She shook her head. 'I can't afford it.'

Blackbirds had been hopping around under the gnarled old pear tree, pecking at the fallen fruit. Now they began to squabble, a squall of bluster that bowled them all over the yard as the sun sat mildly in the sky.

Charlie said, 'Would it help if we talked to him?'

'And say what?' demanded Liam. 'We get rid of the guy—that's what would help.'

'I don't know,' their mother said miserably.

21

Yes, you do, Charlie thought. 'I think you feel scared.'
She wouldn't look at him.

'Not a healthy way to live, Mum. We'll help you get rid of him,' Charlie said. He checked with Liam: 'And help you with the rent until we find someone more suitable.'

Liam nodded.

Their mother worried the top joint of one thumb with the ball of the other. 'I can't ask you to do that.'

'You didn't ask: we're offering. When does he get home from work?'

Her watch was loose on her thin wrist. She shook it into place, glanced and said, 'Mid-afternoon.'

It pained Charlie to see some kind of hope build in her as she looked at each of them. 'Can you both be with me when I tell him? In case it gets awkward?'

'We'll do you one better,' Liam said. 'You drive over to see Grandma or Karen Wagoner for the afternoon. Charlie and I'll pack up his things and when he gets home we'll tell him he has to find somewhere else to live. You don't have to face him at all.'

She agonised. 'What if he comes back when you're not here?'

Liam gave Charlie a look. 'You keep a spare uniform in your car, right?'

4

LIAM DROVE CHARLIE to fetch his car and Charlie followed him back to Longstaff Street, where they emptied Shane Lambert's room, stacking his belongings into cartons and a Kmart suitcase. Charlie expected a foetid bog, but Lambert was man who'd pared his life to the bone: few possessions and obsessive neatness. Decent quality clothing, a spare range of toiletries. No private papers but for an employment agreement with the timber merchant dated November 2019. A serious-looking Canon camera in a well-travelled case. Charlie couldn't work the guy out. Jail time? A bit footloose, so he rented a mailbox somewhere? A creative streak—he liked to shoot sunsets, driftwood, faces on the street?

They wheeled the motorbike out of the carport and onto the footpath, next to the cartons, then Charlie changed into his police uniform and they sat and waited. They barely talked; they never did, which would flummox Jess sometimes. 'What is it with you two? You're not strangers, you have common ground.'

Some common ground. Not enough of it.

Time passed. They consumed tea and cheese sandwiches and watched the street, deckchair canvas complaining under them, the veranda iron flexing as the sun poked in and out of banking clouds. This close to the farmland that trapped the town along the shoreline, there was little traffic. Longstaff was a stubby street. A handful of other tired weatherboards, one or two cramped new places trying to be townhouses and overreaching, and a nearly vacant block at the end, just a concrete slab and plumbing pipes, waiting for bills to be paid. A stillborn street.

And that was it until a sun-faded white station wagon drew up at the front gate. The man in the passenger seat gazed at the boxes and the bike, then at the brothers on the veranda, and Charlie imagined him instructing the driver: 'Stick around, I might need a hand with my stuff.'

The car crept forward again and pulled into the kerb a few metres beyond the house. Charlie memorised the numberplate.

The brothers stepped off the veranda and out onto the footpath, waiting as the motor shuddered and died and two men got out. The driver, a pudgy, anxious-looking man, closed his door softly, as if unwilling to disturb the air. The passenger gave his door a casual slam. Nodded and said, unhurriedly, 'So she called the cops on me.'

'I'm her son,' Charlie said.

'Great.'

Charlie looked hard for bad faith but saw only a weary figure brushed in a fine layer of sawdust. Shorts, a work shirt and dirty, steel-capped boots. Short hair; work-abraded hands browned by the sun; one earring.

Eyes flat, Lambert lifted the tailgate and told his mate, 'Give us a hand,' as he turned to the closest carton. The driver, soft, confused and unformed where Lambert was hard and economical, tripped over his own feet as he stepped onto the footpath, hand outstretched. 'Kevin-Maberly-pleased-to-meet-you,' he babbled, then stared helplessly at the cartons. Finally he bent to pick one up.

There was a thrumming tension in Liam, as if he found Lambert's polite, even manner disconcerting. He coughed. 'Look, Shane—can I call you Shane?—I hope you understand, our mother feels it would be better if you found another place. It wasn't working out.'

Lambert paused. He seemed to stretch his spine to the sky, then sneezed explosively. 'Sawdust.' He continued bending, hoisting, stacking, a tidy dance that had his mate stumbling.

'She's prepared to overlook the rent,' Liam continued. 'And just to let you know, we've booked and paid for two nights at the motel in Hastings.'

'Just to let me know,' Lambert said, eyes dark, knitted. He grabbed the final carton and stowed it. He murmured to his mate, who glanced apprehensively at Charlie before getting behind the wheel. The car wouldn't start, and then it did, pulling away from the kerb and performing a U-turn like a wallowing boat in the narrow street, trailing smoke. Lambert watched it go, shaking his head. He strapped on his helmet, mounted his Ducati and burbled off in his contained way. Seconds later the engine pitch altered as he reached the main road, a howl coming to them on the wind.

Liam slumped. 'Boy, am I glad that's over.'

Charlie deflated, too. But he felt stained, somehow. The way he'd postured in his police uniform—bullying behaviour. It left a taste in his mouth.

5

EIGHT DAYS LATER, the last week of January and the first week of the school year, Charlie was back in Swanage, bussed to the grounds of the youth camp with twenty other probationary and newbie constables from the south-east region. A kid had gone missing.

And there was no mucking around. As soon as he stepped off the bus, he was directed to join a motley group of Emergency Services volunteers, shire rangers and camp staff, all of them shuffling their feet under one of the massive gum trees. A few minutes later, a Rosebud leading senior constable named Frances Bekker was briefing them. She held herself tensely, as if time was wasting and everything was going wrong. Sunglasses were perched on her forehead; her red hair was frizzy in the humidity. She held a bottle of water and shook it for emphasis.

'In a moment we'll form three search parties: one for the town, one for the beach in each direction and one for the creek and wooded area between here and Balinoe Beach.'

She waited, as if expecting some idiot to split hairs with her. 'We're looking for Billy Saul, aged nine. Olive skin, dark hair, small for his age. He's here with a bunch of upper primary school kids from Berwick. They arrived yesterday, staying for two nights. He was seen at beach activities this morning, and he answered the roll at lunchtime, but didn't show up for afternoon activities.'

She looked at her watch. 'That was two hours ago. It took everyone a while to check the campground and the immediate beach area before calling triple zero.'

A young woman standing behind her seemed to shrink a little.

'This is Miss Jaffe, Billy's teacher,' Bekker said. 'Apparently Billy is picked on by the other kids, so it's possible he ran away.'

Bekker's tone suggested that if Jaffe had been doing her job, Billy might not have run away or been snatched by a paedophile or washed out to sea. Then she switched gears, assigning everyone to a search party, simply by pointing and saying: 'Beach', 'Town' and 'Creek'. When she reached Charlie, she said: 'You're with me.'

Why him? Did she know him? He didn't know her. He stood to one side and waited as leaders were appointed, instructions issued. The sunlight freckled the ground at his feet. He was damp with perspiration. He hadn't brought water or a hat and heard an old voice from his childhood: *You don't have the brains you were born with.*

Then Bekker was there in his face. 'You're Rhys Deravin's son.'

'Correct.' God knows what she'd heard.

'Spitting image.' She paused. 'Mark Valente says good things about you.'

Charlie found himself concentrating furiously. Valente was a detective, but Rosebud wasn't a huge police station: there would be crossover between the uniform and plain-clothes branches, opportunities for water-cooler chats, tearoom gossip. That didn't explain why he'd come up in conversation, though. Had Lambert lodged a complaint: his landlady's son using his cop muscle to evict him? Charlie shifted his weight from one foot to the other and told Bekker he was only a probationer.

'Did you think to bring water? A hat?'

Charlie shuffled uncomfortably. 'We only had a few minutes' notice.'

Jaffe had been waiting dispiritedly. 'There's water in the dining-hall fridge,' she offered.

The dining hall was cool, echoey, empty, tables bare.

As if on firm ground now, Jaffe hurried to a refrigerator behind the service bench and returned with two bottles of water. 'The lost property office might have a hat that would fit you.'

'Lead on,' Bekker said.

Jaffe took them to a hallway cupboard, where Charlie grabbed the biggest towelling hat he could find. It was like being at school again, like being a no-hoper kid. *Pull your socks up.* He was relieved when Bekker said, 'Right, Miss Jaffe, tell me more about Billy Saul. Is it Billy or William?'

'Everyone calls him Billy. Please call me Melissa.'

She's older than me, thought Charlie, but not by much, and she looks ready to crack from side to side.

'And the other kids bully him? You've witnessed it?'

Jaffe looked miserable, a woman stippled with freckles and moles. Looking past them she said, her voice muddled, too hurried: 'He comes from a mixed…His father's Thai.'

'And that's why he's bullied?'

'I try to stop it, but I can't be on the spot every minute of the day. He's not very big and he's a bit…a bit…he doesn't stand up for himself.'

Then she seemed to hear herself. Aghast, she said, 'Of course, that's no reason…Would you like to see where he sleeps?'

She hurried to the door and took them across a patch of powdery dirt to a weathered cabin block, their shoes kicking up dust and gum leaves and twigs. 'He's in number two.'

Bekker stopped her at the door. 'Was he bullied this morning?'

'There was a bit of pushing and shoving on the beach.'

'And?'

Jaffe gave up. Hunched her shoulders. 'I tried to stop it but there's only so much you can do, and sometimes it's so covert...'

Bekker grunted. 'Let's see what's missing and what's been left behind—it might tell us what he had in mind.'

The room was small and stifling. A set of bunk beds against one wall, a chest of drawers, two wooden chairs draped with beach towels, two sprawling backpacks spilling clothes onto the floor. Billy Saul's was marked *Billy* in black marker pen on the top flap. Bekker knelt and began pulling out and sorting the contents: underpants, socks, a pair of jeans, two pairs of shorts, two T-shirts, a windcheater, a pair of runners and a toiletries bag containing a toothbrush, toothpaste, sunblock and a bar of soap in a Ziploc bag.

'Does this match the checklist of things the kids were expected to pack?' Bekker asked.

She's a parent, Charlie thought.

'Yes.'

'Where are his bathers?'

'He's probably still wearing them; it's what the boys do. Boardshorts.'

Charlie followed Bekker's gaze. On each mattress a bedsheet, a sleeping bag and a pillow. 'What shoes was he wearing at the beach?'

'I'm not sure. Thongs or sandals, probably.'

Bekker glanced at the scattered clothing again. 'The kids carry their togs to the beach by hand?'

Jaffe thought about it. 'They had little daypacks.'

'There's no daypack here.'

'No hat or water bottle either,' Charlie said.

Jaffe winced. 'You're right.'

The preliminary search had been panicky, Charlie thought. No cop-thinking. He fingered each of the beach towels. The one marked with Billy's name felt expensive to Charlie: thick cotton; dolphins in a vivid sea; a gold fringe top and bottom.

Bekker was looking at him oddly. 'Right,' she said. 'Thanks for your help, Melissa. You can go back to your kids. Constable Deravin and I will have another look around the camp.'

'It's been searched.'

'I understand that, but if we don't double-check, it's my head on the block.'

They stepped out into hot air scented with eucalyptus and the sea, just as a police car shot in, its dust chasing the tang away. The driver powered down his window. 'Hop in, Fran, we've found something.'

Charlie rode in the rear, looking back at Melissa Jaffe, who seemed stiff with misery in the shifting light beneath a gum tree. Then they were tracing the road along the shoreline, out to the other side of the town. He glanced left, reflexively, as if he might spot his mother or his mother's house. He had phoned her every day. 'I'm fine, dear...He hasn't been back...Not a peep...I'm fine, Charlie.'

The driver took them down to a cramped parking area above the beach. They got out and took the steps to the sand and crossed to where a handful of men and women stood around a blue daypack, a sun hat and a water bottle on a beach towel. Two more metres and the tide would have claimed it all.

Bekker knelt in the sand and unzipped the front pocket of the daypack. A wallet—five dollars and a student card in the name of Billy Saul. Then a pair of underpants, a pair of shorts and a T-shirt from the main compartment. Items that made sense to Charlie. The beach towel didn't. Ratty-looking, threadbare, too small.

Charlie had little to do with Bekker after that. With the search now concentrated along the shoreline and out to sea, he was sent with two other probationers to find eyewitnesses. They talked to a woman sitting bowlegged under a blanket, nursing a baby, then a man fishing dejectedly for flathead and two teenage girls focused on nothing but browning themselves on their beach towels. None had been on the beach for longer than an hour. None had seen Billy. And the girls were astonished to realise how crowded and urgent the beach had become while they'd been flat on their stomachs.

After that they climbed to the road above the beach to doorknock and take down numberplates. No answer at most of the houses; no useful information anywhere else. No one had seen a boy with a backpack walking along the street. 'What's he done?' they wanted to know. Or: 'Is he all right?'

They walked on, knocked, walked on. Charlie could hear a spotter plane and a helicopter now. He imagined small craft out on the water, volunteers eyeing drifts of seaweed, sea wrack, sea rubbish.

And, all the while, he felt the pull of his mother's little house on Longstaff Street, uphill of the sea-view houses and the long road that anchored the town along the shore-line. She didn't have a view of the sea, only of other houses, a few scrubby trees and the water tower. And she would be at work. He checked his watch: god, almost 6 p.m. She'd be home by now.

They rejoined the search. Evening darkness deepened. At 9 p.m. Bekker wound everything down. 'We'll resume at first light.'

Charlie boarded the bus again and was back in the Frankston police station carpark by 9.45, addled with tiredness, sunburn and dehydration. Not ready for the men in suits who stopped him before he could get behind the wheel of his Subaru.

'Probationary Constable Deravin?'

Charlie recognised them from the corridors and the canteen—Elliott and DaCosta, CIU detectives. 'That's me.'

Elliott was about fifty, DaCosta thirty, deeply fatigued

men who had been in their clothes throughout this hot day, and the day wasn't finished.

'We need a word with you,' Elliott said. 'Inside, if you please.'

He was lean but sagging under the chin, his shoulders slumped, a man who had reached the loosened-tie-and-undone-top-button stage of life, and Charlie felt a leap of panic. 'Is it my wife?'

'It would be best if we could talk about it inside,' DaCosta said gently. He was solid and, in a few years, he'd be bulky—an impression reinforced by his shaved skull, which he rubbed now, as if for reassurance.

'My daughter?'

'They're both fine, as far as we know,' DaCosta said, with a glance at Elliott that seemed to say, *We'd better double-check.*

Charlie followed them into a hot, airless briefing room with a long table that took up most of the available space. He slumped into a chair at the end, where he'd be able to observe both men with the least effort. 'What's going on? Have I done something?'

Shane Lambert reported me, he thought.

'Where were you today?' Elliott said.

He told them.

'All day?'

Charlie shook his head. 'I was on foot patrol with Senior Constable Gosling this morning, Karingal shops.'

'Where were you at lunchtime?'

'The tearoom. I was sitting with the others when we got the call.'

'You didn't see your mother?'

Charlie was confused. 'Here?'

'In Swanage.'

'This afternoon? No, I was part of the search. I wouldn't just sneak off, if that's what you're implying. What's going on?'

'You didn't see her car anywhere?'

Charlie felt a dread coldness. 'No. Why?'

'According to the school, she slipped home at lunchtime to fetch a training video.'

'I was here at lunchtime. We didn't get to Swanage until early afternoon,' Charlie said. He paused, a hard truth sinking in. 'She didn't return to work, is that what you're saying?'

Elliott nodded, assessing Charlie. Not unsympathetic, just dogged. Just doing his job.

I'm police, I deserve better, Charlie wanted to say.

DaCosta folded his arms. 'What about your father? See him at all?'

'No.'

'Your parents are getting a divorce, I believe?'

Charlie said, 'So?'

'As we understand it, the house will have to be sold?'

Charlie stood and said, 'I'm not doing this. You've found something. You wouldn't give me a hard time if all she did was not go back to work. Is she dead?' By now he was at the door. 'I'm going to go home now and talk to my wife and talk to my father and talk to my brother.'

His hand was on the knob when DaCosta said, 'Your mother's car was found abandoned this afternoon.'

Charlie tensed. 'Where? Just her car?'

'Over near Tooradin. Does she know anyone out that way?'

'Not that I know of.'

'It had been driven into a gatepost and abandoned,' Elliott said. Still watching Charlie he added, 'Blood on the keys still in the ignition, driver's door open and things from her handbag strewn up and down the road. Lipstick, purse with no money in it, tissues…'

Eyes flat, DaCosta asked a cop question: 'What can you tell us about that?'

DECEMBER 2019 – FEBRUARY 2020

6

TUESDAY, CHRISTMAS EVE, and dolphins were arcing in the glassy sea.

They were right there in a straight line between Charlie Deravin, who was standing at the base of the beach steps, and the Nobbies, humped at the end of Phillip Island. He watched and nothing else moved in the half-light of the dawning sun. His best time of the day. The pinks and greys and windless clarity, everything etched, and the deep peace he needed in his life just then. All for him, the rest of the world missing out, asleep behind doors hung with

Christmas wreaths and veranda beams strung with fairy lights and tinsel.

He dropped his towel on the sand and kicked off his beach Crocs and waded in and the sea was shockingly cold around his shrivelling thighs. He cleaved the water neatly, resurfaced and pistoned out to the buoy, then parallel to the shore in each direction until he thought of grey-pointer jaws restless and hungry somewhere below him, and spooked himself. But he'd swum his daily kilometre, he reckoned. He was set up for the day. He was set up, and on suspension from the police force, and back living in the ancestral home and his daughter was asleep in Liam's old room, unlikely to emerge until noon. Pretty damn semi-perfect.

Charlie waded out of the shallows just as an elderly couple came in on his right flank, striding with the help of their sticks, the tips inscribing dashes in the sand. They cut across his path before he reached his towel, saying hello from under their sunhats. The world lost its sharp stillness and became a busy, irregular place again, soft at the edges. He had been staying here for a month now and saw them every morning. No idea where they lived.

He towelled dry, slipped his sandy feet into his Crocs and climbed the steps up to the banksias and tea-trees, then through them to his street.

Emma had tied a hand-painted *Say No to AGL* sign to the post that supported his letterbox. He straightened it. She'd pasted a *Save Westernport* sticker inside the back window of his Skoda and another on the sliding front door of number 5 and was disappointed in him, in her fierce way. 'It's not enough to pay lip service, Dad.'

His morning routine was this: a swim at dawn, breakfast under the flowering gum in the front yard—his muesli bowl at a tilt on the warped and weathered tabletop—the 7 a.m. ABC news scratching from the radio at his elbow. Then a ride along the beach to the Balinoe newsagency or even as far as the Swanage general store to buy the *Age*. Home for morning coffee: sports section, news, cryptic, and then a shower and a shave. That was his life now—except that Emma was visiting. And he'd had some encouraging news: a Facebook post by Shane Lambert's second cousin in Dromana, announcing that she was arranging a family reunion in the new year.

Somewhat encouraging news. Possibly she'd been in touch with Lambert. Perhaps he would attend.

There had been a handful of such leads over the years, and Charlie followed up on every one of them. No one else seemed to be looking for whoever had snatched his mother.

It wasn't Lambert. His police record showed he'd been arrested in Rosebud that day and locked up overnight for public drunkenness. But why hadn't he been seen for twenty years? Did he know something? Had he seen something he shouldn't? Been warned to stay away? He might be dead. But otherwise…A word with him, that's all Charlie wanted.

He pegged his towel to the nylon rope strung between

a pair of flowering gums, then kicked off his Crocs, turned his feet under the garden tap and stepped into the house. Into a sense of slumbering daughter. She altered the air. There was a powerful sense of her warmth spreading unseen and filling every room—modernised since the old days, for the Airbnb crowd. Later today, after he'd taken her to catch the city train, the house would miss her.

He opened the fridge. Grapes, a mango, strange foreign beer: so that's where she'd gone last night, dumpster-diving at the Aldi in Hastings. Tipping muesli, blueberries, yogurt and soymilk into a bowl, juice into a glass, Charlie break-fasted under the trees, his bushies' hat on his head, his boardshorts already dry. The birdbath was empty. He filled it, returned to the table and watched the blue wrens at their crazy pool party, spraying water everywhere as the ABC reported on the bushfires.

Food inside him, Charlie switched off the radio and checked the news feed on his phone. SBS was reporting on a virus, originating in China, that was possibly deadlier than SARS…the *Sydney Morning Herald* on the increasing bushfire devastation…7News on a two-dollar Kmart hack that had gone viral because it promised to halve your bathroom cleaning costs.

That was the world, right there.

Charlie lost himself to dreams as the world awoke around him. Mrs Ehrlich next door deadheading roses. Margie across the street calling back and forth with her husband. Alby the aircon mechanic strapping a ladder to his ute and clattering a toolbox across the tray.

They had all been here when Charlie's mother disappeared, and Charlie wondered if they ever thought about that. If they knew anything. If they thought about Rhys Deravin, who had lived here back then, and if they still suspected him of murder.

Other people did. Most people, it seemed to Charlie. And the suspicion had driven his father out—or so Charlie supposed, for Rhys refused to talk about the past. And because Liam thought their father was responsible, Charlie had rarely been able to discuss his mother's fate with anyone. A twenty-year no-go area. Anyway, Rhys could not—or would not—sell Tidepool Street, so the house had been a short-stay holiday rental for twenty years until a few weeks ago, when it all went wrong for Charlie and Rhys handed over the keys. 'All yours, son.'

Charlie rinsed his breakfast dishes, brushed his teeth and shoved on his bike helmet and sunglasses before walking his bike over the bone-rattling grit and potholes of Tidepool Street. The leaf mould silenced the racket as he wheeled through the banksias and tea-trees. Reaching the steps, he carried the bike down onto the sand. It was only then that he decided he'd fetch the *Age* from the Swanage general store rather than the Balinoe newsagency. He climbed aboard and powered off, the tyres crisp in the sand.

The dolphins again. He dismounted and took out his iPhone. Zoomed in and snapped them and messaged the best one to Anna. It was new between them, but he knew her phone wouldn't be far from her elbow. Sure enough, a minute later she replied: *Wish I was there xxx.*

Rather than mount the bike again, he walked it, eventually overtaking a woman leading three very old dogs, one small and yappy, one mid-sized and nervy, one a lumbering old wreck. Pretty sure that she and her dogs had lived in Menlo Beach back when he was a kid, he gave her a sideways glance as he passed, inviting a connection. 'Good day for it.'

She stopped. 'A good day for striding out,' she said, looking down at the dogs, resting exhaustedly on their hindquarters. 'As you can see, I'm limited in that regard.'

Charlie considered introducing himself. They stood shoulder to shoulder, looking across the water to Phillip Island, until, above the soft sea and wind, came the labouring of a small motor. Charlie turned his head towards the bend that concealed the next curve of sand. 'The ranger?'

'Oh, yes,' the woman said; something rueful in her tone.

A little all-terrain vehicle with fat tyres and a quivering sunshade was steaming towards them, Noel Saltash at the wheel. He wore vaguely official khaki shorts and shirt, a cloth badge on each shoulder. He cut the whining revs to a fumy rattle and braked a couple of metres from them. Leaned his forearms on the steering wheel, a man weighed down, as the woman murmured to Charlie: 'It pains me to say this, but...'

'Pat? What have I said? No dogs on the beach between nine and seven at this time of the year. It pains me to say this, but the rules are there for a reason.'

Saltash shot glances at Charlie as he spoke, complicated expressions flitting about his face. He recognises me; knows why I've come back here to live, Charlie thought. He's left it too late to greet me properly. He feels silly in his little beach buggy. He knows the woman named Pat doesn't respect him; he suspects she's not the only one.

Was he going to issue a fine? Saltash glanced again at Charlie and acute self-consciousness seemed to come over him. 'Look, Pat, I'm prepared to overlook this, this... infraction, but please, do the right thing. This is a family beach. Little kiddies...'

And they all looked down at the panting, toothless mutts where they sat dreaming of cushions and long-lost bones. 'I understand,' Pat said.

Saltash made a wide turn and trundled back the way he'd come. Pat stared sourly up the slope of the beach to a low ridge of tussocky grasses above the high-tide mark. Here the sand was soft, and a few people were sunbathing on towels or sitting cross-legged in nylon shelters. A teenage girl anointed herself with sunblock, utterly lost to the flow of her fingers. Her boyfriend or brother lay flat on his back beside her.

'I expect,' Pat said, 'some good citizen tipped him off.'

Charlie doubted it. Clearly, Noel had had run-ins with Pat before. She went on, 'He seemed to recognise you.'

Charlie didn't want to go into it, his childhood informed by the family or cabal or conclave of Menlo Beach cops. 'I grew up here.'

'You know he used to be a policeman?'

A sergeant, in fact, an arms instructor at the police academy, but her subtext was clear: old habits die hard, and Noel Saltash was still a jumped-up despot. Charlie made an inadequate noise, leaned over to knuckle the skull of each dog, mounted his bike and said goodbye.

His tyres whispered over the damp sand, avoiding the tips of rocks, seaweed, a dog-poo plastic bag, neatly tied, sitting on the sand like a floppy-eared black rabbit. A few Christmas-holiday early birds were out walking, others swimming, and a tinnie carved a white wake in the flat water. Then he was on the last stretch to Swanage, leaving behind the Balinoe Beach yacht club and the horse-churned sand.

Reaching the youth camp on the outskirts, he stopped, hoisted his bike onto one shoulder and carried it through to the long main street, then mounted again. The speed limit was fifty here, but no one observed it: he felt the wind of three cars passing and smelt the toxins hanging. Two bold hand-painted signs a few hundred metres apart: *Koalas crossing slow down*. A kind of community activism that hadn't existed when Charlie was a kid.

He bought the *Age* at the general store, nodded to the coffee-and-croissant crowd on the sundeck, and, because he was here and because he had a lead on Shane Lambert, he rode on through the town and up to his mother's old street near the water tower. He wondered what he'd feel. Rode in and along it and didn't feel her anywhere. A gap, an absence, that's all.

He'd revisited Longstaff Street several times back then—with the investigation team, with Liam, with his father. In search of answers, first. Then, under apologetic pressure from her landlord, to clear out her things. But he hadn't been back since and could see changes. Not so many shacks now: here, too, the old holiday places had been tarted up or replaced. The trees were higher, denser; front fences had been replaced by shrubberies that spilled out onto the nature strips. Audis, hybrids and small SUVs these days, not creaky, sun-damaged Corollas. But the road surface was still unsealed, and Charlie juddered past his mother's old place.

New paint, bigger windows, an umbrella tree on a cropped green lawn and a mezzanine built into the roof. He rode to the end. The house slab was still there but no longer abandoned: a man wearing a yellow helmet and a hi-vis jacket was comparing the slab to a blueprint on a clipboard, another was churning the soil with a bobcat and a third had propped his backside against the bonnet of a twin-cab plastered with a builder's logo.

They stopped to stare at him. He saluted and wobbled back to the main road and coasted right to the bottom, where he parked his bike against a fence and took the steps down to the beach where Billy Saul had drowned. Billy

Saul: the name instantly there in his head.

Others hadn't forgotten him, either. Halfway down a cross had been stuck in the sandy dirt, two sun-faded white sticks hung with a faded Berwick Ballet School ribbon, along with fresh flowers in a murky little vase and a tribute board pinned with Christmas cards. How do you send wishes to a dead kid? He'd never been found. Maybe someone still hopes, thought Charlie, itching to read the cards.

He skipped with confused, unfinished thoughts to the bottom step and onto the sand. Pretty much unchanged in twenty years. The same little fingernail curve of sand, weathered boatsheds and an impression of houses and money brooding behind the banksias, pines and buttressing fence. Not, he thought, a beach you visited for riotous times. A shuttered, keep-out place, a good place to drown.

Time to go home. The tide was up, sealing him left and right, so he rode back through the town and out along the road to Balinoe then down past the Balinoe Beach store to Tulum Court. The usual mix of vehicles parked there: local cars, high-end city SUVs; an old Kombi with South Australian plates and a sticker reading *Visit Coober Pedy: a Sunny Hole in the Ground*. Here Charlie carried his bike through to the beach, then rode it along the narrow strip of hard sand.

The sea air was in him, and the sun was high. Plenty of people about. A big guy, overdressed in jeans, with a hippy beard and a metal detector; kids, parents and grandparents in the water, busy with buckets and turrets and moats. Charlie watched an old geezer with gappy shorts and explosive white hair help a little girl pat seashells into castle walls and his first thought was 'paedo'. Why was that? The change that police work had wrought in him, seeing everyone as a suspect. Catching the man's eye, he said, 'A grandad's work is never done,' and got an affirmative grunt.

The job, and the mistakes he'd made in it. He'd be reinstated; maybe transferred to Traffic somewhere out in the Mallee. Or sacked. Or he could quit. All he was doing now was licking his wounds and waiting. And looking for Shane Lambert, as he'd been doing for twenty years. The thread that remained untugged. All those fruitless leads…

And if he couldn't find Lambert, or if Lambert couldn't help, if there were no new developments, then people would continue to believe his father was guilty. Even though no body had been found. Even though there was no history of violent behaviour—barely even a cross word, since his parents had stayed clear of each other, letting the divorce paperwork trickle through the system. Even though Rhys had been investigating a security van hijack that day. Just a couple of unaccounted-for hours when he was working alone, since, as he'd said at the time, 'I didn't know I'd need an alibi.'

Despite all that, the theories came thick and fast. Rhys Deravin had murdered Rose Deravin because he'd have to sell Tidepool Street and give her half of the proceeds. Or he'd blown his top and killed her in the heat of the moment.

Or he'd killed her and hoped suspicion and blame would fall on her difficult lodger, Shane Lambert. None of these theories accounted for why her car was found abandoned out near Tooradin with a crumpled bumper, the driver's door open and her possessions scattered up and down the road. Unless...Unless Rhys Deravin, the wily out-thinker, had staged a confused and confusing crime scene because, as anyone acquainted with him could confirm, he was too smart to leave loose ends.

7

CHARLIE HAD DISMOUNTED to steer his bike through the rocks at the last bend, and there was Mark Valente, shaking seawater from his hairy ears, his vitality unchanged in twenty years. Retired now, and Charlie had heard from Mrs Ehrlich that he spent his winters up north on the Gold Coast, his summers here on the Peninsula. Best of both worlds.

'Heard you were back,' Charlie said.

'Heard *you* were back,' Valente said.

'Yeah, well...'

'Thumped your inspector, apparently.'

'Didn't thump him.'

'All right—gave him a friendly nudge that sent him arse over tit.' Valente grinned. 'God has left the sullen and the wicked behind.'

'Yeah, yeah, yeah,' said Charlie. He waited to be grilled or criticised, but the old cop had apparently lost interest and was looking around the beach disparagingly. Families with sun shelters and beach carts, Frisbees, teenagers on towels: even Charlie could see a difference in the place. He wanted to say, 'Things change, Mark.'

Valente shook off his blue mood and fixed Charlie with a look from under water-beaded brows. 'What's on for you tomorrow?'

Christmas Day, he meant, and Charlie saw a hollowness in the old detective. Long divorced, like the others, he'd never remarried. No children. Never a girlfriend to speak of. Alone on Christmas Day and for god's sake don't ask me around for Christmas Eve drinks, Charlie thought.

'Spending it with Dad and Fay,' he said.

'Liam?'

'I'll catch up with him tonight,' he lied.

'That lovely girl of yours?'

He didn't mean Jess. And presumably he didn't know about Anna. 'Em? She's been staying with me for a few days.' Charlie checked his watch. 'Still asleep, probably,' he added, knowing it would disarm the old bruiser.

Valente chuckled. 'Typical teenager. She'll be with you for Christmas?'

Charlie shook his head. 'Spending it with Jess. I'm taking her up to the train this afternoon.'

'The lovely Jess,' Valente said. 'Don't know what you were thinking, letting that one go.'

Charlie wanted to say: Fuck you, what would you know? She was the one who let *me* go. But he shrugged.

Before he could wheel his bike to the steps and up them and home, Valente said: 'By the way, be careful who you speak to in the next few days.'

'Sorry?'

'A couple of cute little ferrets in town, knocking on doors. Doing a podcast, they said.'

'About?'

'Oh,' Valente said, one slab of a hand stirring the air, 'local history.'

'Local history.'

Some of Valente's hard old manner resurfaced. 'Mind what you say to them, Charlie-boy.'

That's how it had always been. Mark Valente the alpha figure, the ultimate father of all those cops' kids back when Charlie was little, kicking a ball around. Throwing, catching, batting, running...Toeing the line.

Charlie went away intrigued. His bike on one shoulder as he climbed the steps, he thought: What could put the wind up Mark Valente?

Reaching 5 Tidepool Street, he stowed his bike on the back veranda and entered through the laundry door. His daughter was on a kitchen stool, tapping at her phone. Toast crusts; coffee dregs in a chipped mug.

Charlie made a show of checking his watch. 'Astonishing. Not yet ten.'

Emma's expression didn't alter: faintly sleepy self-satisfaction, irony and confidence. She was used to his routines. 'The coffee's fresh.'

Charlie perched himself on the adjacent stool and poured. Em leaned sideways, bumped shoulders with him and continued scrolling down the screen: Frankston line timetable for 24 December.

She pointed. 'There's a train at three-thirty. Will that give you time to drop me off and get to your appointment?'

He was seeing the therapist at four. Fifteen minutes from the station to Mount Eliza...'Perfect.'

She had shown no curiosity about his appointment. The great adult–kid divide. Her world comprised university, housemates and friends: friendships betrayed, friendships confirmed. Her nails and her hair. Climate change. Instagram, never Facebook. Shit boyfriends and potentially okay ones; nothing serious. Shit retail jobs. *Schitt's Creek*. Her old man's inner life—even his surface one—didn't register.

'While I've got you...' Charlie said. He slid off the stool and through to his bedroom, returning with a parcel he'd wrapped in beautiful paper using his thumbs and two left feet. He plonked it at her elbow, saying, 'Happy Christmas, darling girl. Hope it's a good one—the year ahead, too.'

She beamed a little, bumped shoulders again. 'We're doing this now? Wait here.'

He waited. Sounds came to him from her room: the crackle, snip and snap of paper, scissors, sticky tape. She reappeared eventually and he saw that it was a book. She knew she couldn't go wrong with a book when it came to her dear old dad.

'Oh brilliant, a tennis racquet,' he said.

'You wore out the one from last year.'

'Your wrapping is a tad more skilled than mine,' he said. He was attempting to extract the book without tearing the paper, while his daughter's unwrapping was more of a great lusty laying bare.

'Dad!'

'It's a wetsuit,' he said lamely.

'I can see that.'

'A spring suit.'

He looked out at the sun-drenched front yard as if to reassure himself, and her, that summer days were not always this hot.

'Perfect, Daddyo.' She looked pointedly at the half-uncovered book in his hands. 'Now you.'

He finished easing the paper away from the cover and spine. 'Hey!' he said in genuine delight. A bird book. 'You've done well.'

'You said the first thing you noticed coming back here was the birds, you didn't know what half of them were.'

'I know. Smart of you.'

Charlie gardened and pottered around after that, then listened to the midday news, ate a sandwich and read the *Age* at the outside table. He was doing the crossword when Emma emerged, kissed his cheek and wandered down to the beach with a towel over her shoulder, a straw hat, stuff in a string bag.

He watched her go. Her self-possession. The loping grace she'd inherited from her grandfather, who…well, she saw him from time to time, but when had she last spent a Christmas with him? When had Liam last spent a Christmas with Rhys Deravin, come to that?

Grief crept through Charlie, sitting heavily. The obligations and accommodations of Christmas. He himself hadn't posted a single card, and he'd only received half-a-dozen—including from the Skoda dealer. He hadn't phoned anyone. Hadn't dropped in with a bottle of wine.

Checking for signal bars, he made his first Christmas call: Susan Mead, his old boss.

The sergeant was guarded. 'Charlie.'

'Just ringing to say season's greetings.'

'Same to you.' She paused. 'How have you been?'

The question seemed sincere. 'Good. Twiddling my thumbs, mainly.'

'At the beach, though.'

'True.' It was Charlie's turn to pause. 'Sue, if you've got time between now and the new year, you should visit.'

Her reply was immediate. 'I can't, Charlie. I promised Don and the kids. And Kessler's new trial starts soon.'

'Fair enough.' Charlie heard the barb in the second half of her answer. It was partly down to Charlie Deravin that Kessler's first rape trial had been abandoned. He found himself saying, 'Good luck with it.'

'Thanks. Look, I'd better go, lovely of you to ring, and I hope you have a good one tomorrow.'

'You, too.'

That put a stop to Charlie's dutiful Christmas calls. Who'd want to hear from him anyway? A question he'd asked himself even before he'd fucked up, even when he'd been a happy husband and father. What did he even have to offer people? It was a nasty, defeatist little pathology—or a *big* pathology—and maybe he should mention it to the therapist. Maybe this Dr Fiske would show him ways to live with himself.

Or not. Why should he tell her anything, come to that? Withholding information had always been his modus. And why was she working on Christmas Eve, for that matter? Because she was going on holiday and wanted to get all her appointments out of the way? Because guys like him were more likely to commit suicide on Christmas Day than on any other? She didn't have to worry about Charlie Deravin: his very irritation at *having* to see her showed that he didn't *need* to see her, right? It was just a formality, the police department covering its arse.

As Charlie sat there, he became aware of movement next door: scrapes, thumps, muttered curses. A man was setting a ladder against Mrs Ehrlich's side wall. Cleaning out the gutters for her? Charlie watched: the man didn't actually get on the ladder; he picked up his toolbox and threw it onto the ground with an arc of tumbling spanners, pliers and screwdrivers, let out a bellow of distress and gave the ladder a hefty shove. It scraped against the wall, gathered momentum and toppled over with a crash. Then he threw himself onto the ground and began to roll around and moan, drumming his heels against the weatherboard side wall, until Mrs Ehrlich came running.

Charlie started the dialogue in his head:

'Oh dear, what happened, are you all right?'

'I don't know. It just slipped.'

'Have you broken anything?'

As Charlie listened, the guy moaned again. 'I don't know. I was pretty high up.'

'Lie still, I'll call an ambulance.'

'Hang on, I'll just see…I can move my fingers and toes okay.'

'What about your insides?'

'I don't know. A strain? Those things can take time to heal.'

'Oh dear, look, best if you don't move, you could make things worse.'

'It's just that everything hurts.'

'I really do think I should call an ambulance.'

The guy ignored her and made more noises of agony. 'Look at my pants. Shirt's ruined...'

Mrs Ehrlich hesitated, as if offered a lifeline. 'I can mend those for you.'

The guy felt it was time to inflect his voice with a little outrage. 'The ground here—it's too soft. You should have warned me.'

Hard as concrete, Charlie thought, if it's anything like my garden soil.

'I'm so sorry,' Mrs Ehrlich said. 'I didn't know.'

The guy groaned, turned onto one hip and propped himself on an elbow. 'The ladder looks like it's had it. Toolbox...'

'Let me pay for those,' Mrs Ehrlich said. She paused: 'Are you sure you don't need an ambulance?'

The man seemed to search for a solution that benefited them both. 'Have you got public liability insurance? Oh, wait. No, you could lose your no-claim bonus.'

Charlie parted the bushes and stepped out onto a lawn in better nick than his own. 'Afternoon, Mrs Ehrlich. Can I help?'

Her grey hair bobbed. 'Oh, Charlie, this poor man...'

Charlie stooped to offer the guy a helping hand and a face-splitting, empty smile. 'Shit, mate, lucky you didn't break your neck.'

The guy lifted a soft, uncalloused hand sulkily. He was about thirty, with inked forearms, buzz-cut hair and stained, fraying khaki work pants and shirt. He creaked upright with Charlie's help, uttering a theatrical little moan.

A guy who plays the odds, Charlie thought. He's betting I won't talk Mrs Ehrlich out of giving him a few bucks.

Brushing himself down, the guy muttered, 'Thanks.' He bent stiffly to retrieve a screwdriver, presenting a skinny arse, and Charlie kicked it. Not hard.

The guy knew. He didn't spin around but moved away, hunched over, braced for more.

'Charlie!'

'It's a con, Mrs Ehrlich. This guy was having you on.'

'Was not,' the guy muttered, sprung like a schoolboy.

'Mate, I saw it. I saw you push the ladder over.'

'What?' The expressions rippled across Mrs Ehrlich's face. Wonder, dawning outrage, embarrassment. She was small, wiry—tough—but artless with it. She took a step, ready for battle. 'Who the hell do you think you are? You're a disgrace.'

'Ah, fuck off the both of you.' The guy rattled a few tools together and took off with his ladder bouncing behind him.

'Look at him run, Charlie,' said Mrs Ehrlich with bitter satisfaction. She shouted after him, 'He's a policeman, you idiot!'

Charlie winced. The community might know he was a policeman, but did they know why he wasn't policing? 'You okay? Anything I can do?'

'Oh, the gutter can wait.'

'I'm busy the next couple of days, but maybe early next week?'

'No, no, that's not necessary, Charlie.'

'No problem,' Charlie said, and eventually he went back through the gap in the hedge. Two hours later, as he was dressing for his appointment with the therapist and waiting for Emma to return from the beach, he heard a knock on the door.

He knew it was Valente's ferrets: the podcast crew. Hipster twins, a man and woman in their twenties, dressed for Sydney Road, not dirt roads and beach shacks. She carried a binder; he had a polished-aluminium equipment case. Sound gear? A yellow Volkswagen was parked in the street.

The girl tilted her little chin up to look him in the eye, nothing to hide, her smile bright and empty. 'Mr Deravin?'

'Depends.'

That stopped her. A tiny flaw between her flawless brows. 'Pardon?'

'Which Mr Deravin do you want?'

'Charles. Are you Charles?'

Charlie couldn't see the point of fooling around with them. 'I am. What's this about?'

The guy answered. He was the cynic. He'd already assessed and dismissed Charlie. 'We're making a podcast. We'd like to ask you a few questions.'

'About?'

'The past.' The young woman again. She was scarcely older than Emma, with a similar look about her. Hoop earrings, clear skin and eyes, limitless buoyancy.

But there was something of the predator in her when she added: 'About your father and his mates and the things they did.'

8

THE AVIDITY IN them, the satisfaction. A business card was
shoved at Charlie: she was Ashleigh Deamer and he was
Will Nadal, and together they were MalPod—*Malcontents
dedicated to rooting out malefactors.*

'Cute,' Charlie said.

'If we could sit down with you and have a chat about
what it was like for you and your brother growing up here,'
Deamer said, her teeth blazing.

'I don't think so.'

'Otherwise we can only present part of the picture.'

They'd have tracked down Dad first, Charlie thought, and he'd have told them to fuck off. And Liam would never speak to this pair of twits, despite the fact he's convinced of Dad's guilt. Clearly Mark Valente hadn't talked to them. Noel Saltash probably wouldn't. But maybe they'd been doorknocking, maybe they'd heard some of the stories.

'What picture would that be?'

'Where to start?' Deamer said, spreading her arms. 'The armed holdup of a Medicare office for starters.'

Not his mother's disappearance, then? Charlie let his bewilderment show, but before he could ask, Emma wandered back from the beach, faintly tanned, sandy, damp, her smile as wide as the world. She'd always greeted the unexpected like that, ever since she was little. The sight of strangers on the doorstep meant adventure.

'Hi!'

Deamer and Nadal turned but Charlie got in first, calling to his daughter, 'Hop in the shower, kiddo, we need to get moving.' And to the podcasters: 'Sorry, you've come at a bad time. I'm afraid I can't help you.'

Full of curiosity, Emma crossed to the garden tap and washed the sand from her feet, as Deamer and Nadal backed away, nodding and smiling, sizing her up and down. 'Don't be a stranger, Mr Deravin,' Deamer said. 'Feel free to give us a call.'

'What was that about?' Emma said as the couple climbed into the yellow Beetle and rattled away.

Charlie shook his head. 'I honestly don't know.'

—

At 4 p.m. he was in a consulting room in Mount Eliza shaking hands with Dr Fiske, who then gestured to a padded chair with its back to the door. Charlie, performing a neat little swivel and pirouette, dodged around her and took the other chair. Now he could watch the door, the desk, the window behind it, the framed certificates between the bookcases.

And he could watch that other chair, which Fiske settled into neatly with a small smile. 'You're not the first policeman to choose that one, and you won't be the last.'

Charlie wanted to joke. *Goes with the job, watching exits and entrances* or *We're all paranoid,* but was afraid that would open a can of worms about his mental state. He waited patiently—for what, he didn't know. This appointment had been mandated by the department; he was required to play along.

Fiske was about fifty, slim in a plain dark skirt, a plain white top and bright blue glasses on a cord around her neck. Suddenly she kicked her shoes off, which Charlie found appealing and then disconcerting. Had she done it unselfconsciously, or did she want to disarm him? Disarm me, he decided. A therapist—one with a PhD, no less—would never do much without forethought.

She had his file in her lap and said, 'We might as well start at the beginning, Senior Constable Deravin. Or may I call you Charles?'

'Charlie.'

'Charlie. Let's start at the beginning. Do you know why you're here?'

'Given that it's Christmas Eve?'

She cocked her head—wondering if he was a joker? 'Given that I'm trying to clear a backlog before I go away for a much-needed break. What's your story?'

Charlie laughed. 'Fair enough. Yeah, I know why I'm here, and even though you also know, you want *me* to say why.'

'Let's not start like that, Charlie.'

Her voice was deep, precise, warm, but she was tired—long days and fuckwits. He said, 'I shoved an inspector in the chest, and he went down and sprained his wrist.'

She revealed nothing. 'Would you care to say why you did that?'

Charlie tensed. He wondered if there would be a trap in every question she asked. 'He deserved it.'

'Is that how you usually resolve issues?'

Now he was irritated. 'I'm the most peaceful guy there is. I've never hit a soul in my life, not even back in my uniform days when some drunk took a swing at me.'

'But something caused you to shove a senior officer in the chest so hard that he fell over his own desk. In front of several colleagues.'

'Yes,' Charlie said and waited.

She waited too. Eventually she said, 'If that push was out of character for you—and nothing in your file indicates otherwise—are you able to say why it was out of character?'

Fiske placed her glasses on her nose as she said this, the neck strap forming a pair of big loops on either side of her face. She looked both professional and startled now, and Charlie searched for something else to fix his gaze on. The room was airy, lit by the westering sun, and might have overlooked Port Phillip Bay if not for the Mount Eliza mansions and trees claiming the sky in their roll down to the sea. He chanced another glance at Fiske. The therapist had her head down, reading his file. We're each playing a game, he thought, against an unfamiliar opponent. She'll lob a ball, I'll return it, and vice versa. We'll each watch the return lob, working out the meaning behind it.

'What does the file say?' Charlie said.

She removed her glasses. 'The bare bones, Charlie. I need to know what you were feeling at the time. What you're feeling now. So we can talk through these feelings.'

'Feelings. My feeling is, I've been suspended from police duties and told to see a therapist,' Charlie said.

Even if—after seeing Fiske a few times—he was cleared to return to his duties, that wouldn't be the end of it. He could see further internal disciplinary actions in his future: performance monitoring, transfers, demotion...

'Charlie, you've described a fact, not a feeling. I'm not the enemy here. I'm here to listen. I offer talk-based therapy, the chance for you to talk about work and personal issues. Clarify them, explore options, develop strategies, be more self-aware,' Fiske said, adding: 'Blah, blah, blah.'

'You're sending up your own profession?'

'It's been known to happen. Charlie, I am required to be thoroughly neutral, opaque even. This is not an interview, I don't intend to be suggestive, my job is to give you space to talk. That said, I have been working with police officers for a very long time and I find that I can help them best if I am not always neutral or opaque. But we will respect each other throughout.'

She was making an effort; so would he. He took a deep breath. 'All right. Okay, this is the world as I know it, right?'

She nodded. 'Of course.'

'The rape of Gina Lascelles...'

She waited, and he realised that he was expected to tell the whole story, as if she knew nothing. 'So. One night a few months ago a hotshot young footballer named Luke Kessler raped his girlfriend in the carpark of his team's clubroom. They were having a party and Gina made the mistake of chatting with another kid, so to teach her a lesson he took her outside and trapped her head in a side window of his car and sodomised her. Please don't go asking me how that made me feel.'

A flicker of tension in Fiske. 'Go on.'

'My squad investigated. My own role was marginal, so I wasn't called to give evidence at the trial. I was tasked with getting statements from some of Kessler's mates, that's all. To a man they said, "He's a great guy, the bitch is lying."'

Fiske nodded.

'The thing is, Kessler is private school, wealthy parents, good looking, popular. He's going places. There's talk he could be taken in the AFL draft; clubs are sniffing around him.' Charlie paused. 'Unfortunately for Gina, and the cause of truth and justice, for a lot of people that's all they care about. People on the jury, for example. And some of my colleagues.'

Fiske looked pretty neutral to Charlie. She said, 'Some people care more about a footballer's reputation than a rape victim.'

It was a cop interrogation tactic, quoting the words of a suspect or a witness back at them. The intention was to clarify a statement, a thought or a belief. Maybe tease out more detail. Charlie waited a beat, then said, 'Yes. But we did get Kessler through a committal hearing and before a judge and jury in the County Court. Unfortunately, not everyone was enthusiastic about that.'

Charlie stopped there. Had he said too much? Was she a department spy?

Fiske sensed the reluctance. 'Charlie, everything stays in this room. Tell me about the inspector you shoved.'

'His son plays for the same club.'

Fiske watched Charlie. If she was drawing conclusions about Allardyce, he'd be the last to know.

'To be fair, he recused himself, and I actually think he'd have said *c'est la vie* if Kessler had gone to prison. It's just that the mood in the courtroom seemed to be going Kessler's way. The prosecution was weak, there was a string of high-powered character witnesses, and the defence made mincemeat of the poor kid who was raped. Gina.'

Charlie paused. 'And then the jury was dismissed, and a new trial announced.'

'Tell me about that.'

Charlie took a breath. 'We got a call from one of Kessler's ex-girlfriends—she was a defence witness, attested to his good character, never violent towards her, et cetera, et cetera. She said she was being pestered by one of the jurors. I was sent to look into it.'

He stopped, reluctant to go on. The juror was Anna Picard and he'd fallen for her, and now they were seeing each other. And he didn't want to disavow any of that in any way.

'Charlie?'

'Sorry, miles away. It's not unknown for a juror to turn detective, but long story short, rather than shut this juror down and report her to the court, I listened to what she had to say. It was troubling. She said there was a victim-blaming atmosphere in the jury room, and she was being pressured to vote not guilty.'

According to Anna, the forewoman was a bully, and the jury was stacked with older women unsympathetic to young women who cried rape when they got themselves into trouble. They'd said things like, 'We all know what little missy gets up to of a weekend.' And that old classic: 'Boys will be boys.'

Fiske was watching him. 'I understand that victim-blaming is not an unknown phenomenon.'

'In this case,' Charlie said, 'the defence made a big thing about how much Gina had drunk and what she was wearing.'

Anna had quoted the defence's line of questioning to Charlie, her voice dripping with disgust: '"I put it to you that you are immodest by nature" and "I put it to you that you went braless in the expectation that your nipples would show."' The judge had admonished Kessler's lawyer from time to time, but mildly, as if he was enjoying the show.

'What was the jury's response?' Fiske asked now.

'Apparently the prevailing mood was: she was asking for it.'

'Apparently?'

'So I was told,' Charlie said.

Perhaps Fiske found that answer inadequate? She said, 'What can you tell me about the juror? What does she do?'

'She's an archivist,' Charlie said, trying to sound offhand.

He could feel Fiske boring into him. He shifted uncomfortably and said, 'There's more to the story. She got an anonymous phone call warning her to get in line and vote not guilty. She didn't, she went the other way— she actually challenged Kessler's ex-girlfriend and found another victim—and, rightly or wrongly, I started helping her. I made a few phone calls, ran some LEAP computer searches I shouldn't have, that kind of thing. Meanwhile the juror and I were seen together, and I was investigated, and the anonymous phone call was investigated, with the result that the judge discharged the jury and so there's going to be a new trial. The team was pissed off because they'd have to go through the whole thing again and some of them, like Inspector Allardyce, feared that a different jury would find Kessler guilty.'

You fucking the bitch? Allardyce had said. *She got you so cunt-struck you go poking around behind our backs?*

Perhaps Charlie should have landed a punch rather than just a shove.

Fiske was watching him. 'And here we are. Was the juror fined or reprimanded?'

'Not fined—after all, she got a threatening phone call. A stern finger was wagged.'

'And you? Do you think they'll fire you?'

'That's my fear, yes.'

She nodded. The sun was streaming in from across the invisible bay. 'Let's talk about fear, Charlie. Would you call yourself a fearful person?'

Charlie had been a good boy so far, he'd engaged with her questions, but this one pissed him off. 'I'm fearful in menswear shops.'

To her credit, she treated it seriously. 'Why is that, do you think?'

Charlie realised that he actually was afraid in menswear shops. 'The fabrics are horrible—strange, stiff, non-natural textures. Brand names everywhere when all you want is something plain. Nothing ever fits right. Nothing ever feels right.'

'Yet here you are, fully dressed.'

'Op shops are my friend,' Charlie said. He held up a finger: 'Crucially, everything they sell has been pre-approved.'

'You're being a smartarse now, Charlie. That, in and of itself, is interesting.'

Charlie scowled briefly, then shook it off. 'Okay then. Ask your questions.'

'Thank you, but this isn't a question-and-answer process. I may suggest topics through initial questions, but the aim is for us to talk and see where it leads. Think of your boundaries as porous. So I ask again: tell me what makes you afraid—or vulnerable, or uncertain.'

Charlie said, 'Let me answer like this. When I was on the beach this morning, I saw an old bloke building a sandcastle with a little girl, presumably his granddaughter. But my first thought was: paedophile. Go on: ask me how that made me feel.'

'How did that make you feel?'

'That I'm in the wrong job or I've been in this one too long. I don't see honesty and innocence anymore, I see hidden motives and filth. Maybe you feel it too, in your profession? When you walk down the street are you thinking, Oh, there's a happy husband, wife and kids, or are you thinking, there's a domestic tyrant, there's a pill-popping wife, there's an abused kid?'

Dr Fiske's expression made a small acknowledgment. She said—as if referring to herself as much as to Charlie— 'It's hard to switch off.'

'Yes.'

'Tell me more about that, as it has affected you in the past and as it affects you now.'

'Now I'm in a kind of limbo,' Charlie said, 'playing a waiting game, which is bad in its own way. But back when I was on the job, the work never let up: emails, texts, phone calls. All hours of the night and day.' He shrugged. 'Being in sex crimes, I often gave my number out to victims and informants. It's part of the job, you want them to feel connected, that they can reach out if they need to. But people do take advantage of that.'

'You found that the work never let up.'

Charlie shifted in his seat. The padding was too comfortable; wrong for the things he wanted to say. He needed a stiff-backed wooden chair. 'The shitty things people do to each other, especially to kids. I couldn't sleep. Always tired and grumpy. On the lookout for the next bad thing. Panicky, sometimes,' he added, shooting her an anxious look. He didn't want her to refer him to a specialist who would dose him up.

She merely nodded patiently. 'A kind of hypervigilance.'

'I didn't choose this chair for nothing,' Charlie said.

'No, you didn't. Would it help you to know that over thirty per cent of your colleagues have a diagnosed mental health condition?'

'You're saying I have?' Charlie blurted—too hurriedly?

'I am not saying that about you. But you are here. Perhaps you might entertain another statistic: ninety per cent of your colleagues have experienced some kind of work-related burnout.'

'Sounds like me,' Charlie said.

She didn't demur. 'Another statistic: most of them don't seek help.'

Charlie knew why that was. Fear that you'd be ridiculed, pensioned off or transferred to some tame desk job. And forget about worker's comp. It was an adversarial nightmare for any police member admitting to mental health issues. The bastards would walk over broken glass to avoid a payout.

Charlie didn't say any of this. Fiske would know it all anyway. He said, 'In my case, I was told to seek help.'

'Yes.'

And she waited. Charlie said, 'That's a cop tactic: force the suspect to fill the silence.'

'It seems to be working, too.'

'Am I a suspect?'

'I don't know, are you?'

'Suspected of conduct unbecoming a police officer.'

'Tell me about that.'

'The more I dug around in that rape case, the more I came to believe that Kessler had raped others and that at least one of his character witnesses—the one Anna tried to talk to—had been paid off.'

He realised, too late, what he'd done, for Fiske said, 'Anna. The juror?'

Charlie shifted in his chair.

'Would you care to talk about her?'

The things he couldn't talk about. The way her hair flamed in sunlight. Her eyes half-closed after lovemaking.

'We've become involved.'

Charlie didn't say that Anna had appeared at a point in his life when he'd been waiting in lonely hope for his future to begin. He'd been in the squad room when the call came in from Kessler's ex-girlfriend complaining that a juror was harassing her—but so had several of his colleagues, and it was pure chance that Sergeant Mead had assigned him to check it out. He'd left the station feeling fired up that a juror should risk jeopardising the trial; was ready to throw the book at her, in fact. But he'd arrived at the ex-girlfriend's house in Hampton to find other police already in attendance: two uniforms from the local cop shop, arguing with the juror—Anna—on the front veranda while Kessler's ex-girlfriend stood behind the screen door screaming abuse.

So Charlie had stood back, waiting for them to finish—and found himself staring at her, feeling a jolt, a little leap, inside. She was tall, with reddish-brown hair in a tight bun, freckles across her nose. Tears in her eyes—indignation or fear. Then she felt his scrutiny and her eyes locked on to his and she gave him the briefest of hopeful, uncertain, hesitant half-smiles.

He looked away. She continued to wrangle with the two uniforms, one moment angry, the next jumpy with nerves that she should be under arrest.

And Kessler's ex-girlfriend continued to scream. Charlie acted: shouldering his way into the house, he shut her down.

When he stepped outside again, the juror was being bundled into the police car. 'I'll follow,' Charlie said. 'I'll need to ask her some questions.'

'Knock yourself out,' the driver said.

Anna was processed at the Bayside police station, then showed into an interview room. She talked, Charlie listened—and in between times they looked at each other.

Thus their origin myth, their foundation myth. 'I couldn't take my eyes off you,' Anna would say now. 'As if I'd been searching high and low and had found you at last.' And Charlie would say, 'You smiled at me, and I was lost.' It would make anyone puke, listening in. But no one was. It was bedroom talk, her hair spread across the pillow, her eyes drowsy when not lit by a playful intelligence.

Fiske brought him back to the present. 'You've become involved…'

She was inviting him to elaborate. He could have gone on to describe the events of that first day, his feelings, how he'd persuaded Anna to alert the court that she was being pressured and threatened, but he merely nodded.

After a beat, Fiske sighed. 'For another time.'

His session was up. Telling Fiske that he'd call to set up an appointment in the new year, Charlie said goodbye and went hunting.

9

THE YEARS HAD been crowded for Charlie—marriage, a child, uniform duties, the move to plain-clothes investigations, including suburban CIU squads, fraud, homicide and sex crimes—and so he'd investigated his mother's disappearance in his spare time. An evening snatched here, a Sunday afternoon there, with the inevitable marriage fallout. The trail went cold from the very start: none of his mother's friends knew anything and Lambert had quit working at the timber yard soon after her disappearance. According to Kevin Maberly, the workmate who'd given him a lift home that day, Lambert was close-mouthed, a bit scary. No one knew who his friends were. He didn't speak about family, or where he'd worked before the timber yard, or where he'd intended to go next. 'Like a ghost,' Maberly told Charlie all those years ago, an expression of surprise on his face, as if something had just dawned on him.

Not entirely a ghost. From his digging, Charlie learned that Lambert had grown up in Hastings, been educated at the secondary college and received training as a locksmith and security-system technician. He'd worked in the security field for a few years until a couple of minor theft and dishonesty offences saw him jailed for a three-month stretch in minimum security. After that it had been labouring jobs. The timber supply yard, thought Charlie. No known criminal associates, though, and no family left but a second cousin and two sets of foster-parents he rarely saw.

'Suits us fine,' one foster-father told Charlie.

'Why?'

The man had looked both ways along the street before murmuring, 'A bit off, if you know what I mean.'

'Off.'

'Yeah, off. A bit empty.'

Charlie kept searching and the years passed, and his marriage failed. Or, as Jess had urged him to see it, their marriage had run its course. She was being kind: he'd been inattentive. He loved her, but his thoughts were always elsewhere. During the fading months she'd said, 'You spend more time trying to find Shane Lambert than me and Emma.'

What she meant was, marriages, relationships, require a kind of ongoing maintenance. Charlie understood that now, too late.

Meanwhile, he'd become better at running down leads. All that on-the-job experience had shown him that you didn't necessarily always look for a man named Shane Lambert, for example, but for people Shane Lambert had worked with, befriended, lived with, fallen out with, gone to school with. And if one of these contacts had meanwhile died, gone to jail, changed jobs, moved interstate or married, how did the ever-widening ripples involve Lambert? Charlie patiently made calls, watched houses from the back seat of his car, ran plate numbers, knocked on doors and listened in pub corners, hoping that someone's workmate, acquaintance or friend might mention a name or a location.

Some of these people he found through Facebook and Instagram. Lambert had no social media presence, but his confirmed and possible acquaintances did, and they all liked to post photos: birthday parties, catch-ups, holidays. But only once had Charlie found Lambert in a posted photograph, and that was on the Facebook page of a man with whom he'd been in foster care years earlier. Lambert was seated at a dining table with others, looking solitary, wary, ready to bolt. Using his police ID, Charlie had gone doorknocking. The result was his contact list widened but he grew no closer to finding Lambert. According to the foster-care contact, the dinner had been a reunion and it was held before Lambert ever moved into Longstaff Street. And everyone at the table, painstakingly identified by Charlie, told the same story: Lambert was an enigma.

'First time I'd seen him in years,' one woman said. 'Never learned if he had a wife and kids or a girlfriend or even a boyfriend, nothing,' another said.

Lambert was indeed a ghost. No recent paper trail: he didn't own a car, house or land; his name didn't appear on lease agreements. The addresses he'd given employers before January 2000 were either false, long out of date or post office boxes. And his last arrest—and overnight detention in the Rosebud lockup—had been twenty years ago, on the day Rose Deravin disappeared.

Today, Christmas Eve, on his way home from the therapist, Charlie's target was a house in Dromana, further down the coast. A part of him thought, Give it a rest, Charlie, it's Christmas, but the spoor was in his nose. He might lose Lambert if he didn't move now.

Making his way through to the Nepean Highway, he found that the world was on the move. Last-minute shopping, last-minute parties to go to or drive home from. No booze buses, but a highway patrol car had pulled over a 4WD near Beleura Hospital and Charlie sensed heightened emotion in the air, a need for people to eat, drink, argue, carouse. He turned off the Nepean and down to the quieter coast road, following it through Mount Martha and Safety Beach, glimpsing the sea now and then, flat and silvery. He wished he were freestyling through it.

At the Dromana shops, Google Maps took him left—the upslope of Arthurs Seat looming above him—and then right, into a region of small houses on unpaved streets. The house at 26 Grace Avenue was small, red brick, with a deck above a carport and a view over gum trees and rooftops. A Christmas tree draped in blinking lights sat in the main window; tinsel winked around the mailbox; three cars were parked on the lawn.

Taking binoculars from the glovebox, Charlie focused on the cars, writing down the numberplates. Then the deck: five people slouched around a table, bottles and glasses on a white cloth. Catching up today because they couldn't tomorrow? A hand negligently waved a cigarette, and Charlie recognised the woman holding it from her Facebook profile: Maeve Frome, Shane Lambert's second cousin. He'd found her years earlier, but back then she never posted—no comments, photographs, list of friends. He'd continued to monitor the page, hoping for a pay-off, and suddenly last week there was a flurry of activity: dozens of photos going back decades and requests for friends and family to get in touch. She was arranging a family reunion. It was as if she needed to define or locate herself before she was left behind by life.

He recognised the two young men as her sons, and presumably the young women were their partners…Frome stiffened and rose to her feet. She'd spotted him.

Charlie started the car. He didn't know what he was doing here, or what he'd do next. He'd never been sure what he'd do if he found Lambert. All he'd thought was, why did Lambert stay so completely off the grid? What was he hiding? Where was he hiding? If there was any validity to geographical profiling theory, Lambert, a Peninsula boy, hadn't strayed far. But he wasn't one of the men up there on Maeve Frome's deck.

Charlie pulled away from the kerb as Frome reached the bottom of the steps. He saw her flick her cigarette onto the lawn as he accelerated. Christmas Eve: what the fuck was he doing here, spoiling it for someone? He glanced in the rear-view mirror: Frome was labouring up her steps again, shaking her head as if the world continued to let her down.

10

CHRISTMAS MORNING.

Charlie was on the beach at 6.15. So was everyone else, the older locals anyway, many of whom he hadn't seen since he was a kid. All were carrying themselves with a kind of benign, slow-moving grace as they blessed the day and each other. The murmurs and the stillness; the hazy colours along the horizon and the perfect glass-like water. Charlie hated to breach it, so he didn't go in, just stood there on the sand with his towel. The beach as a cathedral, he thought. Morning prayers and benedictions. Usually the beach was implicit with loss: lost coins, lost jewellery, lost virginity, lost lives. Sandcastles, footprints and hopscotch ladders lost to the clawing tidewater.

Then the old woman from Spray Street waded in and the world rippled, and Charlie woke up. He dropped his towel and followed her, swam his one kilometre until his muscles burned. When he got out, he saw that the beach had emptied, everyone had gone up for breakfast and kids and grandkids and presents. He rued the past strongly just then: Jess and Emma on Christmas mornings…

Home at Tidepool Street, he sluiced the sand from his feet and ate at the gnarly garden table, listening to the news. At dead on 7.10, after the weather forecast, Anna called. She knew his routine.

'Merry Christmas. Or season's greetings if you prefer.'

'General happiness,' Charlie said. 'How's the family?'

'Fine. Not at each other's throats yet.'

The family in question was her parents, and her siblings and their families; she'd been married briefly a long time ago and had no kids of her own. She'd told him a lot about her nieces and nephews and about the various fault lines along which family gatherings tended to fracture, but he was yet to meet any of them, so he couldn't visualise what her day would be like later, or what it had been like in the past. And this year they were all in Sydney, where her grandparents lived, which put the whole thing at a further remove.

Chatting helped, and they did that until he heard the clamouring of small voices at her end.

'Got to go, love you, bye!' she said.

She'd said, 'love you' and hung up before he could echo it. Before he could process it. The words sat there in his head: 'Love you'. Not 'I love you' or 'I am in love with you.' Was this something you said on the way to love? Sometimes Charlie could feel her retreat even as she advanced. Right now he felt like a teenager, heightened feelings fluttering inside him. Grabbing at straws and hoping he could build a mansion with them.

He went inside. The only cure for what he was feeling was a shower and a shave. Tart himself up for Christmas lunch.

Anna would be gone until mid-January and god he hoped she didn't intend to drive back through bushfire country. When she'd called yesterday to say she'd arrived, she sounded teary, shaken by what she'd seen on the trip up, the ash and the blackened stumps. She said it was the world running down, and that's what Charlie had been thinking for weeks, as he watched the evening news with a kind of dread. The fires were catastrophic. Bigger than anything he'd known before. And, even as he felt powerless, he felt angry. Climate-change deniers in control; the fires a photo opportunity for politicians.

A couple of hours later, wearing chinos and a sleeves-rolled linen shirt, the Skoda laden with presents, Charlie drove up to the city. When it all fell apart twenty years ago, Liam had taken their mother's surname, Chivell. Now he lived with his partner in a Northcote weatherboard on a leafy street near the Westgarth Cinema. Ryan answered when Charlie knocked. He was a few years older than Liam, stockier, with the gleaming vigour of a wrestler. They'd met at Melbourne High, where Liam taught English, Ryan phys. ed. 'We never bring the job home with us,' they liked to say.

A hug and a kiss at the door, then through to the kitchen, a region of deep porcelain sinks and whispering white drawers and cupboard doors. Depositing a Montalto pinot grigio, mince pies, irises and a scrappily wrapped vase on the table, Charlie crossed to Liam, who was shelling prawns at the sink, his smooth cheek tilted. Charlie pecked. 'Happy day,' he said.

'Happy day, happy year,' Liam said.

He was slender in shorts, a T-shirt and bare feet—a flexing tautness in him as he worked. 'Finished in a tick,' he said.

'Take your time.'

'Bubbly?' said Ryan, a man of supple smiles.

'A small one, I'm driving,' Charlie said.

Registering the minute stiffening in Liam—*Charlie's driving to see Dad*—he sat at the table. Liam might have said, 'Pass on my best wishes,' but he didn't. He placed the shelled prawns in a large bowl, covered it with a tea towel and stowed it in the fridge, then washed his hands and slipped onto the third kitchen chair—the signal for Ryan to heave from the table in his forceful way, disappear from the kitchen and reappear with a parcel wrapped in thick, silvery grey paper crisscrossed with twine. 'The great unveiling begins,' he said, plonking it in front of Charlie.

'Almost hate to unwrap it.'

Liam touched his forearm briefly. 'Speaking of which, if we could recycle the paper...'

'Sure,' Charlie said. He eased off the wrapping paper, revealing a food mixer. 'Actually, this will be really useful.'

Ryan and Liam had rarely visited any of the houses Charlie had lived in. They wouldn't have a clue what he did and didn't own. But they'd hit the spot here.

Meanwhile Ryan had unwrapped the vase. 'And this is not too ugly.'

'Yeah, thanks for that. When have I ever given you ugly?'

'Come to think of it, never,' Liam said.

The to-and-fro of our Christmas mornings since Mum died—disappeared—thought Charlie. He cocked his head at the vase. He thought he'd done well. It was a slim half-metre in height, the glaze pearly white. He watched Liam fill it with water and nudge the irises into shape.

'Forgot the bubbly!' Ryan said, pushing back his chair, poking his head into the fridge and rattling out a bottle while Liam took the irises through to the sitting room sideboard.

Charlie could see a Christmas tree in a corner of the sitting room, carefully wrapped presents arranged beneath it, a simple run of tinsel along the gas fire mantelpiece.

He felt that he didn't fit. There was a neat choreography to the lives of the men. They had been together for nine years. They took trips, went to concerts, and, for all Charlie knew, were actively a part of the gay scene. Scenes? Or they were just a suburban couple at the younger end of middle-age. He rarely saw them. He called them sometimes, they called him. Ryan called him.

Two minutes later, as they sipped small glasses of Moët & Chandon and munched on Liam's rumballs, Ryan said, 'How's your dad doing? And Fay?'

Liam didn't flinch. He probably wouldn't even have words with Ryan later. Everyone knew that Ryan was the peacemaker. One day he might even succeed in securing peace between the Deravin men.

11

BY LATE MORNING Charlie was in Warrandyte, a hill town as different from Menlo Beach as you could get. Steep woodland slopes with no bodies of water, apart from the Yarra and some boutique dams tucked into the ever-duplicating gullies. No run-down shacks or weekender mansions. No patched or stained boardshorts, salty T-shirts or worndown Crocs; no sea-air rust pitting; garden centres every five hundred metres.

Retired Detective Senior Sergeant Rhys Deravin and his second wife lived in a house perched on a slope overlooking hairpin roads. 'So I can see what's coming for me,' Rhys liked to say.

The couple had moved around a fair bit in the past twenty years. Fay's house in Prahran first, then East Bentleigh, Williamstown and even Portland, in the far west of the state—wherever Rhys's job had taken him. Admin duties rather than crime-fighting, mostly. To keep an eye on him, given the circumstances surrounding his wife's disappearance. Charlie had visited them whenever an occasion called for a get-together: Christmas, Easter, a birthday. Sometimes Emma accompanied him; mostly not. Liam hadn't been to a single one of those houses, those reunions.

Charlie walked in with a ham, beer, bubbly and badly wrapped presents—a Nigella Lawson for Fay, a Gideon Haigh for his father and Belgian chocolate for Fay's sisters and their partners. By now it was noon and Rhys wanted everyone out of his kitchen. 'Ready in an hour,' he said.

The kitchen was broad and airy, with long stone bench-tops and European fittings. Water splashes where he'd been washing potatoes and carrots; three knives side by side on a chopping board. He was a traditionalist: roast turkey, roast vegetables, plum pudding. 'Out,' he ordered. 'Scoot, the lot of you.'

The energy in him was forced today, Charlie thought, realising his father had ceased to be sleek and toned. His grey hair was thinning, his bones knobbly under dry skin. And he was tired. Ill? wondered Charlie.

'Let me slice and dice for you, Dad,' he said, glancing through the window above the sink at treetops islanded with terracotta-tiled roofs.

'Scoot, I said.'

Fay tugged gently at Charlie's forearm. 'Leave the master chef to work his magic.'

She took him into the hallway and past the door to the dining room, where her sisters were laying the table. Down to the study at the front of the house. 'Sit a moment, dear, I need to have a word before the day gets away from us.'

She wore cargo pants, a sleeveless top, hoop earrings and subtle eye makeup. He'd always liked her—her looks and warmth and capability. She was sixty and looked fifty. His father was sixty-three and looked seventy-three.

'A word about Dad?'

'You might have noticed he's lost a lot of weight.'

'He's been losing it all year.'

Fay was silent awhile in the little room—a room without character, and Charlie always wondered what they did in it. Bookcases, a reading armchair and a desk with a laptop and a printer, but no grooves worn into it by life. Emailing, he thought. That's about it.

'He gets tired easily. He's lost a bit of his spark. He's making an effort today, but he'll slip away for a sleep later.'

'Tests?'

'A *battery* of tests. Enlarged prostate, but that's to be expected, given his age.'

She worried the rings on her fingers. She's ageing, too, Charlie thought, noticing her bony knuckles. She caught him looking and placed one hand over the other in her lap. Her eyes were moist. 'A lot of it is simply the ongoing harassment. He hasn't had a moment's peace in twenty years.'

'What harassment?'

'Phone calls in the middle of the night. Occasional emails and letters. All anonymous.'

'But not police harassment?'

'Oh, sometimes the police,' Fay said testily. 'It's a cold case, after all. Some time-server digs out the file every few years. But mostly it's the calls and the letters. We got the most recent one yesterday, saying basically the same thing as the others, but pointing out this was the twentieth anniversary.'

She was in the desk's swivel chair and swung out of it to reach for a cardboard box on the top shelf of the bookcase. Deposited it in Charlie's lap. 'Have a read of that lot.'

A heap of letters and email printouts. 'Might take a while.'

'Just read a selection. You'll get the gist.'

Filling his lap, placing the box on the floor beside him, Charlie began to read, often skimming. 'The handwritten ones look like they're from the same person—that cute little cross instead of a dot above the letter *i*...'

'Always the same thing,' Fay said. 'You killed and buried her. Everyone knows you did it. Do the decent thing and own up to it. So on and so forth.'

Almost word for word with the first letter Charlie had picked up. He read it, then another, feeling certain that a man had written them—a man who'd possibly forged a new life for himself but still held on to strong old feelings.

'Curious,' he said. 'Not nasty, exactly—kind of imploring.'

Fay was awkward. 'Don't take this the wrong way, heaven knows I can't pass judgment, but there was a rumour Rose was seeing someone.' She put up her hands as if to ward him off. 'I know nothing about it, none of my business, but I've often wondered: if she *was* seeing someone, could he be the one making calls and sending letters? Sorry to bring it up.'

Charlie made a don't-worry gesture. 'That's okay.' He paused. 'But you don't know for sure she was seeing someone?'

'Just a rumour. If there's any truth to it, perhaps someone she was teaching with?'

'Not her lodger, that's for sure,' Charlie said.

'The creep? The one you and Liam chased off? Unlikely. And as I said—just a rumour.'

I'd like to talk to Lambert all the same, Charlie thought, ask him who Mum was seeing, who was visiting. He returned his attention to the sheets of paper in his lap. Only a scattering of emails, probably from untraceable addresses. Most of the correspondence was those handwritten letters. Not threatening, except in their anonymity and persistence.

96

'It's getting him down,' Fay said.

'I'm not sure I can do anything,' Charlie said. 'As you know, I'm a bit persona non grata with Victoria Police at the moment.'

She touched the back of his hand with her warm fingers. 'It might help you to know that your dad thinks Inspector Allardyce is, quote, a complete prick.'

She leaned back. 'Sorry, forget it, I understand there's nothing you can do. I just wanted you to know, that's all. It seemed important.'

'I'm glad you told me.'

She smiled and rose from her chair. 'Back to the fray, before my sisters and their better halves start bothering your father.' At the door, she turned to him. 'Did we tell you we're going on a cruise in the new year? Asia. Japan, Hong Kong, Vietnam and Taiwan, mostly.'

'No one tells me anything,' Charlie said—and instantly, in his head, his ex-wife's voice: 'No, Charlie, it's not that you don't get told, it's that you don't listen.'

'We'll send you photos,' Fay said. 'We'll Skype you.'

12

BETWEEN CHRISTMAS DAY and the new year, Charlie swam, surfed, walked, cycled. Emma came to stay; he barely saw her. Rhys and Fay flew to Japan. Two days later, the first WhatsApp photos arrived. A shot of the cruise ship moored at Yokohama, their cabin, the shoreline on departure, a line of tables groaning with seafood and wine.

Otherwise he spoke to Anna—yearned for Anna. Phone calls every afternoon, Messenger morning and evening. *Hope your day goes OK* or *Sweet dreams* and a row of kisses. Or a photo, with some good-natured winding-up.

Or just a photo: Charlie's feet in his best or his everyday Crocs—he knew she hated both pairs. More dolphin pics, to which she responded *Nice driftwood.* She had sent him a stack of photos on Christmas Day—her parents, grand-parents, siblings, nieces and nephews grinning madly in paper hats. One day he'd know their names and their place in her life—if she was still talking to him next year, the year after, five years down the track.

He wondered exactly what part of that he'd stuff up. He had an acute brain for criminal lives, criminal connec-tions, criminal behaviour, but seemed to zone out when it came to parsing the links between the innocent.

It had driven Jess nuts. 'I told you,' she might say, teeth gritted: 'He was the one who used to go out with my sister.'

Charlie would say, 'Right, got you now,' but he usually hadn't.

What struck him most, now that he wasn't hunting rapists, flashers, stalkers, molesters and perverts, was how long the days were. There had never been enough time when he was working, and now there was too much. And he wasn't accustomed to civilian life, civilian ways of thinking. He was free to follow his instincts and cast his investigative net wide without being answerable to senior officers, partner, DPP. He didn't have to brief anyone, seek approval, submit expenses or overtime. The rules and procedures of evidence no longer applied to him. No need to fear that every move he made, statement he gathered or thought he scribbled in his notebook might be reviewed or criticised by a senior officer or used against him in a courtroom.

Free. But he didn't feel free. He had no licence to practise as a detective. He had no backup, no partner, only hostile ex-workmates. No access to phone, tax, banking and vehicle registration records. As for cold-case access, no way would he be allowed to view any files that remained of the investigation into Rose Deravin's disappearance. And the average Swanage house or business wouldn't have had CCTV back then. Mobile phone towers had been scarce. Dashcams didn't exist. No freeway cameras or toll records—Eastlink and Peninsula Link were just pipedreams.

I'm just marking time, he thought. But Fay's remark about his mother seeing someone stayed with him so, on a Saturday morning in early January, he decided to resume his investigation into Rose's life and probable death. Two lines of investigation: who his mother was, and what Shane Lambert knew. If he could be found.

Rose first. Her best friend at the time of her disappearance was Karen Wagoner, a teaching colleague who, with her husband and kids, sometimes attended the Menlo Beach barbecues. Years later, Charlie had tracked her down to Cowes, on Phillip Island, but she'd professed not to know much about his mother's private life, thoughts, heartaches or aspirations. 'I just had to get away after it happened,' she'd said back then. 'You know, to escape memories.'

Maybe this time she'd be more forthcoming, or remember more, or be less affected by sad memories.

'Thanks for seeing me again,' he said that afternoon.

'You're very welcome. But the pain never goes away, does it?'

There were many responses to that, most of them trite. Charlie nodded and sipped watery plunger coffee and wondered about the pain of her memories.

Her house, on a back street, looked out on a heat-struck garden and sagging side fences, but if she simply walked to the shops, the jetty and the beach, she'd have clear views across the water to Swanage, where her best friend had last been seen alive. Maybe she liked to put a dramatic spin on things, thought Charlie. And perhaps that was necessary: she was an inert lump on the sitting-room sofa otherwise.

He reached for a discoloured Tim Tam on the chunky coffee table that divided the chunky room. 'You still teaching at Inverloch?'

She nodded. 'For another year or so.'

'And the kids?'

Karen Wagoner seemed to expand. 'Geoff's in Perth, high up in the Commonwealth Bank.'

'And Hazel?'

Wagoner deflated. Wriggled her pillowy shoulders against the plump cushions. 'My daughter was married for a while.'

And there she stopped. 'Okay,' Charlie said, thinking: odd response.

'She's a teacher. Geelong,' Wagoner said. After a pause: 'In a same-sex relationship now.' The words were squeezed out.

Charlie nodded as if he understood, then Wagoner brightened again. 'But Ash, my granddaughter, she's the light of my life. She's something to do with TV.'

Treading carefully, Charlie said, 'Do you stay in touch with Alan?'

She frowned. 'Not really.'

'Sorry, none of my business.'

'Oh, it's not that, Charlie. Divorce was always on the cards. When Rose…That was the tipping point, really.'

Tipping point. But what had tipped? As she talked, Charlie recalled Alan, the husband, a genial, bulky guy who carted water, swept chimneys, dug fence posts, did a bit of bobcat landscaping and even shore sheep for the hobby farmers of the Peninsula. An uneducated man who had married an educated woman and expressed a simple delight in her brains and looks—*sketchy* brains and looks, according to Charlie's father.

Charlie kept up his nods and when he was sure she'd stopped, he said, 'Like I told you on the phone, I've been doing more digging, trying to work out what happened to Mum.'

She frowned again. 'Not sure what I can add, but you're police, you'd have all the resources, wouldn't you? But I expect there's restrictions on what you're allowed to look into?'

Not stupid, then. 'On temporary leave,' he said, not wishing to misrepresent himself. 'Do you mind if I go over old ground?'

'Like I said, dear, I'm not sure what I can add. But I'm happy to help.'

'What sorts of things did the police talk to you about back then?'

'I don't think they talked to me specifically. I remember they came to the school and asked everyone about Rose's movements, that's all.'

'What about cold-case detectives over the years?'

'Nothing.'

'Did you have your own theories what might have happened to her?'

'That man in her house.'

'Shane Lambert.'

A shrug. Perhaps she'd never known his name. Charlie said carefully, 'Turns out he was in jail that day. Meanwhile, everyone else seems to think Dad had something to do with it.'

She went pink. 'Ridiculous. Your dad wouldn't hurt a fly.'

A strong response. Had there been something between them? Charlie tried to recall the undercurrents at the barbecues, picnics and dinners. The play of looks and touches. But all he could see was his father tolerating the Wagoner family for his wife's sake.

'If not Dad or the housemate, was there anyone else

who might want to hurt her? One of the teachers? One of the kids at school? A friend we didn't know about? Was she dating anyone?'

'If you're looking at my ex-husband, forget it. Alan's a bit rough around the edges, but as gentle as a lamb.'

Interesting, thought Charlie. Perhaps she fancied Dad and thought—hoped?—her husband fancied my mother. A nice little rearrangement. Except everyone lost and she's been living here in spite and misery for twenty years. 'I'm not looking at anyone,' Charlie said.

'She did say to me once how the minute she separated from your dad, all kinds of creeps came out of the woodwork.'

'Creeps.'

Karen Wagoner shifted to get comfortable, fighting the sofa's soft grip on her back and thighs, and made a casual gesture. 'People's husbands. A couple of the teachers. Even a man in the post office.'

'Did she spend time with any of them?'

'One. And he got physical with her one day, she said.'

Why didn't you tell me any of this a few years ago? Charlie wondered. 'Was she hurt?'

'I didn't see any bruises, if that's what you mean. But I believed her, she wasn't a liar like some of these women. Waiting a year or two to see how the wind's blowing before they come forward and make their accusations.'

Men betray women, thought Charlie. But oh boy, some women give it a red-hot go, too. He wanted air. He wanted to get in his car and drive. The room was too blonde, too cushiony, the ceiling too low. There was nothing in Karen Wagoner's house to welcome its inhabitant, let alone any visitor. It was too highly polished, too hostile to fingermarks.

'This man: did she stop seeing him?'

'Yes.'

'Do you know who he was?'

Charlie saw Karen Wagoner gather to herself the world's wickedness. It was ghastly to see. 'I can't be certain,' she said, 'but I think it was one of the English teachers. Drew Quigley.'

13

'I HAD A SOFT SPOT for your mother,' Alan Wagoner said. 'Lovely lady.'

One of those old-fashioned guys who didn't use the word woman. A lady was respectable, wife and mother material; a woman was more independent. She'd be trickier.

Charlie thought these things as Wagoner popped the tops of two lager cans and, with a yank of the cellophane sleeve, spilled crackers onto a plate. Twenty crackers? An outdoors man unused to kitchen finesse.

'A real shame,' he went on. 'To think, all these years and no one knows what happened.'

It was late the same afternoon and Karen Wagoner's ex-husband had been easy to find. A falling-down weatherboard on the outer edge of Tyabb, dead grass rather than garden, with half a hectare to park a listing caravan named Loserbago, his old tip truck, a bobcat and a F100 pickup—Wagoner's Wagon scrolled in gold on both doors. In retrospect it would have made more sense to track down his mother's sometime lover first; but the hours were closing in, and Alan Wagoner lived only fifteen minutes from Tidepool Street.

'I've been trying to find out for twenty years,' Charlie said. 'And just now I have some time on my hands so I'm talking to everyone who knew her back then.'

Wagoner hunched his shoulders as if he'd been caught in a high beam. Still a solid-looking man, he said he hadn't been home long when Charlie arrived. Dust and grime barely sluiced away, a faint whiff of perspiration, and he still wore shorts, a blue singlet and oil-stained steel-capped boots. 'I think Karen's the one you should talk to. She knew your mum better than I did.'

'I've just come from her place, in fact.'

Wagoner said nothing, did nothing, but there was pain behind it. He took a delicate sip of beer, the can a squib in his frying-pan hand, and said, 'How was she?'

Charlie couldn't say 'fine' or 'good' or 'inert and sour' to this man, so he nodded agreeably and said, 'She was helpful, but just as much in the dark as anyone else.'

More pain in Alan Wagoner's eyes, there and gone again. If Charlie was any judge, the guy had only partly resolved his life since Karen left him unmoored twenty years ago.

As if to underscore that, the house creaked just then, responding to a late-afternoon wind coming across the flats, and the chipboard cupboard doors and kickboard were dark, swollen, as if never proofed against the wet slap of a floor mop. Wagoner was tidy, though: no dust, clutter or dirty dishes, just the order of a man still learning to tame his indoor life.

Charlie said, 'She told me what Geoff and Hazel are up to. I haven't seen them for yonks.'

Another shift in Wagoner's face. Uneducated, but no dummy, he suddenly peered into Charlie, and behind Charlie, for the truth. 'Charlie, I don't know what happened to your mum. I was never really part of that crowd.'

Charlie went red. 'Sorry. I didn't mean you to think I have doubts. I'm just digging around. No one else is looking.'

'And I hope it pans out,' Wagoner said. 'I really do.'

The silence was awkward, and clearly still pressing on Wagoner. 'I have a lady friend now,' he said suddenly. 'I'm happy.'

Charlie reached for one of the crackers. 'I'm glad.'

'You want anything on that? I've got some cheese slices in the fridge.'

He's giving himself time to compose the rest, Charlie thought. 'I'm fine, thanks.'

'Karen. Well, Karen made my life hell.'

Charlie tongue-chased a cracker fleck from his teeth. 'Okay.'

'You know what? For a very long time I thought it was your dad she was sleeping with. No offence.'

Charlie hated to hear that. The old times were uncomfortable enough already. He shifted uncomfortably on the kitchen chair.

'Not sure who it was,' Wagoner said. 'Not your dad, but one of them.'

He means the Menlo Beach cop mafia, Charlie thought, and saw a shy, unworldly man elbowed aside by the dash of faster people, careless people. 'Is that why you split up?'

'Yes. And the divorce practically ruined me. We had a nice house, you remember.'

Not a nice house but a big one, a sprawling brick veneer on Hendersons Road. 'I remember.'

'She took the kids with her but that didn't last long. They barely speak to her now. Not a nice woman, Charlie.'

Wagoner picked up a cracker. It snapped, the pieces rolling like a coin trick around his big fingers, and he frowned at it. 'Fool of a thing.'

'Karen told me she moved away because Mum's disappearance upset her.'

'It upset everyone,' Wagoner said, licking the salt from his fingers.

'It frightened her, she said.'

'There's frightened and there's frightened,' Wagoner said, then simply watched Charlie.

Charlie heard, above the wind, a vehicle crunch in on the gravel, stop, switch off. The slam of a door. 'Care to elaborate?'

But a change had come over Wagoner. Ease, relief, simple joy. 'That,' he said, 'would be my lady friend.'

Charlie shook hands with a small, brisk, smiling woman and drove home, thinking about Karen Wagoner's fear. He'd supposed she meant a general, unnameable fear, but Alan Wagoner had seemed to indicate something more specific. She'd been afraid of the Menlo Beach crowd? Which ones? Why?

All he wanted to do when he got home was walk along the beach, a salve for the events of the day and a means to clarity of thought. It helped to pace the sand, see the same people doing the same things. It even helped to see Noel Saltash issue a fine to a dog walker; to spot the metal-detector guy again, the old hippy casting where the holiday-makers might have lost coins, phones, Rolex watches. Charlie watched him stop, stoop, sift, check a bottle top, toss it away. Keep it, you prick. Put it in your pocket. There's a bin at the top of the steps.

Charlie walked on. One certain decision: he really

didn't want to visit Karen Wagoner again, to learn more about her fear. Police work, of course, mostly entailed going over old ground but all he wanted to do was move forward, over new ground. In this case, Drew Quigley, the teacher who might have been his mother's lover.

He went looking when he got home and found Quigley after about five seconds of googling. A headmaster now, at a secondary college in the Dandenongs, Quigley's Facebook likes ranged from the Carlton Football Club to a microbrewery in Mornington and a Queensland beach resort. Married with two children. 326 friends. And he read Raymond Carver, watched *The Wire* and listened to Chris Smither.

Not all bad, then.

But Quigley would have to wait. School holidays—the Quigleys were in New Zealand, according to Facebook.

What couldn't wait was a call to his old sergeant: Luke Kessler's new trial was about to start.

Susan Mead was abrupt. 'Charlie.'

'Just wishing you luck next week, sarge.'

'It's not luck we need,' she said.

That put Charlie on the back foot. 'It's good you can put a second victim on the stand.'

'Remains to be seen. Remains to be seen how well she stands up to questioning, Charlie. She's a bit shaky.'

As if it was all Charlie's fault there was a second trial, a second victim prepared to testify. 'Sorry,' he said.

So just as damn well Anna was coming down tomorrow.

14

THE NEXT DAY. His sitting room, soon after lunch.

They were still in that mad first stage of instant igni-tion and hadn't seen each other for close to three weeks, so it was not until they were slackly tangled on the carpet that Anna said, 'Charlie?'

'Right here.' He pressed his lips to her damp shoulder.

'You don't think Kessler would come after me, do you?'

He jerked in her arms, his drowsiness vanishing. 'Where did that come from?'

She shrugged and her skin moved over his. 'Just a feeling.'

'He's in jail.'

Luke Kessler had punched a court official and screamed at the judge when the judge dismissed the jury and announced a new trial. His bail was revoked.

'His family isn't,' Anna said. 'His friends aren't.'

'They wouldn't be mad enough to try anything,' Charlie said, even as he wondered if that were true. Judging by the TV news, the Kesslers and their friends had seemed aggressive and entitled all through the first trial. They made pronouncements on the steps of the courthouse; gestured at the cameras; shoved reporters aside.

He propped himself on one elbow, a signal for Anna to roll onto her back and look up at him. He was sun-browned, she pale, and at that moment the contrast fascinated them, Anna lifting her head to look along the variable planes and swells of her body as his fingers cupped, traced and pressed. She flopped back with a soft moan.

Presently her voice came from far away. 'When I got back from Sydney,' she said, 'there was graffiti sprayed on my front door: *Watch your back bitch.*'

Charlie froze again. Lay with her, pressing hard against her. 'Jesus, Anna. Did you report it?'

'Not yet. All I wanted to do was come down here.'

Charlie kissed her. 'Someone getting back at you? Blaming you because there's going to be another trial?'

'Maybe.'

The fact that the prosecution had a second victim who was prepared to testify against Kessler would worry his lawyers and supporters, even if Sue Mead considered her too wobbly to make a good witness. Doubtless this woman would be traduced, too—slut-shamed, like Gina Lascelles. Charlie knew it was an old defence tactic to attack a rape victim's moral character while praising the accused's and ignoring the circumstances of the crime—as if a young woman's being sodomised with her head trapped in a car window could be called a case of he-said, she-said.

But maybe this time around the jury wouldn't be top-heavy with middle-aged housewives. They were a godsend to defence counsel, apparently—unlike nurses, who might have cared for rape victims, or teachers, who might be bolshie and feminist. A barrister had once explained it to Charlie: 'Your older housewife's been around, she's seen a lot, not easily swayed, not afraid to doubt people. And if you're lucky she's brought up daughters who wouldn't in a million years have got themselves into that kind of situation.' Daughters, in other words, who were sober and conservatively dressed at all times. Who would not have been raped, and if they were, would not have known their assailant. Who would have fought back: shown some spirit rather than freeze, as so many women did. Who would have gone straight to the police instead of waiting a day, a week, a year. Who, more than anything, would have been emotional in the ways that onlookers would consider appropriate.

Charlie hadn't attended the first trial, but he'd followed the squad's water-cooler chatter. The prosecutor had been inexperienced and not very effective. The defence team was hard-hitting and persuasive. They'd trotted out a priest, local businessmen, a doctor, an ex-girlfriend and other good-character witnesses for Kessler. They'd painted his victim as a loose, untrustworthy, possibly money-grubbing slut.

'I seemed to be the only one taking notes during the trial,' Anna had told him, the day he met her. 'Then when we started deliberating, people were nodding off or cracking jokes. And whenever I said anything they'd roll their eyes—egged on by the forewoman, who kept cutting me off and telling everyone what she thought really happened and how we should vote. It was like it was all decided. It was as if I was the only one aware of the gravity of what we'd been asked to do—if that doesn't sound too pretentious.'

Charlie didn't get to meet many people with principles in his line of work. He felt chastened.

Meanwhile, she said, it had been hot and cramped in the jury room. 'No windows; awful coffee. My chair was really uncomfortable, and the toilet door banged against it every time someone went. And I kept seeing Gina's family in my head, the way they stared at us as if begging us not to believe the things being said about her, and the way Kessler's lot was so intimidating.'

There must have been a spy on the jury, too: someone

feeding information to Kessler's friends and family. Anna got a call one night, a male voice: 'If you don't vote to acquit, you die.'

Charlie had encountered his fair share of bad juror behaviour over the years—a woman who'd done Sudoku puzzles during witness testimony, for example—and he knew that it was not uncommon for jurors to bully, grandstand, get bored, google names, second guess the evidence and make judgments based on the looks of the victim or the accused. He hadn't struck jury intimidation or tampering before, though.

Unfortunately, Anna had turned detective rather than report any of this to the judge or the prosecution. She hadn't been the first juror to do that; she wouldn't be the last. And in Anna, it wasn't surprising. He'd seen her stubborn side right from the start. Driven. Confident that she knew best. Coming on top of the jury-room bullying and slut-shaming, the phone call warning her off had been like a red rag to a bull. She'd visited the crime scene, taken photographs, run internet searches and questioned witnesses in her efforts to find new evidence and other victims.

Charlie rose onto his elbow again. Ran his gaze over her, circled her stomach with the palm of his hand. A couple of private eyes, that's what we are, he thought: she was on the Kessler case and I'm on my mother's. That wasn't the only congruence. Their birthdays fell in the same month; their mobile numbers both began with 0406; identical thoughts and observations kept popping into their heads simultaneously.

Charlie flopped an arm across her middle; nuzzled her neck.

That lasted about a minute. Anna huffed and grunted and pushed him away. 'Jesus, Charlie, when did you last have this carpet cleaned?'

'Er...'

'That's what I thought.' She uncoiled neatly, her skin pink where she'd rested against him and inscribed where she'd rested against the weave of the offending carpet. She strode into the kitchen unselfconsciously until she spotted the naked glass all around her—'Oops'—and drew the curtains. 'Tea?'

'Thanks,' Charlie said, climbing to his feet and dragging on his shorts.

The kettle mumbling on its base, Anna came back with her sleepy-eyed face on and wrapped him up, angling for a kiss. Charlie obliged, and she skipped away. 'Quick shower first.'

He trailed after her. 'There's just about room for two,' he said.

Tea was insufficient. They scratched together bread, olives, cheese and hummus and sat at the garden table, shaded by the umbrella. Anna turned Charlie's wrist to peer at his watch. 'Three o'clock. Is this a late lunch or afternoon tea?'

'It's a post-coital snack,' Charlie said, and saw a flicker in her. She could be bawdy with the best of them, but right now she didn't think 'coital' applied to what they'd just been up to. Too clinical.

She caught his eye and smiled. She knew that he knew what she was thinking, and reached her hand to his across the weather-gnarled table, her fingers warm. Charlie Deravin felt a wave of gratitude. And she was staying for three days.

'Anna,' he said, 'you need to report the graffiti.'

She curled her lip. 'I'm not convinced anything will be achieved by that.'

Charlie tightened his grip. 'It's important to have it on record.'

She withdrew her hand. 'In case things escalate and they attack me, not my door?'

Charlie shrugged helplessly. 'I've seen all kinds of shit, you know.'

The tension left her. She patted his wrist and helped herself to an olive. 'I'll be fine.'

It occurred to Charlie that he was a target, too. 'No strange cars followed you down here?'

'Charlie. Come on.'

'Okay, okay. Last question: have you been told who might have tried to warn you off?'

She shook her head. 'The police hate me. I'd be the last person they'd tell, don't you think?'

Charlie shrugged. 'Maybe,' he said, thinking that normally there'd be a full-on investigation if a juror was threatened. Perhaps it was still ongoing. Or perhaps not much effort was being expended.

15

THE DAYS PASSED, Anna returned to the city, and Charlie resumed his hunt. Until Drew Quigley returned from New Zealand, there was little he could do to follow his mother's story. That left the search for Lambert.

He started with the timber yard in Hastings, ten minutes' drive from Menlo Beach and on a side street in the industrial area past the Kings Creek hotel. The place had not altered in all the years he'd been away. A low-slung admin building at one end of a large shed, surrounded on three sides by stacked planks of varying width and thickness, seasoning away in the sun and the air.

Charlie parked around the back next to a display of ready-made picket fencing. As he crossed the yard, an eddying wind drew the smell of sawdust past his nostrils. Saws screamed unseen within the shed; a truck trundled out, another in. A forklift shot its tines under a stack of merbau decking boards.

He discovered that Kevin Maberly was now the manager, and found him behind a desk covered in invoices, order forms and timber samples. 'Sorry to turn up again like a bad penny,' Charlie said.

Maberly grimaced but was too polite to complain. Shaking Charlie's hand, he said, 'Always keen to help.'

'How long have you been the manager?'

'Five years. That's what happens if you stick around long enough. Please, pull up a pew.'

He waited for Charlie to sit, then collapsed into the chair behind his desk. 'Not sure how I can help you, though. Is it the anniversary? Are they reopening the case?'

He struck Charlie as a mild man, trying hard. 'Just loose ends. But I'd dearly love to talk to Shane Lambert. Has he been in touch at all?'

'Shane? No.'

Maberly was wary now. As if to hide it he rocked back in his chair and laced his hands behind his head, revealing sweat marks under his arms. He was plump, constructed of overlapping rings like the Michelin man.

'Just thought I'd check,' Charlie said. 'You seemed to

be the only one he was friends with, and I was hoping he might have returned to the area.'

'Friends is stretching it, as I said before. I lived in Swanage back then and somehow found myself giving him rides to and from work.'

Found myself: Maberly had used those exact words before. What was the implication? That Lambert was manipulative? 'Hope you don't mind, but if we could rehash things, maybe you'll remember something I can run with?'

'I am busy...'

'Just a few quick questions. Shane quit around the time you helped him move out of my mother's house?'

Maberly was curt. 'A few days later, from memory.'

'How did he quit?'

'Called in sick but didn't show up again.'

'When, exactly, did the police come here?'

'I can't remember the exact date, but it was soon after your mother disappeared.'

'What did you tell them?'

'That I didn't really know him and certainly didn't know where he was.'

'They haven't contacted you again? Cold-case detectives over the years?'

'No.'

Slack, thought Charlie. 'You say you weren't friends with him. But you must have formed an opinion?'

Careful, Charlie told himself. You sound accusing.

Maberly thought so, too. He said stiffly, 'We've been over all this. Shane was the type of person to take you over. Manoeuvre you.'

'A powerful personality.'

'Not really. Quiet. Hard to read. But in a way that you'd be careful what you said and did around him.' Maberly paused. 'I can see why he made your mother feel uncomfortable. No one liked him really.'

'Did he have any other friends in the yard?'

'No. And like I said, I wasn't really friends with him, it's just that people thought we were.'

'What about friends outside the yard?'

'We've been over this. I have no idea.'

Feeling frustrated, Charlie said, 'So you never saw him with anyone at all?'

Maberly frowned. He sat forward, damply serious. 'Actually, now you mention it—a couple of blokes were here once. I thought they might have been police, they had that look about them. But if they were, they didn't hassle him. Had a quick word and shook hands and clapped him on the back and then they left.'

New information. Charlie thought about it. Got nowhere.

'What about where he went to live after the motel? He only stayed one night.'

Maberly shrugged. 'Couch-surfing, maybe? Not on my couch, though. Ask his cousin.'

'His cousin?'

'She came tearing in here a day or so after he quit, wanting to talk to him. Management passed her on to me.'

'See?' Charlie said. 'You didn't mention this before.'

Maberly shifted uncomfortably. 'I saw her in the street the other day, that's all. Not to talk to, but it reminded me.'

'What did she want when she came here?'

'She said something about he'd left her a message saying he needed to crash in her spare room for a while, but she couldn't get hold of him.'

Charlie trembled. 'And she wanted to tell him he could stay?'

A decisive headshake. 'No. The opposite. She was all steamed up, even had a go at me, as if I'd put him up to it.'

Maybe Lambert had more than one cousin. Charlie took out his phone, tapped the Facebook icon. 'Is this her?'

Maberly peered. 'Looks like her.'

On an impulse, Charlie swiped the screen again. 'How about these two?'

Images of Nadal and Deamer. Maberly looked and said, 'What's going on?'

'You know them?'

'They came here but I don't know them.'

'When?'

'A few days ago.'

Now Charlie had a part-explanation for Maberly's wariness. 'What did they want?'

'Same as you. Wanted to know about Shane. But I don't know them, so I didn't tell them anything.' Maberly looked troubled now; reluctant. 'Look, this is all getting a bit too strange for me. Who are they?'

'Making a podcast, so they say.'

Maberly clenched in alarm. 'About Shane and your mother? Why would I know anything about that?'

Charlie held up a hand. 'I believe you. I'm not sure what their podcast is about.'

Maberly subsided. He twisted his mouth. 'They showed me photos too.'

Charlie stiffened; waited.

'Four or five men, like I was supposed to know who they were.'

'And you didn't?'

'I didn't. Well…' He paused. 'I did recognise two of them. They were the ones who came here to see Shane that time.'

Charlie felt the creep of something nameless and alive. 'You recognised them after twenty years?'

Maberly backpedalled. 'I think it was them.'

Charlie didn't press the matter. 'Did you tell the podcasters you recognised them?'

Maberly winced. 'No. Was that wrong?'

'No. In fact, if they show up again, don't tell them anything,' Charlie said.

Maberly hunched miserably. He didn't want to get involved.

Charlie continued: 'So they gave no indication who these men were or why they were interested?'

Maberly pouted. 'It was like I was supposed to give and get nothing in return.'

'That's how the media operate,' Charlie nodded.

Same as the police, really, he thought, as he left the timber yard.

16

LATE MORNING NOW, Charlie heading out along Bittern–
Dromana Road and down through the cuttings to the
flatlands and Port Phillip Bay. The sea was glassy, two
container ships etched against it, and with his window
down Charlie could smell the salt air, laced with vehicle
exhaust and fried food.

He drove parallel to the shore, then left and uphill
again into the system of paved and unpaved side streets
where Maeve Frome lived. One car on the lawn this time, a
white Hyundai. No one on the deck. Rather than pull into

her driveway and have her recognise his car, he drove past her house and parked behind a dumpbin in the next street. Switched off, got out, walked.

Frome's house seemed to offer no ground-floor access, except possibly through the garage, which was closed. He climbed the steps to the deck and caught a glimpse of the Bay over the tops of the nearby trees. Melbourne floated there, too. No dreaming spires, just hazy glass tower blocks shirtfronting each other. The sun was high and hot; Charlie could almost feel it leaching the colour from the outdoor furniture. He rattled the glass sliding door with his knuckles.

A moment later it was swept open. 'Yeah?'

Maeve Frome wore shorts and a baggy white T-shirt. Solid legs and her feet were bare. Chipped scarlet nails. Watery eyes and springy grey hair. She was smoking; she took a drag and jetted the smoke at Charlie. 'Help you?'

Charlie decided on a mix of directness and evasion. 'I'm Charlie Deravin and it would mean a lot to me if I could have a word with you about Shane—Shane Lambert, your cousin.'

She stared at him, still expectant, but then slumped. Touching the tips of her fingers to her lips, she rubbed vigorously as if to seal them. I've lost her, Charlie thought, getting ready to leave, but she gathered herself and said, 'One, I haven't seen Shane for years. Two, I know who you are.'

Charlie felt awkward. 'Oh. Okay. Sorry to bother you.'

'Come in. I can give you a couple of minutes.'

Really? Feeling a kind of wonder, he followed her across an island of cream shag on a glossy wooden floor. She gestured at a bloated red leather sofa, took the matching armchair and rested her feet on a misshapen pouffe. Picked up a glass; rattled ice at him in a kind of toast.

Vodka? Gin? Giving her a grimace more than a smile, he said, 'You said you know who I am?'

'Deravin. Not a name you'd forget.'

Her voice and tone were harsh, but her face was sifted with traces of sadness and sympathy. She'd remembered the name for twenty years? Charlie realised he didn't know where to start.

She sensed that. Her voice was flat: 'You want to speak about Shane because he rented a room off your mother.'

'You've got a good memory.'

'My memory's fucked. But two reminders in one week?'

Charlie stared at her. Me, he thought, and the podcast twins. 'You had visitors.'

She shot him a suspicious look. 'Yellow VW. You sent them here?'

'God, no. Did they want to speak to Shane, or about Shane?'

'Both. What he was up to back then, where he was living. I told them I hardly ever saw him.'

A pause. Maeve Frome was awkward, looking for the words she wanted. 'I didn't like them. They were full of themselves, and they tried to get me to say I knew Shane was doing burglaries, like I was some kind of low-life. I told them to fuck off.'

'You did the right thing,' Charlie said. 'They've had a go at me, too.'

She nodded. 'Don't know what their game is, but it got me thinking about what happened to your mum.'

Charlie waited a beat. He said carefully, 'Shane worked in Hastings back then, and went to stay in a motel after… after he left my mother's place. Did he ever talk about that?'

Frome drew deeply, sustainingly, on a fresh cigarette. 'No. All I know is, after your mother, you know, went missing, he rang me to say the police might want a word— which they did—and could he stay a few nights.'

'And did he?'

Another bite of her cigarette. 'No. As soon as he said about the cops, I told him I didn't want his shit in my life, not with a couple of kids still at home.'

Charlie decided not to tell her what Maberly had said. 'Are they still living with you?'

'No. And you leave them out of this.'

'Are they in touch with Shane?'

'*Leave them out of it.*'

'Sorry.' Charlie held up his hands.

'They don't know anything. Wouldn't even remember him, it's been so long.'

'Okay. So the police contacted you…'

'Yeah, well, they wanted to interview Shane again and

couldn't find him and thought I might know where he was.'

'What about in the years since then? Any cold-case detectives been to see you?'

'Not a peep. Far as I know, Shane dropped off their radar.'

Charlie felt glum. Frome picked up on that and said, 'Look, he was a no-hoper. Still is, probably, but hurt someone? No way. Plus, he was in the Rosebud lockup the day it happened—I know, I had to go and pick him up the next morning.'

'All I want to do is talk to him.'

'Yeah, well, good luck finding him,' Frome said. She waved the smoke from her eyes. 'You don't mind? Should of asked you first.'

'It's your house,' Charlie said, gasping for breath in it.

'Yes, it is my house, and Shane's never lived here, no matter what them podcast people said.'

Charlie tensed. What had Nadal and Deamer heard? He said, 'But you used to hang out with him sometimes?'

Maeve looked into her glass as if hoping it had been replenished. 'Not that often. Maybe if I had've, things would've turned out different for him. He was in foster care when we were growing up. Our whole family was a bit fucked, actually, excuse the French.'

Treading carefully, Charlie said, 'When the podcast people said Shane was into burglaries, what do you think they meant by that?'

'I have no bloody idea.'

'Did you ever meet any of the people he hung out with?'

'No. Look, if he was stealing, it wouldn't have been hardcore, he just had trouble making good decisions. But he might of known people who'd hurt other people.' She wriggled her shoulders uncomfortably and added: 'The kind who might've hurt your mother. Why? No idea.'

Charlie nodded. His smile was sad. 'So you haven't seen him for twenty years? No letters, phone calls, Christmas cards?'

'No. He just disappeared. Maybe he was into something dodgy at the same time and got spooked when the police came sniffing around. He went walkabout.'

'For twenty years.'

Maeve drained her glass. 'He'll be up north somewhere. Andamooka, Lightning Ridge. Might be an opal millionaire by now.'

'Did he respond to your family reunion invitation?'

She gave him a look. 'You're a fucking sneak, aren'tcha? Is that how you found me? Facebook?'

Charlie shifted awkwardly. 'Something like that. Sorry.'

'No.' She was shaking her head at him. 'No, he hasn't responded.'

One last move. 'Do you have old photos I could look at? Shane with friends or family?'

Another look. 'If it'll get rid of you…'

She left the room, returned with a photo album and sat beside him. The sofa complained softly, tipping her thigh against his. 'These are the only ones I have.'

Her cousin as a small boy; as a teenager; at work. Charlie peered. 'That's the Hastings timber yard. His last job.'

'He had a friend there, don't know his name.'

17

WAS KEVIN MABERLY lying when he'd said Lambert wasn't his friend? Maybe. What was more likely, Lambert had lied about having a friend.

Charlie walked around to his car and drove it into the deceptive shade of tall gums at the bottom of Maeve Frome's street. Ten minutes later her Hyundai backed timorously onto the street and then uphill and left at the intersection. For all Charlie knew, she was headed down to her local Woolworths, but the Hyundai turned right at the end, then a short distance upslope to the freeway on-ramp.

That didn't tell him much: she might stay on it until Eastlink and the city, or take an exit to one of the intervening towns. Lunch in Mornington; the Kathmandu outlet in Frankston…

He tailed her for several kilometres, keeping well back, separated from her car by an Australia Post van, an SUV and a small truck hauling a ride-on mower. The sun beat down. He flipped the visor; fumbled in his shirt pocket for his sunglasses.

Frome exited the freeway inland of Mount Martha, down to a roundabout that led to Mornington in one direction, Balinoe in the other. She turned right onto Balinoe Road. Tailing her would be trickier now: one lane, fewer cars, a lower speed limit, so Charlie pulled over to the side, waited an agonising half-minute for another car to pass, then pulled out behind it. A few minutes went by, the road bending and dipping in and out of hollows, so that he thought he'd lost the Hyundai, but then, at the bottom of a hillslope near the Balinoe sportsground, a flare of brake lights: Frome was turning right, onto a street that formed the northern border of the town.

The intervening car also turned right. Charlie followed confidently until near the end, when it wheeled into a driveway, leaving him exposed. Holding back, he slowed and pulled to the side of the road, watching the Hyundai, now two hundred metres ahead. It turned right onto a narrow, potholed dirt road leading to an area Charlie had always found anomalous in such a prosperous beach town.

On one side of the road was a poultry farm with a rusted corrugated-iron roof and a ramshackle piggery which—literally—got up the townspeople's nose when there was a northerly. On the other side was a defunct boatbuilding yard and a collection of fibro shacks that housed a half-hearted experiment in communal living: a few grubby dreadlocked kids growing wizened vegetables and spinning wool for weekend markets. It was a local-traffic kind of town outcrop; even in mid-summer everything here seemed chilly, damp, untouched by the sun.

Charlie slowed at the road entrance and watched Frome turn into the boatyard. Then she was swallowed up by tin sheds and rusted hulls on blocks, so he drove on down the road and past the boatyard to where the track wound up into scrubby trees and a paddock of depressed alpacas. Here he stopped and fished out his binoculars. Frome had parked beside an old Kombi and a mould-streaked caravan skirted by dry grass.

He focused on the numberplates to be certain: South Australian, and there was the Coober Pedy sticker on the rear window. As he watched, a man stepped out of the caravan and gave Frome a quick hug. Charlie recognised him, too: the guy who'd been sweeping the sands of Balinoe Beach with a metal detector.

Charlie did a five-point turn on the narrow track, drove down to the boatyard and knocked on the caravan door. When the guy peered through the gap at him, he smiled. 'Shane?'

—

They got the recriminations out of the way—Lambert dismayed with Frome; Frome angry with Charlie—and invited him in. They both seemed tired: tired of life, and, maybe in Lambert's case, tired of hiding.

'Shane, I've been trying to find you for twenty years,' Charlie said.

'Why?'

'Just, you know, wanted answers.'

Lambert was smoking. He took a final draw on his cigarette and mashed the tip in a brimming ashtray. 'You along with everyone else. So, I pissed off out of here and up to Coober Pedy—where they don't ask questions. Kept my head down.'

Maeve Frome was sitting beside her cousin, separated from Charlie by the caravan's fold-down table. 'And don't you go reading anything into that,' she warned, leaning over the table, jutting her chin at him.

He raised his hands. 'I won't.' Turned to Lambert again and said, 'But you didn't need to leave—or hide. You were cleared.'

'Cleared, yeah.' Lambert narrowed his eyes. 'Something bad goes down, it's just safer for a bloke like me to be somewhere else. The cops had a second go at me—like everyone, they thought I knew things, saw things, knew the wrong kind of people…That's why you're here, isn't it?'

Time hadn't been kind to Lambert. The ungainly bulk

of late middle-age; sun-damaged skin and work-damaged hands; sunspots on his bald dome and greasy hair to his shoulders. Watery eyes. And he was hunched protectively over his ashtray as if the life he'd led was one where you guarded your possessions. Prison behaviour. But the guy hadn't been arrested since the day Rose Deravin disappeared, according to police records.

Lambert lit another cigarette and now Frome lit up too. The air thickened, already superheated from the midday sun beating down on the thin metal skin of the caravan.

'Why did you come back?'

'Getting too old for that kind of work. This here's like a caretaker position.'

Of a defunct boatyard. Frome saw the doubt in Charlie's face and said, 'The owner's a friend of mine. The place doesn't look like much but there's equipment and stuff locked in the sheds and Shane keeps an eye on it.'

'Free rent,' Lambert said.

Charlie nodded. 'Plus you do a bit of metal detecting down on the beach? I saw you the other day. Didn't recognise you, though.'

'I recognised you,' Lambert said. 'Thought, fuck, here we go. Beer?'

Charlie blinked. 'Sure.'

Lambert edged out and stood stiffly, the toll of hard physical labour. Charlie watched him limp to the fridge and bend into it. The metal detector leaned against a cupboard. There were few other possessions. Everything was neat and clean, but it was a place of faded laminex and swollen MDF. The hopelessness of poverty and ill health, he thought. Of a life put on hold.

Lambert returned with three cans of Foster's. They popped them and drank.

Charlie said, 'I won't stay long, don't want to hassle you, but if I could just ask a few questions…?'

Lambert shrugged. 'Knock yourself out.'

But Maeve intervened. With a glance at her cousin as if assessing his ability to look after himself, she told Charlie, 'Shane was questioned for hours back then. When I got there to collect him after his night in the lockup, detectives from Frankston showed up. I waited all day, practically.'

'Tell me about the arrest,' Charlie said.

Frome answered. 'He never done nothing to anyone. He went on a bender and got aggro with a cop and they locked him up.'

Lambert smiled at her, patted her hand. 'It's okay, I can tell it.'

He turned to Charlie. 'No hard feelings about you and your brother asking me to leave your mother's house, all right?'

Charlie nodded.

'I wasn't the best tenant,' Lambert said. 'And it was good, you blokes paying for me to stay in the motel. But, you know, I was a bit of a mess back then, drinking and whatnot. Plus, I couldn't stay on in the woodyard, I was stoned half the time. I nearly cut my own hand off once. So

I quit. I couch-surfed for a bit, then went over to Dromana to ask if Maeve would put me up.'

He shot her an apologetic look. 'She wasn't there, but the kids were. Troy, the eldest, shut the door in my face and so I went to the pub and started drinking and the rest, as they say...'

Charlie let him talk. It was all useful context, but he knew he'd soon outstay his welcome. Maeve Frome was clearly protective of her cousin this time around. She'd lied to the podcast twins, lied to Charlie, and Charlie reckoned he had until she reached the last mouthful of beer before she told him to wrap it up.

'Before I go,' he said, 'could I ask about the last few days and weeks you were renting from my mother?'

'Sure. Don't know what I can tell you, but.'

'Was she seeing anyone?'

'Anyone like a boyfriend?'

'Yes. Or anyone she spent time with.'

A shrug. 'Me and her went our separate ways, really.'

'Anyone, man or woman, friend or otherwise. Anyone you heard her on the phone to.'

'I wasn't there that long. Started renting...what? A week or two before Christmas? She went to a couple of school break-up sessions in the pub, I think.'

'She told you?'

'Just chatting, you know.'

'Which pub?'

'No idea.'

'Anyone come to see her at the house?'

Lambert grew guarded. 'Couple of teacher mates.'

'Do you remember their names?'

'Sharon…no, Karen something. And a bloke, once, after Christmas.'

'A bloke.'

'Mate, I don't know. It was her life, and it was a bloody long time ago.'

'But a bloke.'

'Yeah, I said.' Lambert was testy now. 'One of the teachers, I think. I don't think she wanted him there.'

'Okay. You said you couch-surfed with some mates after you left?'

The watery eyes went flat, and Charlie saw the Lambert of twenty years ago: the powerful ease of him, a man unimpressed, as he'd stood in the road and stared at the Deravin boys. 'Mate,' he said, 'I know where you're going with this. I grew up in foster care. I never got close to no one. Never hung around with no one would do what you're thinking.'

Maeve Frome set her empty beer can down with a sharp metallic this-interview-is-finished slap.

18

TO SHAKE OFF his feelings of uselessness, Charlie kicked a garden edging stone when he got home, then a weed clump, then decided to trim the side hedge. The satisfying snap of the blades, the tendrils falling victim at his feet.

Mrs Ehrlich leaned over and said, 'Didn't know you had a green thumb.'

Charlie peered at her through the hedge. 'I don't. My approach is strictly slash and burn.' He paused. 'My mother was the cultivator.'

'That she was,' Mrs Ehrlich said. She paused. 'Actually, Charlie, if you're so keen on slashing and burning, the Foreshore Preservation mob's having a working bee on Sunday.'

Anna was coming down on Saturday. 'I might be busy...'

'She can help us, too,' said Mrs Ehrlich—the witch.

Late Sunday morning saw Charlie and Anna on the clifftop overlooking the sea with a dozen other volunteers, planting indigenous grasses, ripping out weeds. Weeds: that was a laugh. As Mrs Ehrlich said, they were toiling away beneath a stand of pine trees, the biggest, most prevalent weed on the Peninsula.

Charlie reached his trowel to the base of a flourishing bit of grass. Hesitated and said, 'This?'

'Charlie, Charlie, Charlie,' Mrs Ehrlich said. 'A weed. It can go.'

Anna, on the other side of her, shot him a grin. Affecting nonchalance, he dug out the weed, shook the dirt from the roots, tossed it into the barrow, then bent and dug and pulled again in the calm, filtered light, an eye open for snakes. He'd never seen one up here on the cliff, but some of the others had. His back ached. He wanted to be out on the water, he wanted to be in Anna's arms, and he wasn't at first aware that Mrs Ehrlich had said something about a cavalcade of police cars.

He rocked back on his heels. 'Say that again?'

'At least a dozen of them,' she said. 'One after the other.'

'Going through Balinoe?'

'Yes.'

'When?'

She looked at him oddly: pay attention, Charles. 'Mid-morning. I was doing a shop before I came here.'

'Did you see where they were going?'

'Not really. I was trying to turn into the Ritchies carpark and had to pull into the dentist's driveway to let them through.'

'Sirens?'

Mrs Ehrlich shook her head and stood to swipe at a tendril of damp hair with the back of her wrist. It was going to be a hot day. Her bony knees were grubby pale orbs under the cuffs of baggy khaki shorts. 'They weren't all police cars. Two had crime scene written on the side.'

Meth lab? Charlie stood to ease the strain in his back. Out there, glimpsed through the bushes and trees, breakers were rolling. Perfect surfing conditions, according to his phone app. Perfect making love conditions. He looked across at Anna, who was weeding efficiently, effortlessly.

He pointed. 'What about that one, Mrs E?'

'It's indigenous, Charles, you may safely leave it in the ground.'

He pointed at a tiny blackberry plant. 'That one?'

She gave him a look his daughter often gave him: he wasn't as funny as he thought he was.

They wound up at noon, went home and ate lunch in the shade. Then Charlie suggested a swim.

'Sounds good,' Anna said.

'I'll check tide times.' Charlie swiped at his phone.

Good: the tide was pretty high. He checked his emails. There was only one, from the police credit union. Finally the news feed.

Skeletal remains found during excavation work at an address in Swanage.

19

THOSE POLICE CARS.

Charlie's first thought: Mum. The remains were skeletal, but if her teeth were intact and DNA could be extracted from the bones...

Notify Dad and Fay, he thought. Tell Liam.

Charlie was clenched. He didn't know enough. He didn't know what his next step should be. And no reason to assume it was his mother, given that her car had been abandoned over in Tooradin.

Anna cut in on his thoughts. 'Charlie?'

He looked up, his mind still racing. Something in his face alarmed her. She reached her hand to his, then jerked back, swearing. 'Splinter!'

He watched her pick and dig at her thumb with the fingernails of her other hand. He watched her bite the flesh. She was a stranger at that moment, remote from him. She said, 'Charlie! Stop it, you're scaring me.'

Charlie shook himself. 'Sorry. Did you get it out?'

She peered at her thumb again. 'All good. What's the matter?'

Charlie passed her his phone. 'I think they've found my mother.'

'Alive?' she said, tapping to wake the screen. 'Sorry, stupid question.'

She narrowed her eyes and swiped up and said, 'Quote: "declared a crime scene."'

Makes sense, thought Charlie. A body buried is suspicious enough. And maybe there were suspicious injuries: broken hyoid bone, crushed skull, evidence of knife or bullet trauma.

He felt Anna's hand slide into his. The world came back to him: the sounds and smells of the sea; the birds; the coins of sunlight on the tabletop and Alby tinkering with his ute again. These were the sounds of Charlie's life as he thought about death. First, the remains would have to be identified. An autopsy to determine the probable cause and time of death. A check of the property records, missing persons files. Doorknock the neighbourhood.

'Earth to Charlie, you're zoning out again.'

He blinked. 'Sorry.'

He realised Anna was kneading his knuckles with her thumb. He checked his phone again—this time they had video.

His mother's street.

He double-checked. The camera panned: a sign—*Longstaff St*—and the road out of Swanage, then the top of the water tower behind the pine trees before returning to a pair of patrol cars parked snout to snout at the entrance to the street. Finally, a long-distance shot along it—and there was his mother's old house at the mid-point.

But the main activity was at the end. The house slab. Forensic vans and marked and unmarked police cars parked outside it. Figures in uniform and plain clothes standing around, observing; others in forensic suits coming and going from a crime-scene tent, evidence bags in hand.

'Charlie?'

He placed the phone on the table, spun it around on its back, tapped the screen. 'That's the street my mother was living in when she disappeared.'

'Oh, Charlie.' She put her nose to the phone. 'Are they at a vacant block?'

As she said it, she exchanged an alarmed look with him, a simultaneous dread, the words 'vacant block' somehow making it so much worse. Seeing him swallow, she reached out her hand again. 'Can you ring someone for more information?'

'Doubt it. I was sex crimes—my old sergeant won't be in that loop. And I don't know anyone at any of the local police stations.'

'You were in the Homicide Squad for a while.'

'Years ago. Things change. People move on.'

'Charlie, why don't you go there.'

'Mum's street?'

Anna was definite. 'It can't hurt. You might see someone there with answers. Don't you want to find out?'

'Of course I do, but I know how things work, I'd be told to stand back or move on. If it's Mum I'll find out soon enough.'

'But what if it takes days before they notify you? What if it's not her body? It could be a man's. It could have been there for a hundred years, or, or…five. What if no one tells you anything and you just have to wait? Go down there, find someone in authority and say who you are and why you have a legitimate reason to be there. I'll come with you.'

Charlie was halfway tempted. 'I know how cops think, though. I'm trying to insert myself into the investigation, therefore I must be a suspect.'

'You have the perfect alibi. Didn't you tell me you were searching for a missing kid when she disappeared? You're her son, for god's sake, they can't deny you.'

Charlie was touched. It had been a while since anyone cared, since anyone had been supportive of him. He glanced down at the phone again. 'I doubt they'll let us

148

in. The street's blocked off. They won't be letting cars get anywhere near there.'

'Ride your bike.'

She grabbed his hand again. They were still getting to know each other, and here she was, in an extreme of emotion on his behalf. What did that say about him, that he couldn't accept it? Was it really such a good thing, the jaded old Charlie? 'Okay.'

Her expression softened; her fingers were mobile in his. 'Can you dink me?'

He gave her a crooked grin. 'Not such a good idea. You can ride Emma's old bike.'

'This is going to test muscles I didn't know I had,' Anna said later.

She was puffing next to Charlie up the stretch of Balinoe Beach Road between the store and the Frankston–Flinders Road intersection, where they would turn onto the road to Swanage. He grunted; his mind was full.

A little Audi overtook them with a neat flick, followed by a bulky Land Cruiser, which laboured by, trailing the stink of its ageing motor. As the sound receded, Anna said, 'Sore bum, sore everything.'

Charlie ignored her and, at the top, waited for traffic before shooting across to join the bike path. He stopped, turned around, watched her catch up. He shook himself into order again. Now that he'd decided, he was impatient to reach Longstaff Street and was behaving like a prick.

'Sorry.'

She touched his sleeve. 'Gentle pace, okay?'

'Okay.'

But a few minutes later his legs were pistoning again as he planned their route to Longstaff Street. Come in from the Westernport end, he thought, not through the town. He rode on, farmland on either side, until he neared the roundabout downslope of the water tower. Here he stopped, one foot on the ground, and looked back. Anna was toiling gamely a few hundred metres behind him. He waited. She pulled up, a complicated expression of hurt, anger and sympathy on her face.

He stretched his fingers to her sweaty neck. 'Sorry.'

She shrugged away the offending hand. 'Can I say something? If you go in all fired up, you're going to piss people off. Be polite. Wait and see, watch for a while, till you know who to approach.'

He took a breath in. 'You're right.'

He touched her neck again and she turned her head, gave the back of his hand a quick kiss and said, 'I'm soaked.'

Charlie reached down, unclipped his water bottle. 'Here.'

He watched her swig from it. 'Good?'

'Better.'

He reclipped the bottle, swiped the sweat from his eyes and pointed to the roundabout a hundred metres ahead. 'That's where we turn. It's not far then, just over the rise.'

But there was a patrol car blocking the way into

Swanage, a uniform diverting approaching traffic around the roundabout and away again. Most of the cars simply rolled through and drove on, but some had parked on the grassy verges of the approach roads: a low-slung, hotted-up car playing loud doof; a station wagon; the leaky Land Cruiser from a few minutes ago; a minibus.

If they've blocked this entrance to the town, they'll have blocked the other, Charlie thought.

At that moment a shout, a whistle. A small SUV marked Peninsula FM had pulled up at the roadblock, the driver gesticulating, the traffic cop shaking his head. 'Perfect opportunity,' Anna said, grinning, streaking down the bike path.

Charlie raced after her, to the roundabout and then up the slope into this back part of Swanage, trailed by shouts and the shrill of a police whistle. Reaching the top, they dismounted and walked their bikes the short distance down to the entrance to Longstaff Street.

It was crammed with outside broadcast vans, cameras, reporters, townspeople and police. Propping his bike against a hedge, Charlie removed his helmet and swigged from the water bottle, Anna joining him. That earned them a cold glance from the woman nearest them: *ghouls; stickybeaks*.

Or maybe it's the stink of sweat, thought Charlie. He smiled at her. 'Have they made any announcements?'

Her expression shifted into distaste now—but she bit down on it and muttered, 'No.'

'Any theories?'

She moved away from him. 'You know as much as I do.'

'Awful thing to happen. You live here?'

Faintly mollified, the woman pointed. 'Next street down.'

The three of them stood there with the others and the minutes passed. Charlie tried to work out how he could slip past the half-dozen constables who formed a cordon across the entrance to the street. Then, a disturbance: a black BMW police pursuit car was drawing up, followed by an unmarked Passat. Cameras swung around, expectant; microphones reached. Nothing happened for a couple of minutes, until the BMW peeled away again and the Passat, edging closer to the side of the road, bumped its passenger side wheels up onto the footpath. Two women got out, one young and stocky, the other slight, middle-aged, her reddish hair turning grey.

Charlie watched them sign the log ready to walk down Longstaff to the crime scene—and something caught his attention, a tilt of the head. He knew the older detective. Except she'd been in uniform…Beckman? Bekker. She'd overseen the search for Billy Saul.

A small world, the police world. Last year, investigating a rape in Shepparton, he'd liaised with a uniformed sergeant who'd attended detective school with him and later switched back to uniform. But now he was sprinting, shouting: '*Ms Bekker.*'

She turned, expressionless.

The younger woman whirled around to face him with one hand raised, the other gesturing wildly to the nearby uniforms. She shirtfronted Charlie, shouting: 'Stop right there. Who the hell are you? What do you want?'

'To speak to Senior Constable Bekker.'

'That's Senior Sergeant Bekker.'

'I need to speak to her.'

Bekker's hard-featured offsider ignored him. At her nod the uniforms came in on either side of Charlie and gripped his upper arms. A voice in his ear: 'Sir, I have to ask you to move along.'

Charlie looked past the stocky detective at Bekker, calling, 'I'm Charlie Deravin. Is it my mother?'

Bekker was expressionless. Then she nodded; she'd made the connection. With a sigh she left the cordon and joined her colleague.

A tired-looking woman with busy eyes, she said, 'What are you doing here, Mr Deravin?'

'Is it my mother?'

Bekker watched him for a long beat, then nodded to the uniforms. 'Let him go.'

'Is it my mother?'

'It is not your mother.'

Charlie almost protested. But that would be stupid. He slumped. 'You're sure?'

'Yes.'

She turned to go. Charlie, badly wanting her to stay, babbled absurdly, 'Are you still based at Rosebud?'

'I joined the Homicide Squad, Mr Deravin. Now, I understand your concern, the conclusion you jumped to, but I must ask you to leave. Go home. We have found human remains, but they do not belong to your mother.'

Hands steered Charlie away, then gently prodded. He stumbled towards Anna; she gathered him in; people watched, gleaming and hungry.

'Let's go.'

'Is it her?'

'No.'

She hugged him. Her shirt was damp, her temples, her face, but he didn't care. Her strength flowed into him.

They mounted their bikes and rode back to the roundabout; turned left for Balinoe. Still the cars were arriving and still the traffic cop turned them away. More were parked now. They pedalled past a line of them, Anna leading, and Charlie saw her slow and wobble alongside the ditch—another cyclist was on the path, streaking towards them. Looked like…yes, it was Mark Valente.

Charlie braked, coming in to join Anna as he heard a clunky engine labour into life behind him and was aware of nothing else before something—solid, inevitable—struck his back wheel and flipped him onto his head.

20

A SPECIALIST WAS hovering in mid-sentence when Charlie opened his eyes.

'Where am I?'

Like specialists everywhere, this one hated to be interrupted. An older guy doing his rounds with a retinue of kids in white coats, he glanced at his watch. 'Frankston.'

Clearly not Frankston Private, thought Charlie. This hospital was a gamely struggling place of noise and underfunding, and he was in a bed curtained off from other beds, other poor souls going into or recovering from procedures and—*pain*. Acute pain. Not skull deep, brain deep—and right now pressing behind his left eye. He put a hand to it, but that strained parts of his torso that wanted to be left alone. He sank back against the pillow, both eyes squinting, spine straight, not daring to risk further movement. 'Was I out for long?'

Another question. With exquisite distaste the specialist said, 'Apparently you recovered consciousness in the ambulance for a short time. Do you recall?'

'No.'

'In addition to a very nasty crack to the head, your ankle was twisted.'

Charlie couldn't make sense of any of it. 'Ankle?'

A new face appeared; she'd been standing beside him at the head of the bed all this time. 'It got caught in the pedal.'

Pedal—bicycle.

Charlie gave her a thankful look. Suzi, according to the name tag. Tatts, half-shaved neon-pink hair, piercings and a sweet smile.

He returned to the specialist. 'But I was wearing a helmet.'

The old patrician tugged back his sleeve again, read his watch face and said, 'Not all bicycle helmets provide sufficient protection from transverse or lateral impacts.'

He waited a microsecond for that to sink in. 'Rest. You will be monitored for concussion overnight and, all being well, you may go home in the morning.'

Charlie wanted to demur, but they all swept out, leaving him with Suzi, who wheeled him through corridors to a private room. Private. Would his insurance cover it? She got him settled and flicked about the room: water jug; patient chart; venetian blinds. Still light outside but light of the long, low kind: late afternoon. He must have lost a couple of hours of his life.

Suddenly Anna was there in his head, behind the pain. He said, a croak in his voice: 'I was with…Did someone…'

Sentences were troublesome, so were sentence fragments. Thought fragments. He tried again. 'I was riding with a friend.'

Suzi gave him a look of sweet regret. 'Sorry, I don't know the circumstances, only that you were knocked off your bike. But you do have a visitor. Just let me finish here…'

A minute later she hurried out. And Charlie thought: Anna, but Emma hurtled in, saying, 'Daddy!' and he thought: How could I have forgotten I have a daughter?

'Careful,' he said, wreathed in smiles and pain as she threw herself against him.

She jerked back, her dismayed face fringed by sun-bleached hair. 'Sorry!'

'It's fine. I'm fine. Sit.'

Thin, leggy, summery, Emma eyed the edge of her father's bed and rejected it, her gaze settling on the only chair, which was against the wall, under the TV, and the same non-colour as the room, upholstered in the same

157

non-fabric as the floor. Swinging it out of its hidey-hole, she sat close to Charlie's bedside cabinet. 'I was so worried.'

'How did you know I was here?'

'Mark. Mr Valente. He called Mum; Mum called me.'

Jess was holidaying on Norfolk Island. Charlie visualised the calls bouncing around the world, across the seas. 'But how did you get here?'

'The train. Mark picked me up at the station.'

Charlie patted the back of her hand. 'I'm glad you're here, but really, I'm fine.'

'Don't be an idiot. Don't be a martyr.'

She's like her mother, he thought. 'Did Mark stick around?'

She nodded. 'He's here somewhere.'

It was a strain on Charlie's neck, looking up at his daughter from the pillow. He scooted back, pushing down on the mattress for purchase, and the world spun. 'Whoa.'

'Here,' she said, helping him.

'I was riding with a friend,' he said.

'I know. Mark told me.'

'Is she okay? No one's told me anything.'

'Mark said her leg was banged up pretty bad. They took her to the Austin.'

Charlie closed his eyes.

'She's the one you've been seeing? Anna?'

Charlie croaked, 'Yeah.'

'I hope she'll be okay.'

'Me too.'

'I told Uncle Liam, but I don't know if I should tell Grandpa and Fay, it would worry them.'

'Yeah, don't tell them, I'm going home in the morning anyway. Somehow.'

'All organised. Mark's taking me home to your place, and I'll sleep there and drive back here in your car in the morning.'

'My god—up before noon again.'

'That's getting a bit old, Dad.'

In the doorway behind her a cop voice spoke. 'Mr Deravin? A few questions, if you please.'

21

PLAIN CLOTHES. A MAN and a woman at the fag-end of a long day. When Emma excused herself, they came in, faces blank, a job to do, introducing themselves as Major Collision Unit officers, a leading senior constable named Grieve and a constable named Ransome.

'Major collision? This was attempted murder.'

Grieve took her time. Younger- and smarter-looking than Ransome, she settled into Emma's chair, first pulling it away from the bed. Ransome meanwhile propped himself against the doorframe and seemed to zone out.

He was racked with yawns that showed too many teeth, accompanied each time by a little recovering shudder; recovering eyeblinks, another yawn.

Charlie yawned. 'I said, this was attempted murder.'

Ransome stirred. 'We heard you.'

Is that how it's going to be? thought Charlie. I have to watch both of them? He focused on Grieve. 'It wasn't an accident.'

'The heart of the matter,' Grieve said. 'What do you remember?'

'Look, before we go any further, I haven't been awake for long and no one's told me what's going on. All I know is, I was knocked off my bike and might have concussion. But I was riding with a friend and I need to know how she is. And no bullshit.'

Grieve pulled the chair closer. Too close. Charlie retreated along the pillow, his head complaining.

'She's in the Austin. Nothing life-threatening—in fact, she was able to give a statement—but she has a broken leg and a possible rib fracture.'

'So I wasn't imagining it, he ran into her as well as me.'

Grieve cocked her head. 'You witnessed it?'

'No. It's just an impression I have. I heard a vehicle start up behind me, the rest is a blur.'

Grieve chewed her bottom lip. 'We think the front bumper hit your back wheel and went on to hit Miss Picard side-on, in the leg. Not a high-speed impact, but enough to hurt you both.'

Memories were returning. 'There were people around.'
Namely, Mark Valente.

'We do have a witness.'

'And?'

Grieve said stiffly, 'This person believes you were run over deliberately. Why would that be, Mr Deravin?'

'Did this witness see the driver? Have you made an arrest? Have you found the vehicle?'

'Steady on, a question at a time. What can you tell us about the vehicle?'

Over by the door, Ransome yawned again, audibly. Charlie wished the guy would just go home. 'Seems like you get to ask questions and I don't. If I'm not mistaken, we were run over by an old Land Cruiser, dirty white, mounted with a bull bar.'

'You saw it?'

'A couple of times.'

'It was following you?'

'Putting words in my mouth, Leading Senior Constable Grieve?'

'Gathering facts, Mr Deravin.'

Charlie pushed the headache away, looking for the words he wanted, clear words, and proceeded to tell Grieve about Anna, the first Kessler trial, the words spray-painted on Anna's door.

Grieve nodded as he spoke but said nothing. She already knows, he thought.

'It'll be one of Kessler's footy-club mates,' he said.

Grieve gave him an empty smile. Charlie knew all about empty cop smiles. This one was replete with intel she didn't intend to share.

'Have you found the vehicle?'

She ignored that. 'What can you tell us about the driver?'

Charlie concentrated. The pain shifted to his right eye socket and hammered him for a while. 'Honestly? Nothing. Didn't occur to me I'd have to ID him later. A youngish bloke, that's the main impression I got.'

Grieve signalled to Ransome, who handed her a laptop from a briefcase. 'Some photos we'd like you to look at.'

Charlie gave her a long look. Quick work, he thought. Mark's description must have meshed with Anna's. Maybe she'd even recognised the driver. 'Already?'

'I can't comment on that, Mr Deravin,' Grieve said, loading the screen and proceeding to recite the arse-covering preamble he himself had recited plenty of times—to rape victims.

He scrolled through a mix of booking photos and candid shots. Young men with attitude, with shaven domes, mullets, crewcuts, designer tousles and unwashed mops.

And Jake Allardyce. Inspector Allardyce's son.

But Charlie was a fair man. 'Could be any of these. I didn't see his face. Maybe try hypnosis on me?'

'That won't be necessary,' Grieve said, resettling the chair under the TV, where it seemed to vanish into the wall paint before she returned to the bed. 'Here's my card. If you do remember anything, however minor, give me call. Hope you get better soon.'

They reached the door and Charlie shouted, 'Wait!'

Grieve raised an eyebrow. 'Yes?'

'Anna, my friend—you going to protect her?'

Grieve nodded as if weighing the merits. Nodded, smiled with some warmth, and left Charlie there, his mind racing.

22

HE WAITED FOR EMMA. She didn't return. He dozed and woke to find a cling-wrapped sandwich and a pot of tea. He picked and sipped, the sandwich stale, the tea lukewarm, and pushed it all away. Anna. Where was his phone? He checked the bedside cabinet. House keys, wallet, phone. The screen was cracked, but it powered up, responded to his touch and reached out to Anna's phone.

Rang and rang. A kind of dread lodged in him, until a strained, last-minute voice snatched a reply. 'Hello? You've reached the number for Anna Picard.'

'This is Charlie Deravin. I'm a friend of Anna's, we were—'

'I know who you are, Charlie. It's Andrea, Anna's sister.'

The tone was neutral. Condemnatory would be better. Or recognition that he had a stake in the whole sorry business.

Charlie floundered on, not knowing where he stood with the Picard clan. 'Oh, hi, just calling to see how she is. Can I speak to her by any chance?'

Gentler now, tinged with regret: 'Actually, Charlie, she's asleep, but I know she'd love to talk to you. Maybe call her in the morning?'

'Will do.'

Time passed again. Still no Emma. He grabbed his phone when it pinged: a string of WhatsApp photos from Fay and his father: the ship again, harbour markets, misty mountains and Rhys singing karaoke, the images shifting and splintering as Charlie tilted his smashed-up screen.

He texted a vague reply, then texted his daughter—*All clear*—and slumped back on his pillow in a flare of pain. He explored it: still deep, still not content to settle in one place, sending warning signals from the outposts. His left eye, then his right. The crown, the back of the scalp, and all through his soul like a full-body toothache.

He squinted, swiped at a tear, and saw that he had visitors again.

'Charles.'

Charlie scooted his spine along the mattress and up against his pillow and the world tilted. 'Senior Sergeant,' he croaked.

Frances Bekker took another step into the room, then to one side, revealing her tough little offsider. 'Charlie, this is Detective Senior Constable McGuire.'

McGuire nodded, filling the doorway as if to stop Charlie from bolting. She was expressionless—if you didn't count the gleam in her eye. A cop on the hunt.

'I've already spoken to the accident people,' Charlie said.

Bekker nodded. 'We saw them in the foyer. They filled us in on what happened.'

Charlie tried to read her. 'What do you want?'

'May we come in?'

They were already in, but Charlie nodded. Regretted it. His hand went to his eyes and Bekker was murmuring, 'We won't stay long,' as she settled onto the edge of his bed, a few centimetres from his feet, a development that alarmed him on almost every level. It seemed intimate, but he doubted that was her intent. It was presumptuous. He was helpless and she knew it.

'What do you want?'

'We came here initially to see if your accident, for want of a better word, had anything to do with your extra-curricular activities.'

Charlie's eye leaked again. He swiped at it cautiously. 'Extra-curricular?'

'We've had a complaint,' said McGuire from the foot of the bed.

'Or rather,' said Bekker, 'a phone call from a man who wanted to know if we suspect him of something.'

McGuire said, 'What can you tell us about that?'

A question Charlie had been asked too many times in the aftermath of shoving Inspector Allardyce in the chest. Mostly he chose not to answer. This time he couldn't answer since he didn't know what they were talking about.

'Who?'

'Fellow called Kevin Maberly. Know him?'

Charlie was astonished. 'He was the one who ran me over?'

Bekker's smile said, don't waste my time. 'You went to see him, Charlie. Grilled him, to use his words. Why would you do that?'

Charlie felt like a schoolkid challenged by a teacher and not up to it. The pain shifted again, lodging behind both eyes, but this time bringing clarity, unblocking his neural pathways. 'I was doing what the police have failed to do for twenty years—looking into my mother's case. It's interesting that you think it might be connected to someone running over me.'

'We did wonder,' Bekker said, 'but for the life of us can't see a connection.'

She patted his sprained foot. He jumped, and she jerked back her hand: 'Sorry!'

Charlie still couldn't read her but knew there was

something else going on. 'You didn't come here just to tell me off.'

Bekker nodded slowly, weighing up her words. 'We think we've found Billy Saul.'

Charlie opened and closed his mouth. For twenty years he'd been seeing Billy Saul's body tumbling as the tides surged, pulled back, surged again. The shredding rocks. The sea creatures nibbling and chewing. He shook that off and said, 'You asked to be assigned to this, right? When you got word it was a kid?'

Her face was neutral: she wasn't going to admit to an obsession with the Billy Saul case. But then she surprised him. 'That's partly true. You could say my antenna was up and working. Then word came in that they'd found a watch with the remains. Billy's name was engraved on the back.'

Charlie shook his head in wonder. 'All these years we thought he'd drowned. So either someone snatched him from the beach or staged it as a drowning.'

'That's for my squad to decide, Charlie. Meanwhile, we're hoping to obtain DNA.'

'Right,' said Charlie absently, thinking about the beach towel. The search for Billy Saul: the vivid day, full of gumtrees ticking in the still heat; the salty sea in his nose; the metallic taste of the water from the youth camp's kitchen tap.

Now he skipped twenty years and visualised the disinterment, the transportation of the remains, the autopsy table, the extraction of DNA for a familial match.

The world receded, flooded back again. He heard electric beeps from another room and the lights were unforgiving, the air super-sanitised. 'How did he die?'

Bekker got to her feet. 'I want you to keep this to yourself, understood? Head injuries. Severe trauma.'

'Accident?'

McGuire gave Charlie the sleepy-eyed look of an accuser. 'Even if it was, someone covered it up.'

An insinuating thread in her tone, and Charlie bristled. 'Is that right?'

'Interesting that your mother's car was found with damage to the front.'

Charlie lifted himself in the bed and everything pulled and twisted. 'Well aren't you a piece of work?'

Bekker intervened. 'Enough, the pair of you.'

She stood, looking down at Charlie. 'Hope you feel better soon, Mr Deravin. I'm glad it wasn't worse.'

Charlie eyed her for the hidden meanings. Found none. 'Okay, thank you.'

'Stop playing detective, Charlie, please?'

And they were gone.

But they hadn't gone far. Charlie heard Bekker's low voice in the corridor. 'If it isn't Mark Valente.'

'And behold, she appeared upon a white horse.'

'Oh christ, I'd forgotten that about you. Thought you'd retired to the Gold Coast. Noosa, somewhere like that?'

'I winter up there, summer down here.'

'All right for some,' Bekker said.

'Heard you'd moved on from uniform, Fran.'

'For my sins.'

A pause. 'You're here bothering my boy?'

'Oh, is he your boy?'

'Known him forever,' Valente said. 'This is his daughter, Emma. Em, Senior Sergeant Bekker.'

Charlie heard tension in Emma's voice as she said hello and asked: 'What do you need my dad for?'

'Just paying our respects, nothing more.'

'I bet,' Valente said.

'Well, better be off,' Bekker said. 'Bye, Mark. Bye, Emma.'

Over his daughter's soft, 'Bye,' Charlie heard Valente say, 'Don't hurry back.'

Then, as squeaky footsteps receded along the corridor, Emma charged in calling, 'Daddyo,' and throwing herself onto Charlie's chest again before she could stop herself.

He gasped. 'Careful.'

'Sorry!'

Looking past her shoulder he saw Mark Valente, a bulky form filling the doorway. 'Mark.'

'Champ.'

Emma swung the chair beside the bed again. 'What did the toe cutters want?' She grinned over her shoulder at Valente.

Charlie was economical with the truth. 'The body they

found. They think it's Billy Saul, a kid who went missing around the time your grandmother did.'

She looked confused. He could see her mind working. And then Valente came further into the room. 'As I recall, you were on the search party.'

Charlie nodded. He stopped doing that when the pain arced behind his eyes. '*Christ.*'

Emma's face creased. 'Dad, you okay?'

Charlie squinted at her, feeling deeply fatigued. 'I'm fine.'

She got to her feet. 'No, you need to rest. Mark will take me home and I'll pick you up in the morning.'

But she was biting her bottom lip. She thinks I'll fall asleep and not wake up, he thought. He said, 'Go. I'll be fine. They'll monitor me all through the night.'

She wasn't convinced, but said, 'Okay.'

Valente gave her shoulder a little pat as he stepped past her and approached the bed, his massive paw out. 'Hope you have a restful sleep.'

He's getting old, Charlie thought, as he shook hands. Almost seventy. Losing hair, losing weight, losing…force. Funny that he hadn't noticed before. 'Mark, I need to thank you.'

Valente waved that off. 'Happy to give her a lift.'

'Well, thank you for that, too—but I meant thank you for earlier, the accident.'

Valente shrugged. 'I was upon that barren street.'

Emma, behind him, rolled her eyes at Charlie. He

fought down a grin. 'You saw it all happen?'

'I did.'

'Was it you who called the ambulance? How was…?'

'She was conscious. In a lot of pain, though.'

Charlie closed his eyes.

'So I, you know, stayed with her and talked,' Valente said awkwardly.

Now Charlie was reluctant for either of them to leave. The world was busy all around him as the wards prepared for the dark hours. 'Did you see who was driving?'

'I gave a description to the major collision team, if that's what you mean.'

'And?'

'Let the experts do their job, sunshine. Get some rest.'

Another spasm behind Charlie's eyes. Emma saw it and said, 'Dad, he's right—get some rest. I'll see you in the morning.'

She kissed him and then Charlie was alone. The evening deepened. Memories returned—urgently, so that he swung his legs out of the bed, placed his feet on the industrial-grade carpet and stood, thinking that to be upright was the cure he needed. But he blanked and swayed and a passing nurse grabbed him. 'Whoa, not a good idea.'

This one was Shireen. Dressed differently from Suzi. Agency nurse? She settled him and raced away again, and he dozed, and the night grew fully dark outside. Dark and deep, he thought. Suzi appeared, flicked around his room and said she was going home.

Charlie was reluctant to sleep. If he slept, concussion would claim him. So he turned on the TV—and realised that he was watching breaking news. Longstaff Street in darkness, men and women working under scorching lights.

A second body, under the first.

23

NO ONE ELSE came for him that evening. No one came to grill him or play cop interrogation games and finally he slept, and in the morning showered, picked at his breakfast and read the news feed on his phone as he waited for Emma. She appeared at 9.15. He was home by 9.45.

The second remains were those of an adult female, according to the news, and Bekker and McGuire were on his doorstep by ten o'clock.

'We called the hospital, they said you'd already been discharged.'

Something solemn about the pair of them there at his door when the morning air was so sweet to Charlie, the pull and surge of the sea so mournful. 'It's my mother, right?'

'May we come in?' Bekker said. She cocked her head to take in the lump, the graze on his temple. 'If you're up to it.'

Charlie looked past Bekker at the street. Mrs Ehrlich, washing her car. Otherwise Tidepool was still. 'You can come in if you're quiet. My daughter's here, she's still asleep.'

She'd gone back to bed, in fact, explaining that she'd barely slept. Worried about his concussion.

'We need a DNA sample, Charlie, you understand— then we'll be out of your hair.'

'You've found my mother.'

'Yet to be determined,' McGuire said, remaining one step behind Bekker. Polite enough, but there was masked elation there. *If I'm collecting DNA from you, you must be guilty of something.*

'Come in,' Charlie said, stepping back, one hand ready to close the door. Bekker slipped by him first, trailed by McGuire, with her little dead-eyed smile.

'Tea?' he said, when they were in. 'Coffee?'

'We can't stay,' Bekker said.

McGuire meanwhile fished a DNA kit from her brief-case. 'Open wide.'

Charlie obeyed and she scraped the inside of his mouth as if his DNA were playing hard to get. He stared at her as she did it: the satisfaction in her eyes.

'All done.'

Suddenly Charlie found himself saying, 'My mother used to say that. Getting cough medicine into me or splinters out—hold up the needle and say, "All done."'

Then he felt embarrassed; they looked embarrassed. McGuire took a step back as she sealed up the sample stick. 'Yes, well...'

Charlie turned to Bekker. 'It makes sense that you'd think it's my mother, but was there something on the body that pointed you in that direction?'

McGuire sparked up. She closed in on him. 'Like what?'

Charlie kept his gaze on Bekker. 'Like jewellery. Her chain.'

In his mind's eye the chain rested on his mother's summertime skin, just below her throat. He didn't want to think of it flopped slackly across her bare bones, the links welded together by the earth and disintegration. 'Dad gave it to her,' he said.

Bekker looked away and said, 'Just covering bases, Charlie.'

That was as close to an admission that Charlie would get. But he felt agitated, on the backfoot. 'Tea?' he said again.

McGuire shook her head, but this time Bekker shrugged and said, 'Why not.'

They didn't sit. They stood on the other side of the

kitchen bench and watched him limp from the overhead cupboard to the electric jug to the tap above the sink. All the time, he was trying to anticipate their thinking. They couldn't assume anything—someone else could have been wearing his mother's chain. Dental records next—but Dr Tidemann had been ancient back then and his surgery on Mornington main street was now a camping shop.

Which leaves a sample of my DNA, he thought: a mitochondrial match.

McGuire cut in on his thoughts, lifting her voice above the sound of the electric jug: 'We were going to talk to your brother, since you're…unwell,' she said. 'We couldn't track him down.' She said it with a tone, as if Liam might be guilty, too.

Charlie said, 'Simple explanation: he took our mother's last name.'

That pleased McGuire. 'Because he thinks your father killed your mother?'

'Detective Constable McGuire,' murmured Bekker.

McGuire was undeterred. 'We tried to have a word with your father, too. No one home.'

'He's away.'

'Apparently so,' McGuire said, bumping against the kitchen bench repeatedly. It was like she wanted to wade through it and attack him.

'Not apparently so, *actually* so,' said Charlie. 'He and my stepmother are overseas.'

'Where?'

'On a cruise. Off the coast of Japan somewhere. They left *before* the bodies were found, all right? A holiday. People do have holidays. He hasn't run away, he'll be back. But sure, if you want to go ahead and mount some major international arrest and extradition operation...'

The heat in his voice delighted her. 'Ooh, touched a nerve.'

'Detective Constable McGuire.' Bekker sounded more tired than remonstrative.

She turned to Charlie. 'Obviously, we'd like a word with your dad, Charlie.'

He shrugged. 'You'll have to wait. Biscuit?'

'Please,' Bekker said, casting McGuire a look that Charlie couldn't read. Knock it off? Keep it up?

They all perched on the sitting-room armchairs and had nothing to say now. No small talk. No needling. They sipped and stared at each other until McGuire had had enough.

'Talk about cut the tension with a knife,' she said. 'Is there anything you'd like to tell us, Charlie—may I call you Charlie? Anything bothering you, any detail you want cleared up, anything that happened back then that suddenly makes sense now?'

Charlie glanced at Bekker. Bekker merely sipped her tea. So he addressed McGuire. 'How did she die?'

'Skeletal remains.'

'Cut it out. Blow to the head, like Billy Saul? Blade or bullet nicks?'

'You'll be notified in due course.'

Bekker broke in. 'Actually, it won't hurt to tell Charlie this: blow or blows to the head, both sets of remains.'

'*Massive* blows to the head,' McGuire said. 'You left- or right-handed, Charlie?'

He smacked his mug down but said, mildly, 'Keep it up. I've got all the time in the world.'

'Actually, you might not have all the time in the world. Life as you've known it might change in profound ways once we make an arrest.'

'Arrest who? My father? On what evidence? And what is this childish fucking game, making me wriggle on the hook?'

'I think both of you should knock it off,' Bekker said. 'Charlie, assuming it is your mother we found, any reason she'd be in the same grave as Billy Saul? Did they know each other?'

'Not to my knowledge.'

'She didn't teach him?'

'She taught high school; he was a primary-school kid. And she'd always taught here on the Peninsula. Billy Saul was from Berwick.'

'So there would be no reason for him to be on her street?'

'I have no idea why he would be there. Like I said yesterday, maybe he was killed somewhere else, on the beach for example, then taken there? You led the search: he was being bullied, remember? He ran away and came across the wrong person. But what's interesting is the lengths this person went to, staging not only a drowning but also my mother's abduction.'

'If it is your mother,' McGuire said.

'Yes, thank you, Detective Constable McGuire,' Charlie said. 'Whoever did it staged two deaths, kilometres apart, so they wouldn't be linked.'

'Misdirection,' McGuire said, in bleak amusement. 'Now, who would be good at that kind of thing? I know—a cop.'

'Good one,' Charlie said. He turned to Bekker. 'Who was killed first?'

'No way to tell.'

'Who was the intended target?'

'Charlie, we don't know. Either they both were, for whatever reason, or one of them was targeted and the other stumbled on the scene by chance and had to be silenced.'

'Paedophile teacher or townsperson or camp cook or—'

'Charlie, we don't know, but rest assured all theories will be looked at.'

'Yes, thank you for your contribution, Charles,' McGuire said.

Charlie wasn't finished. 'Just to be clear: they were found in the same grave?'

'One on top of the other,' Bekker said.

Charlie was desperate for the facts that would form a picture in his head. 'Just left there? Any belongings? Were they wrapped in anything?'

That alerted McGuire. She leaned towards him. 'Wrapped in anything? Why would you want to know that? Did a blanket or a rug or a tarp or bedsheets go missing back then?'

'Get out of my face, Detective Constable McGuire.'

'Glad to, Mr Deravin.'

Charlie took his mug to the kitchen and rinsed it. It was a signal that he was through, and shortly after that he was showing them out, distracted, thinking: Tell Dad. Tell Liam. Tell Anna. Tell Em...

They all stood for a moment on the veranda, Charlie looking past them to the street, where Mark Valente was walking by, heading for the beach. The old cop knew an unmarked car when he saw one. He gave Charlie an abbreviated nod and walked on in his hard, imperious way.

Bekker noticed. She turned back to Charlie with a smile. 'That man does get around.'

'Meaning?'

'The hospital last night, now here.'

'You knew him at the Rosebud cop shop, right? Maybe you should run after him and pick his brains.'

'Very droll. We'll speak again, Charlie.'

'As soon as the results come back, let me know.'

She shrugged, declining to commit.

24

THE HOUSE SLUMBERED around him, but Charlie was twitchy. Should he notify everyone now, or wait for the DNA results to come in?

The twitches won. Still framing his approach, he called Liam, who headed him off, saying, 'Are you okay? Emma rang me last night; I was going to call you later today. Are you home?'

'Yes.'

'How are you feeling?'

'A bit battered and bruised,' Charlie said.

'Want me to come down? Run errands?'

'Em's still here. I'm fine. Or not fine: Liam, I've just had the police here. They collected a DNA sample from me.'

Liam absorbed that. 'It's Mum, and they need to be sure,' he said.

'They *think* it might be Mum.'

'It's her,' Liam said on a savage note. 'How did she die?'

'Head injuries. Same as to the other one, the boy.'

'Will they want a sample from me?'

'Unless my sample proves I'm adopted, I doubt it.'

They were silent until Liam said, gentler now: 'I remember the day you were born.'

He'd have been five years old, Charlie thought—but who would have taken him to the hospital? 'I was cute, right?'

'In a damp, red-faced way.'

More silence. Charlie looked through the window at the garden table and saw again how warped the boards were when viewed side-on. One day he might do something about it. Or not. The wood was grey with age. Sun-warmed now. And a blackbird landed and hop-pecked around the surface, hopeful of lingering crumbs.

Liam broke into his thoughts. 'Grandma looked after me while Mum was in hospital. I don't remember where Dad was. Work, presumably, like always.'

Charlie didn't want to get into it. 'Anyway, just thought I'd let you know. I suppose I'm saying, expect the worst.'

'Oh, I've been expecting the worst for a long time now. I saw his car there. He did it.'

Charlie wondered if he'd misheard. 'Pardon?'

'Dad's car. I saw it.'

'What are you on about? When?'

'The day Mum went missing.'

'Why didn't you tell me?'

'Because you were so fired up about her lodger.'

'Yeah, until I found out he was in jail that day. What do you mean, you saw Dad's car? Did you see him?'

'Pay attention. I drove to Dad's, loaded the mower, and was on the way to do Mum's lawn when I saw Dad's car. He was coming from Swanage and turned onto Balinoe Road before I reached the intersection.'

Charlie was rattled. 'The day Mum went missing?'

'Yes. Early to mid-afternoon from memory.'

'Why weren't you at work?'

'Still on holidays—we started a week later than the state schools.'

One of the perks of teaching at a private school. 'But Dad would have been at work.'

Liam snorted. 'So he kept saying. Some security van hijack. But he worked solo that day. Not much of an alibi.'

A familiar sensation rose in Charlie: frustration, panic, inability to draw enough air in. Asthma brought on by stress, the family doctor had said when he was a kid. There was a bit of stress in the family back then. A lot of asthma attacks. He slowed and deepened his breathing. 'Plenty of cars like Dad's on the road. Was it him at the wheel?'

When no reply came, Charlie snorted inwardly: That's what I thought.

And then Liam said, 'Look, let's not fight,' and at once the bands loosened, Charlie's breathing eased.

'Okay.'

The pause was uncomfortable until Liam said, 'Let's assume, for the sake of argument, that the second body is Mum's, okay?'

'Okay.'

'They were killed in the same way, probably at the same time, and buried in the same grave.'

Charlie knew where this was going. My brother's channelling McGuire, he thought. 'So?'

'So whoever did it then went on to stage one death as a drowning and the other as a possible abduction. Who would think like that? A cop.'

Charlie was clenching the phone. 'It always comes back to Dad with you, and I'm sick of it.'

Liam said nothing, a silence that presaged another fight. Charlie took a shuddering breath. 'Look, Liam, I'll try to meet you halfway. Consider this: if it was Dad, how did he get home again?'

'Pardon?'

'Mum's car was found in the middle of nowhere. If Dad drove it there, how did he get home again?'

Liam digested that. 'He had help.'

'Like who? Fay? Don't be ridiculous.'

'Well, you raise a good point—either he was picked up by someone or he had his bike in the boot.'

Their father, the cyclist.

'A bloody long way to ride,' grumbled Charlie. 'And how could he be off the radar for so many hours? He was running a major case. Someone at work would have wondered where he was.'

'He was pretty senior, not some junior constable you'd need to keep tabs on.'

'But why hurt Mum?' Charlie said, unable to say *kill*.

'Wounded pride,' said Liam promptly. 'Nobody leaves Rhys Deravin.'

'He was never like that, and you know it.'

'Okay, she was going to get half of everything in the divorce. The house had to be sold, and that was really getting to him.'

'How do you know?'

'It's divorce law, Char—'

'I mean, did he say he was upset about having to sell the house?'

'Stands to reason.'

Charlie thought Liam was probably right, but said, 'You weren't around back then, remember. You'd stopped having anything to do with us.'

'But not with Mum.'

'Did she talk much to you?' Charlie needed to know more, and Liam seemed less inclined to be combative now.

After a pause Liam said, 'Apparently Dad was trying

to find a way to keep the house. Buy her out, for example.'

'There you go. They were being civilised about it.'

A kind of silence from Liam. It said: Except Dad got impatient.

Move right along, Charlie told himself. 'What do I tell Dad? *Do* I tell Dad?'

'At least wait until you know for sure,' Liam said. He paused. 'Fay sent me some WhatsApp photos the other day.'

Charlie was surprised. 'Fay did?'

'She's always stayed in touch. Not often. My birthday, things like that. Messages from Dad.'

'Liam, they care about you.'

Liam said a mild 'Fuck off.'

They kicked that around silently until Liam said, 'If the DNA results prove it's Mum, the police are going to question Dad when he gets home—maybe even arrest him.'

Charlie was frustrated again. 'What I want to know is, how come no one's looking at other people in Mum's life?'

'Like who?'

'Was she seeing someone, for example.'

The notion offended Liam. 'She'd barely left Dad.'

Charlie felt disgruntled. 'I tracked down Shane Lambert the other day.'

Liam took a moment to process the name. 'Her lodger? Wasn't he in jail?'

'Yes.'

188

'What, you're thinking he had a friend kill her? Because he got kicked out?'

'In my world,' Charlie said, 'five bucks is motive enough.'

'Oh, *your world*,' Liam said; the old nastiness between them.

'Okay, how about this: can you honestly, hand over heart, see Dad killing a kid?'

He waited. Liam said, 'Maybe if he was desperate enough.'

Charlie was fed up with his brother. He said, 'Anyway, I thought I'd let you know,' and finished the call.

That afternoon he went against Liam's advice and alerted Rhys and Fay, who had just returned to the ship from a bus tour of Kagoshima. His father, inept with any IT software and hardware, filled the Skype screen with his nostrils and said, 'Sorry you're bearing the brunt of all this, Charlie.'

'Dad, not so close. And don't sit with the porthole behind you.'

Rhys looked taken aback, then he was struck by a tsunami, the cabin tilting, his face wrenched violently from view. His hoary old toes filled the screen, the carpet, Fay's elegant feet, until it all settled down and his father's face reappeared, unreadable in shadow. 'Is that better?'

'Much,' lied Charlie.

Suddenly Fay was there, her face in close-up. 'Charlie, your face is all bruised.'

'Fell off my bike.'

'You poor thing.'

She retreated and Rhys was there again, one side of his face queerly half-lit, the other the dark side of the moon, with one eye gleaming, doubting, disbelieving. 'Do you know how she died?'

'If it is her? Head trauma, same as the boy.'

'Any weapon found?'

'Don't know, Dad.'

'Buried one under the other?'

'Yes.'

'We'll need a funeral,' Rhys said worriedly. 'We don't get back until mid-February.'

'Dad, it could be weeks, months, before they release the body,' Charlie said.

And Rhys shook his head, not knowing what to say, until Fay—subtle, perceptive—cut in with a few traveller's tales to make them all laugh.

25

NEXT DAY, IMPATIENT to visit Anna in hospital, Charlie drove his daughter home to the townhouse she shared with Jess in Coburg, near the Merri Creek. Here they had on the doorstep one of those conversations: the child concerned for the parent, the parent for the child. In her shorts, T-shirt and sandals, an old Country Road cloth bag hanging from one shoulder, Emma said, 'I'm worried about you.'

Charlie kissed her cheek then gestured at his Skoda, parked at the kerb. 'Did I veer off the freeway? Cause a pile-up? Embarrass my fellow road users? I'll be fine.'

'There is a phenomenon known as a relapse, Dad.'

'I'll relapse when I get home this afternoon.'

She kissed him. 'Promise?'

'Promise.'

'Minor relapse?'

'Cured by a glass of red.'

She frowned. 'Should you be drinking?'

'One glass,' Charlie said. 'Meanwhile, I want you to be careful. When's Mum home?'

'Tomorrow.'

Charlie looked up and down the street for young footballers waiting in old 4WDs. Muggers. Rapists. He saw only a guy who couldn't decide if he was a hipster or a contestant on *Farmer Wants a Wife*. 'Maybe stay with a friend tonight?'

'I'll be fine, Dad.'

'Be careful who you open the door to.'

'You be careful on the roads.'

A hug and a kiss and Charlie returned to the car, feeling Emma's gaze all the way. Both of them worried. Unable to do anything about it.

Twenty minutes later he was at the Austin hospital, hesitating with short-stemmed roses in Anna's doorway. Flowers everywhere; the sister, Andrea, seated beside the bed; Anna with a bruised and swollen face, plastered right leg and bandaged left wrist. He felt his eyes fill and swiped at them. 'Thought you'd be hooked to machines, braced for take-off.'

Anna grinned to see him there. 'What you see is what you get.' She beckoned with her good arm. 'Come here.'

The sister scooted out of the way, took his roses adroitly, and now there was only Anna's face tilting to him. He leaned in gingerly; her lips moved dryly over his.

Behind them a voice: 'I'll grab a coffee and leave you two to get on with it.'

Charlie turned, straightening his back with a few creaks and ticks. The roses were clumped in a drinking glass and Andrea was throwing him a grin as she gathered her bag and twinkled her fingers goodbye.

Good-looking women in this family, Charlie thought, returning his attention to Anna. Her poor face: the gritty ravages of pebbles and asphalt, and slightly misshapen. He felt the full force of his guilt. 'Anna, I should've put a bomb under someone as soon as you told me about the graffiti on your door. It might have—'

'Don't.'

'I should have paid more attention.'

She grabbed his hand and tugged until he was seated on the edge of the bed. 'Don't.'

But he'd run out of steam anyway. 'Okay. How are the aches and pains?'

'I do get reminded of them from time to time,' she said. Then, peering at him, a twist of affinity on her face: 'What about you? That's quite a graze.'

Charlie's hand went to his temple. 'Could have been worse.'

'Me, too.'

They both thought about that, but Charlie, at a loss, looked away first. He was in a hospital room, that was about all you could say about his surroundings. The sounds and the smells and the thrum of low-level anxiety.

He caught Anna looking at him. 'I know what you're thinking,' she said, 'and I want you to stop it. He went after both of us. He was going to hurt us sometime or other, whatever we did.'

She was probably right. A home invasion. A bull-bar nudge on the freeway. A bullet through a window.

'Still.'

'I'm alive, you're alive,' she said.

Charlie accepted that. He found that he was holding her right hand. 'I'm told you saw him?'

She nodded. 'When he hit you, I turned around and got a glimpse before he hit me.'

'And you recognised him.'

'From the trial. He was a character witness,' Anna said. 'A teammate.'

'Do you remember his name?'

'No.' She shook her head; pain hit. 'Ouch. Remind me not to do that again.'

They sat there, her warm hand in his. She dozed. His mind drifted.

She stirred and her voice came drowsily. 'Did you have concussion?'

Charlie blinked. 'No, but they had to monitor me.'

'Your friend Mark was worried about it, but he didn't want to move you.'

She's talking about the scene immediately after the accident, he thought. 'You talked to him?'

'He sat with me until the ambulance came. You weren't moving and I wanted to hold you, but I couldn't stand or even crawl.' She paused. 'Mark checked you over then sat with me and held my hand and talked to me. It was...I don't know, there was something lovely about it.'

Charlie nodded, trying to reckon that with the Valente of his childhood. The uncompromising character who had always pushed him, who had never let him get away with half-measures. A stern father, really. Stern with me, stern with my actual father. A man who holds a woman's hand until the ambulance gets there.

'Complex guy.'

Anna looked at Charlie, wanting more.

'He's kind of a friend of the family.'

'Lucky he was there.'

Charlie needed to think about that. 'Yeah.'

'He dropped in to see me yesterday.'

'Really?' Another thing to think about.

The afternoon passed. Anna's brother and his wife visited, twin daughters racing to their aunt's side, riven with drama, trailed by a small boy, shyly smiling. Anna catered to her nieces in a jolly, practical way but clearly felt something deeper for her nephew. Charlie wondered, is this what family life is like? There were fault lines in his own, going back twenty years.

Then her parents arrived with a forcefield of love that drove Charlie to a corner of the room before they brought him back in with their curiosity about the man in their daughter's life.

He was there, and that meant he must be important to her. If she liked him, so would they—unless or until he proved himself unworthy of their regard. Charlie felt dazed. All the shit I've seen over the years, he thought. You forget about simple goodness.

Eventually, alone with her again, he told her about the second set of remains, the DNA test.

'Oh, Charlie.' Puzzled, she shifted in the bed. He almost heard her bones scrape. 'Did she know the boy?'

'Not that I know of.'

'So how come they were found together? Why were they killed? Why there?'

'You sure you're not a cop?'

She tried a smile on him, then flopped back on her pillow. 'Have you told your father?'

'Yes.'

'How did he take it?'

'He seemed bewildered.'

'When's he due home?'

'Couple of weeks.'

A voice from the doorway said, 'Miss Picard? If we could have another quick word?'

Charlie turned: Grieve and Ransome from the Major Collision Unit. 'Can it wait?'

'It's okay, Charlie,' Anna said, slipping her hand from his, pushing herself upright.

Grieve stepped into the room. 'Mr Deravin, I need to talk to Miss Picard alone,' she said, a hint of polite apology in her voice. 'Just to keep things simple.'

'And uncontaminated,' Charlie said. 'I'll grab a coffee.'

'We won't be long,' Grieve said.

Charlie stepped into the corridor and realised he was starving. Finding the cafeteria, he scoffed down coffee and a chocolate muffin as he paged through an abandoned *Herald Sun*, which managed to be at once overexcited, salacious and sombre about the second set of remains found in Swanage, without saying anything new. Halfway through the crossword, he looked up and saw Grieve and Ransome cross the foyer and leave by the front door.

He found Anna with her eyes closed. In repose, her poor face showed not freedom from strain or pain but a blade twisting. He settled gently into the chair beside the bed— wanting to take her hand, unwilling to disturb her.

She opened her eyes and smiled as if he'd come to save her. 'Hello.'

'What did they want?'

'To show me pictures.'

'Didn't they already do that?'

She shrugged and clearly that was a mistake. Her eyes

scrunched in pain; glistened when she opened them. 'I have no idea what's going on. They said they needed to be sure.'

'The same photos or a different lot?'

'The same.'

'You identified the driver again?'

She was frustrated. 'I did, and they said I must be mistaken.'

'Why?'

'They said he has an alibi; I must've seen someone else.'

26

TWO DAYS LATER, early light, the police were on Charlie's doorstep. Uniformed search officers, forensic technicians in oversuits and Bekker and McGuire, the latter smirking as she shoved a warrant into his hands.

'Searching for what?'

McGuire ignored the question. Turned to the search team and issued commands. 'House and shed, you know the drill.'

Charlie turned to Bekker for answers. 'Search for what? And why forensics? What forensics?'

Bekker opened her mouth to reply but McGuire muscled in. 'I'll ask you to step aside, Mr Deravin, and let my officers go about their duties.'

'You really love this, don't you?' Charlie said. But he stepped aside and, as the search team filed past him into the house, he cast a last glance out at the street: police vehicles; neighbours gathering and getting an eyeful. He waved to Mrs Ehrlich, who returned the wave with a grimace of sympathy.

The morning was windless again, full of a thin, curative haze. Charlie breathed it in, face tilted to the sky, eyes closed.

Bekker touched him on the shoulder. 'Walk with me.'

Not quite an order, but she expected obedience. Charlie slipped his feet into his beach Crocs and walked beside her down Tidepool Street to the path through the tea-trees. She rolled her shoulders as she walked; rolled her neck; took deep breaths. 'Fresh air,' she said. 'I really needed this.'

She wasn't his ally, exactly. A fair woman burdened— by life, the job, maybe simply this case. Then she was skipping ahead of him, down the steps, the sea air working on her soul, a woman in her fifties who spent all her hours at a desk or in a car. He saw her slip off her shoes at the bottom, tuck them behind a scrubby dune bush, stride out onto the beach and inhale again, her face greeting the boundless sea and sky. She even curled her toes in the sand.

Charlie was disarmed—as far as it went. Joining her,

he said, 'The DNA has come back? It's my mother?'

She gave a little wake-up shudder. Resurfacing, the public world replacing the private. 'Sorry, Charlie. Yes, it is.'

'Can I ask why you need to search my place?'

'Walk with me,' she said again.

She wheeled to her right and headed in the direction of Point Leo. The sand was firm, the tide halfway on the turn, and people were swimming. She halted abruptly. 'Gets around, doesn't he? Mark Valente again.'

Valente had been chopping through the water. He stopped to adjust his goggles, stared at Charlie and Bekker. 'I reckon you two should catch up,' Charlie said.

'I don't think so,' Bekker said. She set off again.

Charlie kept pace with her. Some people were fast walkers, others favoured something closer to ambling; a smaller sample—Anna tended to do it—would keep veering into you. Bekker liked to stride.

'I repeat, what are you looking for?'

'Think about it, Charlie. Your dad is a suspect and—'

'He's always been a suspect. He was questioned and cleared back then but the stink never left him.'

'...he's a suspect and there might be evidence of some kind.'

'He was cleared.'

'No, he wasn't cleared, not exactly.'

'What do you mean?'

'I'm telling you this because I don't want you playing

201

detective with only half the facts. Better still, don't play detective at all, understood?'

Charlie said nothing.

'I mean it, Charlie. Let us do our jobs. We have been re-interviewing everyone, believe it or not—including Mr Lambert, who was in jail the day of the murders and has nothing to add—and wherever we go, you've been there, too. Or you've come along after us. It has to stop. People are getting cranky.'

'Like who? I haven't...'

Bekker scowled. 'To continue. Your father's alibi was... it wasn't solid. He said he spent his entire shift running down leads on an armoured car hijack, but it turns out he was by himself most of the day.' She paused. 'He was a man with powerful friends, Charlie.'

Charlie knew full well that an experienced cop like Fran Bekker would never reveal her thinking or investigative findings to anyone as involved as he was in one of her cases. *She's hoping I've been harbouring doubts all this time*, he thought. *Hoping if she gives me titbits, I'll repay her with gold.*

Charlie walked on glumly. 'Okay, for the sake of argument, let's assume he did it. What do you expect to find after twenty years?'

'Legal and financial documents that might speak to motive. Photos, old diaries, letters...'

'But forensics? Come on.'

Bekker gave him a look and Charlie knew he was being

naive. What if his mother had been killed at Tidepool Street and transported to the house site in Swanage? He visualised the forensic team quartering the house metre by metre, looking for blood traces on the carpets, floorboards and walls. Blood spots; blood pools; blood that had been mopped and sponged. But everyone steps on broken glass at some point. If they find Mum's blood, he thought, let's hope they keep that in mind.

'Be careful of tunnel vision,' he said.

'*You* be careful of tunnel vision,' Bekker replied, and they walked on in silence. Gulls wheeled above the sea or bobbed in it. There had been a rising wind last night, a tidal surge, so the beach was flecked with seaweed.

'Another thing I shouldn't be telling you: it seems the original investigation was less than thorough.'

'Meaning?'

'Meaning that we are retesting old trace evidence and testing for new trace evidence. Talking to original witnesses again. And there are a couple of witnesses who called and wrote to us back then but were never followed up.'

'You're kidding.'

Bekker said nothing. Charlie said, 'Can I look at the original files?'

'Don't be stupid.'

'It's not that Dad had powerful friends, it's that you lot didn't do your job. You know what he told me? No one came to talk to him properly for at least five years, not until the cold-case unit reopened the investigation. Hopeless.'

'I share your concern,' Bekker said, stomping along.

'What trace evidence are you retesting?'

A quick sideways glance: did he deserve to know? 'Her car is long gone,' she said. 'Sold as scrap for all I know. But we swabbed the keys, steering wheel, dashboard, seats and seatbelts back then. And we still have her handbag and everything in it—lipstick, purse, tissues…Let's hope we find new DNA.'

'Let's hope,' Charlie agreed. 'She had that car for a while. Dad drove it sometimes.'

'We're aware of that. We're also aware that even if new DNA does crop up during retesting, it could have got there innocently. Maybe she was in the habit of giving lifts to colleagues.'

Drew Quigley? Charlie wondered. Should he tell Bekker? No. It was just a rumour. He said, 'Could I look at photos, at least?'

'Charlie, I'm not letting you look at anything.'

'Can I ask what you have photos of?'

She was suspicious. 'The car. Her house. Her handbag and the other stuff—in situ and before and after testing in the lab.'

'I was told the car had run off the road and into a fence post.'

'Gatepost.'

'Staged to suggest an abduction.'

'Or an accident,' Bekker said. 'She hit her head, got disorientated and wandered off into the bush.'

No bush there, thought Charlie. Farmland.

Bekker was striding out again. She seemed to toss her next question on the run: 'Charlie, when's your dad due back?'

'Mid-February. Why, you going to arrest him?'

'We just want a word.'

Charlie was stubborn. 'Can't you leave him alone? Tunnel vision.'

'Telling me my job. Love it,' Bekker said. 'Did your father ever hit your mother?'

Charlie halted. 'Beat about the bush why don't you? No. Never. They never even argued much.'

Bekker chewed on that. 'He didn't attend the inquest. Were you aware of that?'

'Did he need to? Maybe he was grieving. Anyway, I assume you've read the coroner's report. On the balance of probabilities, Mum was killed by a person or persons unknown.'

Bekker simply forged on. '*Was* your dad grieving, though? People remarked on his apparent *lack* of grief back then. And within a short while he'd moved in with Whatshername...'

Her voice trailed away. She grabbed Charlie's arm. 'What *is* that?'

A humped shape, brownish black, was stretched out on the sand ahead of them. 'Not a homicide victim, if that's your thinking—it's a seal,' Charlie said, drawing ahead to make certain.

He looked back at her; nodded his confirmation. 'Seal.'

She joined him, a bundle of distress, awe and curiosity. 'Poor thing.'

'There's a colony of them on the Nobbies,' Charlie said, gesturing across the water to Phillip Island.

She wrapped herself in her arms. 'What happened? How would it have died?'

Charlie shrugged. When he'd lived here as a kid, he'd seen at least one dead seal a year. He crouched to examine the remains. 'I can't see any injuries. Sick? Old? Disorientated? There was a bit of a storm last night.'

And as he looked at the bedraggled seal he thought unaccountably of his father—like this seal, all of his old sleekness gone.

Bekker stepped around the carcass, walked a few paces ahead; returned. 'Let's go back. That's enough for now.'

She was brisk again, Charlie hurrying alongside her. 'Like hell that's enough for now.'

She glanced at him, not breaking her stride. 'Elaborate.'

'You said it yourself, the original investigation was botched. Maybe my mother was seeing someone.'

Bekker increased her pace. 'Is that you saying you have someone in mind? I need you to back off, Charlie. Stop hassling people.'

'Well, if you did your job…'

She stopped, a hostile intensity in her. 'I have done my job. Butt out, Charlie. Don't let this become another Kessler.'

'Whoa,' Charlie said, hands up, backing away.

Bekker went to pursue him, but regret took over. She touched his forearm, a complicated expression clouding her face. 'Sorry, unwarranted,' she said. But walked on.

After a beat Charlie caught her up. 'Do you at least have a theory of the case?'

'Charlie, don't...'

Charlie was clutching at straws. 'Like I said the other day, maybe my mother wasn't the intended victim, Billy was. Some paedophile grabbed him, and she intervened, and he had to kill them both. Do you know who was killed first? Just because Billy was found first, that doesn't mean he was killed first.'

'Or,' said Bekker, 'your mother was the intended victim and Billy happened along.'

'Did you even check for perverts back then? Are you checking now?'

'Perverts. Love the terminology.'

Charlie felt a clutch of frustration. His fists tightened.

Bekker, flicking him a glance, noticed the tension and again softened her stance. 'Charlie, we're doing a thorough job. We've been thrashing out likely scenarios and we'll thrash out new ones as they arise. Trust us, okay?'

She stopped suddenly. 'Tell me about your family. Your dad, your mum—your dad with your mum.'

That boiled down to one question, really, and it was too big for Charlie. But she didn't seem to be asking for dirt—she was curious, she deserved a reply. Nodding at a neighbour from Spray Street, who passed with a keen glance at Bekker, he said, 'What can I tell you? Peninsula born and bred, boyfriend and girlfriend since the first year of high school.'

'Where?'

'Dromana—where Liam and I went.'

'Tell me about Liam.'

'I don't think so. You already know Liam thinks Dad's guilty and I don't.'

Bekker switched topics again. 'Was the divorce acrimonious?'

'They weren't divorced. They were separated.'

'*Getting* divorced, though.'

'Yes.'

'Which would have meant selling the house.'

'Has the original file got photos of the house? So you'll have seen the For Sale sign stuck in the lawn.'

'How did your father feel about that?'

'We were *all* sad.'

'Your parents split up because your father was…' About to say, *sleeping around.*

'He met someone else,' Charlie said. 'You know all this.'

'I'm interested in your take on the matter.'

'What do you want me to say? People fall in love with others. Marriages run their course.'

'Tell me about Fay.'

'She's lovely,' Charlie said promptly. 'She was single

when Dad met her—he'd gone to the police credit union for a loan. She didn't force the breakup; my parents were already kind of remote with each other.'

Was that a lie? Not quite the truth. He didn't elaborate.

'Your dad moved in with her pretty quickly.'

'He didn't have anywhere else to live.'

'Yes he did. The house you're in now.'

'No,' Charlie said stubbornly. 'He was driven out by memories and public opinion.'

Bekker almost snorted. 'Have you ever considered that your mother was an impediment to his relationship with Fay?'

Charlie's police-work mantra was: Believe no one, accept nothing, until you had proof otherwise. He wasn't surprised by Bekker's theory. But he was curiously offended.

'You'll be checking Fay's movements too, I imagine.'

'She was cleared at the time—and I mean properly cleared, she was in Sydney, a conference.'

Charlie let the sarcasm in. 'But perhaps she was establishing an alibi for herself. Perhaps there's an unexplained nine thousand, nine hundred and ninety-nine-dollar payment to an identity known to police in her January 2000 bank statement.'

Bekker punched him lightly. 'One never knows. Like I said, we're going over everything again. What did you think when they got married?'

'I was pleased for them. It took a while—Mum had to be declared dead first.'

'And she *was* dead all along,' Bekker said.

'That wasn't very nice.'

'Sorry.'

He saw that she probably was sorry. She looked spent. He said, 'When are you going to release her body?'

'It can't be soon, Charlie, you know that. I know you'd like a proper funeral, and there's no reason why you can't have one, but it could be weeks. I have no say in it, sorry.'

'No one has any say in anything,' muttered Charlie, feeling sour. Wondering if he'd been played by Bekker as he trailed after her to the Tidepool Street steps. She was slipping on her shoes as Mrs Ehrlich descended, sunblock smeared over her nose, her sandals clapping the soles of her feet. She said nothing, merely smiled nervily.

'All my neighbours will think *I'm* guilty of something.'

'You have an unshakeable alibi for the day poor Billy and your mother died,' Bekker said. 'You were with me.'

Charlie followed her up the steps, thinking: Have you talked to Liam? Has he told you he saw Dad's car?

He wanted to tell Bekker that she should be looking for a cold, exacting mind. A mind able to anticipate the steps in every narrative, able to steer and misdirect by staging the drowning of one victim and the violent abduction of the other. But if he told her that, he'd be inviting only one response—everyone's response: 'A cop mind, for example?'

27

CHARLIE WAS LEFT alone by late morning, but reporters, photographers and media vans soon replaced the search team, crowding Tidepool and Bass streets, trapping him indoors. Some of them walked across the parched lawn to tap on the sliding door; saw Charlie in there, stony-faced, and would mouth words, gesture, smiles splitting their faces. And they all had his phone numbers, so he took the landline off the hook and muted his mobile when he wasn't calling everyone: Liam, Anna, Em, Jess.

Mid-afternoon he confirmed the identification with

Rhys and Fay. Rhys, looking troubled, lost and very far away, said, 'Why search the place? What the hell did they expect to find?'

Charlie didn't know what to say, with Fay there, listening in. That the police expected to find blood where her husband had hacked his first wife to death? 'Covering bases,' he said.

Rhys started coughing, bent over with it. 'God. Excuse me.'

Fay inserted her clever face. 'Did they find anything?'

'Left empty-handed, as far as I know.'

Then Rhys was there again. 'You need us to fly back, son?'

'Nothing you can do,' Charlie said. 'Enjoy the rest of your holiday.' He paused. 'But they might give you a hard time when you get home.'

The day drew on, eventually softened by afternoon shadows. Whenever his mobile buzzed, he monitored the caller numbers and listened to voicemail. Mark Valente was sorrowful, sharing a couple of memories and saying, as he signed off: 'And so the sullen and the wicked are left behind.'

Charlie smiled to himself, then saw Sue Mead's number come up. He hit reply.

'Hi, sarge.'

'Charlie. I just wanted to say how sorry I am, we all are.'

All? Half of his old sex-crimes squad hated his guts. 'Thanks. Means a lot.'

'If there's anything I can do…'

'I'm fine,' Charlie said. He paused. 'How's the Kessler trial going?'

'It's going,' she said. 'Sorry, Charlie. Got to go.'

Hopeful reporters still lingered in Tidepool Street as the sun disappeared behind the trees, so Charlie left via the laundry door, over the side fence and across Mrs Ehrlich's backyard. She was there at her sink, backlit by her kitchen light. She saw him and wagged a friendly, yellow-gloved hand at him before he ducked into the laneway behind her house. He felt her eyes on him all the way: godspeed, Charlie.

The tide was halfway out, the water still as glass, mirroring the fading light, barely lapping the little rock islands where the cormorants liked to spread their wings to a drying wind. He stood for a while, letting himself grow, his chest or his heart, that part of him that was a vessel for feelings. But what feelings? His mother had been lost but now was found. Only it was bones they'd found, not his mother. Beaten to death—but in his mind's eye a skull had been beaten in, not his mother. She was still missing. Her absent face: he couldn't bear to visualise an assault on it. She was a smiling woman; she mostly smiled. Patient, loving—transformed into a loud-voiced termagant whenever she had a vacuum cleaner in her hands. Best avoided. 'Flee the house, boys,' Rhys would say. And she'd snap, '*You* do it, then.'

Where had that image come from? Slowly there

213

clarified in Charlie's head a real woman, her quirks and character, and he was weeping. He headed left blindly, around the bluff towards Balinoe Beach and wondered what he was weeping for. His mother, yes, but also for his lost years. The fruitless search. The useless suspicion, energy and effort.

He would have to start again. Butt out, Bekker had said. Trust us. Charlie did trust her, but that wasn't the point. Being expected to sit around and twiddle his thumbs was the point.

He tramped along the sand, his eyes drying and the sky and the water and the perfumed air flowed into him. He was a solitary figure, but he wasn't alone there. A cyclist overtook him, hissing by on fat tyres, and a fisherman stood with three rods in the sand, each one bending tautly to the sea. He'd never seen one of these guys catch a fish. They must have some other reason for being there. Escaping home; embracing thoughts.

Two black swans bobbing. Now, that was something. From the nature reserve near Swanage, probably, a place of abundance and safety—but even a swan needs to get out and about sometimes, test the boundaries…the porous boundaries.

Where had that phrase come from? Something Dr Fiske had said. Charlie walked on as the sun spread across the horizon and wondered what to do about his therapist. If he quit the force—or was sacked—he needn't see her again. But he'd liked her. Little things in him that she'd teased out and nudged into view. Things for him to contemplate.

Okay. Plan of action. Speak to his mother's friends and acquaintances again; discover who owned the slab house; look into Billy Saul's life, see what might still be undiscovered there.

He passed a woman and two children sitting in the sand, fish and chip scraps beside them. The children patted the sand despondently while their mother muttered into a mobile phone. Charlie saw it every time he walked on the beach. Children who wanted to play but didn't know how.

Finding a drift of beach garbage further on, he veered towards Tulum Court and its rubbish bin, and Noel Saltash was coming down the shallow dune with an old labrador on a lead. He and Charlie were about to pass each other with the abbreviated nods of abbreviated men when Saltash stopped, looking shy and awkward. Damn, thought Charlie.

'Hi, Noel.'

'Charlie,' Saltash said. He was one of those older men who seemed cobbled together from many men. Little pot belly, skinny shanks, eyes wide apart, gristly ears and a neat nose; pianist's fingers. Out of his ranger's uniform his forehead was ghostly white, his forearms and legs like old leather. As old as my father, Charlie thought. As old as Mark Valente. But he'd be the ranger for as long as the shire let him stay. He would be lost without the beach; it was his realm.

'Didn't know you had a dog—'

'Charlie, I just wanted to say how sorry I am. She was a lovely woman.'

Charlie paused, taken aback. 'Thank you,' he said.

Saltash almost said more but thought better of it and nodded an abrupt goodbye. Charlie, watching him step down onto the sand, amused himself with an image of Pat the dog-woman coming along at that moment. It was not quite 7 p.m., the hour at which dogs were allowed on the beach in summer, so she'd be within her rights to call the ranger a hypocrite.

Dumping his rubbish scraps in the bin, he waited a couple of minutes, half-concealed by the kayaks and surfboards left amid tea-trees and dune hollows all year round, never stolen or vandalised. When he was sure Saltash had a head start, he stepped onto the beach and darted a look each way: thank Christ, the old geezer had headed around to the left. Charlie headed right, back to Tidepool Street.

'Lovely woman,' Noel had said. The words conjured Charlie's mother again. Trite words, the sort of thing you said, but also, just then, the simple truth.

28

HOLIDAY-MAKERS RETURNED to work and schools opened. Mid-afternoon on Friday, 31 January, Charlie steered the Skoda up steep, switchback roads and through little hill towns to finally settle, engine off, in the visitor carpark of the high school where his mother's possible lover was now the headmaster. He checked his phone, wound down his window, got comfortable as parents collected their kids, buses trundled off, teachers left for the day.

Drew Quigley appeared at five-thirty. A tall, thin, nervy-looking man. Balding—he had more hair on

Facebook—and wearing a white short-sleeved shirt and tie, he was unlocking a Golf station wagon when Charlie intercepted him. 'Mr Quigley?'

A tired face turned, resigned to be flattened further by some kind of parental grievance. 'Yes?'

Charlie stuck out his hand. 'Charlie Deravin. Rose Deravin was my mother.'

Quigley shook automatically as emotions flickered behind the tiredness: surprise, unease, calculation. Releasing Charlie's hand, he calmly opened the rear door, stowed his briefcase, shut the door—giving himself time, Charlie thought. The story, the facial expression he needed.

He settled on a sombre face. Leaned back against his car, folded his arms, gave a little headshake. 'I heard on the news. An awful story. Tragic. All those years of not knowing, and now this?'

Charlie tried to imagine what his mother must have been thinking if she'd been involved with Quigley. What might she have seen in him? What would any woman see? He was nondescript, buttoned-down, almost prissy in his mannerisms. Good voice—the sonorous voice of a born instructor—but even so, an unlikely lover. The kind who was bound to get his heart broken. Had she needed someone safe and colourless for a change? Maybe Quigley was a kind man and she'd needed a listener. Charlie heard Jess's words ringing in his head: 'I just want someone who'll listen. Even when you're here you're not here.'

Still: an unlikely lover. And his reaction...Why wasn't

he more surprised? Puzzled? Annoyed? Twenty years had passed; he'd never met Charlie; there was no reason why Charlie or anyone else would track him down. Had he spent twenty years waiting for the hammer to fall? Did he always keep his cards close to his chest? He should have been utterly thrown. He wasn't even spluttering.

'Sorry to intrude,' Charlie said, 'but I wonder if I could have a word?'

Quigley glanced right and left, then past Charlie's shoulder and around at the admin building, as if mapping a dash through the long shadows forming up here, in the land of mighty trees and a late afternoon sun. Then he turned to Charlie and said, 'I must confess I have no idea what you want with me, and things are always hectic at the start of the school year. I have a stack of reports to write when I get home.'

Charlie ignored that. 'You were friends with my mother.'

Quigley winced and checked the exits again. He said, dragging the words out: 'We worked at the same school…'

Charlie said, '*Close* friends is what I heard.'

'I don't know where you're getting your information from. I can't help you, I'm afraid.'

'Very close friends.'

The hunted look returned. 'A group of us…we'd have a drink after work sometimes, that's all.'

It was a word picture for Charlie. He visualised a single woman, lonely, looking for a kind ear. Quigley responds, she responds in turn. They contrive to stay on in the pub when the others leave. Knees touch. Fingers.

'You're a grandfather now.'

'I beg your pardon?'

'Meaning twenty years ago you had a wife or a partner at least. Did my mother know about her? Were you separated at the time?'

'Mr Deravin, I've been married for thirty years, happily married. But what that has to do with anything—'

'It's understandable,' Charlie interrupted. 'My mother had left my father by that stage. He had himself a new girlfriend, in fact, so she had every right to seek male company, and you—'

'Do we have to do this here?'

Charlie hadn't been expecting that. He'd been pushing, expecting Quigley to push back, hoping that in the heat of it he'd make a mistake. 'There's a pub down the road.'

Quigley gave him a look that said, 'Don't be ridiculous, I don't hang out in pubs,' and gestured to the admin building, rattling his keys. 'My office.'

It made more sense to Charlie when he saw what Quigley had seen: a van marked Dandy Cleaners rolling in from the main road. It pulled up outside the main building and two women got out wearing headscarves and grey overalls. Slid open a door and reached in for buckets, mops, dusters. Useful witnesses in case I get agitated or violent, he thought.

He followed Quigley into the foyer—Quigley calling

a jolly, 'Ladies!' to the cleaners—and past the reception desk to a corridor hung with posters and naive paintings of trees, houses and stick figures. Odours hung in the air: cooped-up, hormonal kids and their industrial deodorants; disinfectant, copy paper, petrochemical carpets and resistance to learning.

Quigley's office was small but overlooked a playing field, white goalposts and fence pickets, trees beyond. Files sat on the desk and the tops of the filing cabinets. Two large monitors faced the swivel chair, and the walls were crammed: a trophy cabinet, timetables; a tourist poster of Neuschwanstein Castle.

Not the worst place for a chat, but Quigley would regain a sense of assurance here, surrounded by the symbols of his authority. And he'd had a couple of minutes to collect himself on the walk from the carpark. Charlie watched him settle behind his desk, then grabbed one of the visitors' chairs for himself.

Quigley regarded him across the desk: This is my ground. 'Now, how may I help you?'

'You and my mother were lovers.' Everything in Quigley's responses so far made Charlie certain of it.

'We most assuredly were not. We were work colleagues.'

And he leaned back and actually steepled his fingers: The ball's in your court.

Charlie nodded absently. Weak; pompous. Perhaps his mother had seen that, finally—or even from the start. Had quickly tired of him. He'd bored her. Too stuffy; too needy.

221

But before he could formulate his next move, Quigley sat forward and fixed him with a headmaster's gaze. 'And for your information, and to head off any nasty little accusation you might have in mind, I was teaching the day your mother disappeared. All day. Sorry to be blunt, but there it is.'

He would have wanted to micro-manage her, Charlie thought. He'd have brought the habits of classroom teaching to sex, to ordinary relating. He'd have laid down the law, satisfied that she couldn't possibly demur because no one else ever had.

'You hit her.'

Quigley blanched. 'I beg your pardon?'

'If I can find that out, so can the police. You hit her.'

'I would never hit a woman.'

'My mother wasn't someone to kick up a fuss or rock the boat. She was a pacifist. Sweet, protective, always looking out for others. But she'd left my father and was having a taste of freedom. She wanted to be happy. But she was still vulnerable. Given time, she'd never have got involved with you. With any married man, for that matter.' He glanced around the room, his voice goading. 'Did you lie to her? Tell her you were separating; your wife didn't understand you?'

Quigley flapped. Charlie ignored him, his gaze taking in the depressing walls again...

Something about the timetable. Coloured inks on a whiteboard, it took up a quarter of the side wall above a row of four two-drawer filing cabinets. Teachers' names: Gittins, Driscoll, DiMaggio...Charlie got to his feet to check. A little *x* in place of the dot above the *i*.

He returned to his chair. 'In any event, she came to her senses, and you didn't like it.'

Quigley seemed ready to prolong his protest, but then he slumped. Said, in a low, desolate voice: 'You've got it all wrong. I treated her with respect. I would never...'

Charlie saw the motions of Quigley's throat as he swallowed, trying to claw back his dignity. 'We parted amicably. I had feelings for her, she for me, but it couldn't continue, we both saw that.' He paused, a calculation behind the eyes. 'She was terrified of your father; did you know that?'

'It was physical: you were lovers.'

'None of your *damn business*.' Almost a shriek. But again Quigley put a brake on his feelings. Avoiding Charlie, seeking answers in the turrets and spires on the poster, he said loftily, 'I was a happily married man—I still am—but your mother and I had a special friendship. It broke my heart, her disappearing like that.'

'Did you tell the police about this so-called friendship?'

'You're a grubby little man, aren't you? Tell the police what, that we were friends? She had heaps of friends. That woman...Karen Wagoner—why don't you talk to her? I was at work all day, like I said.'

'Did the police talk to you?'

'They talked to everyone.'

'Have they talked to you again?'

'No. Why should they? As I said, your mother was afraid of your father. Join the dots.'

Charlie stood; Quigley flinched.

'Don't be an idiot, I'm not going to hurt you.'

'I'd like you to leave now.'

'I'm going. And by the way, stop sending my father those anonymous letters. They're as pathetic as you are.'

29

CHARLIE SPENT THE weekend regrouping. Time now to work on the possibility that it was not his mother but the boy who had been the intended target.

After his swim and paper run on Saturday morning, he googled 'Saul' and 'Berwick'. The family hadn't moved. Tania Saul, now divorced, would see him on Monday.

Saturday afternoon he surfed, Point Leo promising onshore waves to 1.5 metres. He loaded his board and was there by 3 p.m., stopping to pay for a parking permit before driving around to the surf lifesaving club, where he pulled onto a grassy verge beside the usual panel vans and SUVs. He wriggled into his wetsuit and the familiar snap of the material against his skin worked with the sounds of the wind and the gulls, the tang and odour of the sea, to bring back the past even as the present was fully alive in him. With his board bumping his right hip, he trudged past the clubrooms and down the dune track to the beach. A few solitary dogwalkers; hunting seabirds tipping onto one wing above the waves; the tiny, patient dots of surfers out on the water; waves that merely rolled uneventfully to the shore but sometimes teased, sometimes reared and broke, if you were patient enough.

He joined them out the back, bobbing lazily, waiting. Then an anomalous wave began to rise. He paddled hard for it, launched into a steep take-off, dropped fast down its face and came through in a low crouch, riding a short barrel section and finally gliding upright until he flopped onto his belly and paddled to the shore. That was all he needed. There'd be no repeating that, not today.

Saturday evening Anna called him. He should have been the one to call—his turn, if anyone was keeping tabs—but some indefinable reluctance had crept into him since he'd seen her lying there in hospital. The grazed and broken skin. The police hovering. The shit he'd brought down on her—things like that.

It was there in his tone now as he returned her greeting. Maybe she sensed it. She started chatting, a little faster than was natural to her. She'd been released from

hospital that morning; she was recuperating at her parents'
house in Ivanhoe and already impatient with the idea of
spending days sitting in the sunroom at the back, all cane
furniture and flowery cushions; a physio had called by to
discuss her rehab; the bushfire news just got worse and
worse...

'I'm babbling, Charlie. How are you coping?'

'All right.' A barely adequate response, and she was
silent. 'Keeping busy,' he added, not quite understanding
why he was being such a prick.

She said, treading carefully, 'Let me know if I can help
in any way.'

'Thanks.'

'Mum and Dad were saying, will there be a funeral?'

'Some time,' Charlie said, 'when they release the body.'
Once they'd finished poking, prodding, scraping and
analysing his mother's remains under magnification. Once
the coroner cleared a backlog of paperwork too, probably.
And what kind of funeral? A celebration of a life or an
interment of dead bones?

There was a silence and Charlie felt Anna reach for
him as she said, 'Or maybe a memorial service? Something
less gloomy?'

Presently Charlie said, 'That's actually a good idea.'

'I can help—you can bounce ideas off me, I mean.'

'Better leave the planning to Liam. Liam and Ryan. If
I got involved, we'd just fight.'

A brief silence.

'Charlie,' she said, 'when you get your head on straight, come and see me.'

And so he felt like a bastard all day Sunday. Not helped when, halfway home from a run to Bunnings, his mobile rang. Bluetooth was hit and miss so, steering with one hand, an eye on the rear-view mirror and CCTV cameras, he snatched the phone up from the passenger seat.

'Deb Fiske here, Charlie.'

Charlie ducked as if a sniper had spotted him. 'Oh, hi.'

'Forgive me, but I saw on the news about your mother. Look, it's not strictly kosher, my calling you like this. But I want to let you know, if you need a session I can always squeeze you in.'

Something like gratitude stirred in Charlie. 'Thank you. Stage two of ironing out my soul and character.'

'I wouldn't necessarily have put it that way.'

'I'm fine, Doc,' Charlie said. 'Yet to fall in a heap.'

Which was probably a lie.

30

ON MONDAY MORNING Charlie surfed then drove to Berwick and parked outside a 1970s brick-veneer house on a busy street. Tania Saul shook his hand warmly and ushered him into an interior of low ceilings and compact rooms as if he were not a stranger but a friend come to give her answers.

'Make yourself comfortable,' she said, gesturing at a tired sofa.

She returned from her kitchen a minute later with a glass of iced tea in each hand, to find Charlie not sitting but peering at framed photographs on a glossy upright piano. As he stepped away self-consciously, she came up and proffered one of the glasses. They stood there looking at the phases of Billy Saul's short life: in Tania's arms; giving a gummy smile from the depths of a stroller; revving a yellow truck in a sandpit; beaming in a floppy hat outside a primary school; onstage at a ballet concert.

It wasn't a shrine—elsewhere in the room were photographs of a daughter, and photographs of both children—but the little collection had a grave dignity to offset sad memories and financial struggle.

'It must be strange for you…It's strange for me,' Billy's mother said.

Suddenly she gave Charlie a quick, unexpected one-arm hug, as if to say, 'We're in this together.' A welcome antidote to some of the victim reactions he'd witnessed over the years: sibling competing with sibling in the suffering stakes, friend with friend, parent with parent.

'Come. Let's sit.'

Charlie settled at one end of the sofa and glanced around the room. Partly open venetian blinds cut the sunlight, striping a child's playpen in the corner.

Tania caught his curiosity. 'I'm a grandmother now.'

He glanced at a photo of Billy with his sister and a scruffy dog. The girl looked a couple of years older. He did a quick sum—she was probably about thirty now.

The passing of the years. Charlie felt awkward, didn't know where to begin, and kept eyeing the room. A sewing machine on a card table in another corner, with a sewing basket and fabrics on the floor beside it.

Again Tania Saul deciphered his gaze. 'I do mending for people. Dressmaking, replacing zips, taking up hems, you name it.'

'Wish you lived near me,' Charlie said.

She smiled, inclined her head, prepared to indulge him, but she knew this wasn't a social visit. For his own good as much as hers, it was time for him to spit it out. He gulped down half of his iced tea and settled the glass on a coaster. 'Now that I'm here, I don't quite know what to say.'

'Take your time.'

'I've had this sense of two, two...'

'Two depleted households,' she said simply, 'apparently unconnected for twenty years, and now this.'

He was relieved. 'You've felt it, too?'

'Since the news came in.'

He glanced at photographs on the wall behind her. She'd been slim when the children were young, lit up inside as if her days were too short, and she'd favoured jeans and T-shirts. She was pushing sixty now, with cropped grey hair, and looked slower and more comfortable in herself, as if grief had burned away the excess energy.

'I'm glad you made contact.' She paused. 'I didn't want to intrude.'

Seeing his gaze go to the piano again, she said, 'If you're wondering about Billy's father, he hasn't been on the scene for a long time.'

'Oh. Sorry.'

'Don't be. We had some good years together.'

'He left after what happened to Billy?'

'I know people do split up when that kind of thing happens...' She shook her head. 'No, he left when Billy was a toddler. He wasn't comfortable here. Didn't want to be a father again. It happens. He went back to Thailand.'

Then she looked at him and in it was a wisp of challenge. 'In case you were wondering about the children's colouring.'

Not to mention their dark eyes and their beauty and grace, thought Charlie.

Still looking at him, Tania Saul said, 'The kids really copped it, both of them.'

Charlie grimaced in sympathy. But his next ungracious thought was: if the father didn't do it, maybe there was a boyfriend?

'Have you told your husband?'

'Ex. We're divorced. Yes, I phoned him a few days ago. I think he was genuinely shocked and sad but after a couple of minutes I got the feeling he thought I wanted something from him, so I just said goodbye. Anyway, he has a new family now. I doubt he'll come to the funeral—whenever that will be.'

'We're having the same issue,' Charlie said, and silence gathered around them until he looked up and said, 'I've had to completely rethink everything.'

'Me, too.'

'All these years I more or less forgot about Billy—no offence.'

'None taken.'

'All I thought about was my mother being abducted and I got it into my head this guy who was renting a room from her knew something about it.'

'Do you still think that?'

A shape passed by the window, a flicker in the gaps of the venetian blind. Tracking it, Charlie said, 'Someone just walked down the side of your house.'

'My daughter. I'm babysitting today.'

'Oh. I'd better go. I don't want to—'

'Stay. There's no hurry. You were saying about a man living in your mother's house?'

In the seconds or minutes left to him before the back door opened and daughter and grandchild appeared, Charlie told Tania Saul he'd finally managed to speak to Shane Lambert. 'He didn't really know anything. Said there was a guy Mum might've been seeing, but...' He shrugged.

'So, dead end? Back to the drawing board?'

'Pretty much.'

'And you're wondering if maybe Billy was the intended target.'

Charlie winced. 'It crossed my mind.'

'Crossed mine, too, except in reverse. They were after your mother and it was somehow wrong time, wrong place for Billy.'

A mild commotion in the rear of the house, a woman's voice speaking babytalk softly, then yelling, 'Mum!'

'In here.'

Charlie waited. He stood as Tania did, watching a reunion that was probably repeated several times a week. Big smiles; the baby lifted from its stroller; the handover; the coos and talking over one another. Except this time a strange man was there, and the daughter, uncannily similar in appearance to the young Tania Saul in the photos, looked quizzically at Charlie, a stranger in her mother's house. Quite a bit younger, so maybe not a would-be boyfriend. Both drinking iced tea, no apparent tension in the air...

So no immediate cause for concern. She finally smiled warmly at Charlie. 'Hi, I'm Nan.'

Charlie shook her hand. 'Charlie.'

Tania Saul, watching on, rocking the baby, peering around the wispy head, said, 'Love, it was Charlie's mother who was buried with Billy.'

The daughter looked shocked. 'I'm so sorry.'

Charlie smiled; nodded. Nothing much he could say.

Then Nan left to run errands and Charlie found himself eating an early lunch with Tania while the baby slept. Radishes, gherkins and cheese on a dense black rye loaf, in the kitchen this time. Over faint noises coming from the baby monitor on top of the fridge, Tania said, 'I googled you after you called on Saturday.'

'I'd do the same.'

'Umm…' She gave him a shrewd look. 'Do people think your dad was responsible? Sorry if I'm stepping over the line here.'

'That's fine,' Charlie said. 'Yeah, people do think that. A twenty-year whisper campaign.' He paused, embarrassed. He didn't want to air dirty linen. 'They were going through a divorce, et cetera, et cetera, but he was never violent to her. He's not like that. And believe me when I tell you he'd never hurt a child.'

She waved that off. 'You'd like to silence the critics.'

'Something like that.'

Tania Saul wet the tip of her forefinger and dabbed at seeds and crumbs. 'A man on a mission. You could say I've been on one these past few days, trying to work out who'd want to hurt Billy.' She cocked her head at Charlie. 'Nan happens to be a Thai name; did you know that? And Billy's real name was Kiet—that didn't last long. Anyway, they were both given a hard time in various ways. Outright bullying, in Billy's case. Insults in the street. People would *cross* the street, in fact. This is—or was—a pretty white-bread town.'

'I can imagine.'

'I doubt it. Sorry, that was rude. Anyway, I got some of the spill-over racism—like I was soiled or something.'

'Rough.'

She looked annoyed: inadequate response. 'Yes, it was *rough*. But Nan and Billy bore the brunt of it, especially in primary school. The thing is, I can't see kids killing and burying anyone, can you?'

Charlie decided not to tiptoe around. 'Kids have older siblings though. They have parents. Was there anyone more than casually racist back then?'

Tania barked a laugh. 'Oh, there was nothing casual about it. And some of them had that look—you know, white supremacy.'

'Yeah. I know.'

'But kill someone? They weren't *bad* like that, if you know what I mean. Just not very bright.'

'What about the kids' teachers over the years. Any of them a bit...'

Tania shook her head. 'You know primary school teachers.'

Charlie didn't, but she seemed to be saying that your average primary school teacher didn't go around killing and burying people. Pretty sure I can prove otherwise, he thought.

But she was moving on. 'Anyway, how likely is it that a parent or a teacher would drive all the way to the youth camp and hang around on the off-chance Billy would run away?'

'And the teachers on duty would have been too busy,' Charlie said.

Tania was constructing a new sandwich. 'Exactly,' she said. He realised that he wasn't bringing her anything new, she'd already thought it all through.

She looked up. 'Which leaves,' she said, 'someone who was already in the area. A local. A paedophile, say.'

'Yes. A line of inquiry that was followed at the time, but paedophiles weren't thick on the ground.'

She snorted. 'I expect there's a lot who never get caught. What about the camp staff?'

'Checked and cleared.'

Tania Saul lifted her sandwich with both hands and tore out a bite as if impatient with Charlie and their conversation. 'His beach towel.'

Charlie went very still. A tingle in his scalp. 'I did wonder about that at the time.'

'Did you? So did I, but no one listened. It didn't make sense to me in the first place that he'd run away from the camp to go swimming—he didn't really like swimming. But take some ratty old towel with him instead of his good towel? No.'

'It was important to him?'

'Very. Nan gave it to him that Christmas. The two of them were very close and he adored it. Right from the start I thought he must have run off because he was upset and intended to come back later. But someone grabbed him, for whatever reason, or he walked in on something he shouldn't have, and was killed. And whoever did it staged the beach scene using that old towel.'

'Yes.'

'A mind at work,' Tania Saul said. 'Clever. Cruel.' She gave a little shudder. 'I can feel him.'

31

CHARLIE RETURNED FROM Point Leo on Tuesday to find a Hyundai police van parked outside his house, two uniforms on his veranda, the male officer in the act of knocking on the glass, the female cupping her eyes to peer through it. Hearing the Skoda pull into the driveway, they turned in unison. 'Mr Deravin?'

'Yes.'

Charlie went about his business as he said it, methodical, his mind racing. He took his surfboard down from the roof rack and rested it on the old garden table, then sluiced the sand from his feet and fetched a tin of wax from the footlocker. Cast looks at the uniforms. They weren't wearing faces of professional regret—no one had died—and seemed too junior to be asking questions on behalf of homicide, sex crimes or major collision.

'Can I help you?' he went on, beginning to apply the wax to his board.

They watched, fascinated, and then the spell broke. They were based at Hastings, they said, and had been tasked with an action.

'Tasked with what action?'

'Your whereabouts on Saturday. Specifically, the afternoon.'

Charlie felt some sympathy for the men and women he'd interviewed over the years. Sometimes they simply lied, but often they were completely flummoxed by the demand to recall dates, places, movements, their days merging and blending.

'I was here early afternoon. Mid-afternoon I went surfing at Point Leo.'

The guy perked up. He surfs, thought Charlie.

'Anyone vouch for that?' his colleague asked.

'Not sure. Hang on…'

Charlie leaned into the Skoda and backed out with the carpark ticket. 'Will this do?'

The examined it expressionlessly. 'You said you were here early afternoon. Where were you in the morning?'

'Here. Reading the paper. Pottering.'

'At lunchtime?'

Charlie pointed at the old table on the front lawn. 'Right there. Can I ask what this is about?'

'Can anyone at all vouch for your movements on Saturday?'

Charlie shrugged. He'd seen Noel Saltash patrolling the beach early Saturday morning, but not to talk to. It was unlikely the Point Leo mob would remember him. 'Sorry, no.'

The woman had been taking notes. She came to the end of her scrawl, pocketed her notebook and nodded at her partner. 'Thank you, Mr Deravin.'

'You going to tell me why you want to know what I was doing on Saturday?'

'Have a good day, sir, what's left of it.'

In what was left of his day, Charlie finished waxing his board, defrosted and consumed a pesto sauce from November 2019 and tried to watch junk.

Unable to concentrate, he finally called Fran Bekker. 'Is your investigation concentrating on me for any reason?'

'Not really.'

'Not really? I had two uniforms from Hastings here today, wanting to know about my movements on Saturday.'

'I have no knowledge of that, Charlie. Perhaps it's related to your other issue.'

Other issue. Kessler. 'All right. Any update, now that I've got you on the line?'

After a longish silence, she said, 'We found your mother's car.'

And immediately the old maroon Corolla, 300,000 km on the clock and likely to last another 300,000, was in Charlie's head. But that car had taken her to her death, or so everyone thought, and been badly damaged in the process. Who would want it after that? After it had been scoured for trace evidence? You'd want to toss it into some big metal-crushing machine, surely? And why hadn't he wondered about that car, all these years?

'Where?'

'In a tractor shed in Leongatha.'

'What was it doing there?'

'Your dad sold it—still registered in his name. He had it repaired and sold it to a dairy farmer, who drove it until it gave up the ghost.'

'You going to retest it for trace evidence?'

'If there is any, it'll be badly degraded by now. But yes, we will, you know that, Charlie.'

His other issue, she'd said. He called Sue Mead and asked for a Kessler update.

'Stay out of it, Charlie.'

'Just asking, sarge. Did you form an impression of the jury, for example?'

'What do you mean, impression of the jury?'

'Well, the last one was overloaded with defence favourites. Football fans, older women.'

'Charlie, good to talk to you, sorry again about your mother, but—'

'If you guys need to debrief me, just say so.'

'Not going to happen.'

'Ms Picard is happy to talk off the record, if that would help.'

'Not going to happen, Charlie.'

'Okay, just thought I'd mention it. What's Allardyce doing?'

A pause, guarded and prohibitive. 'Why do you ask?'

At once, Charlie was on the back foot. 'Sorry, sarge, none of my business.'

'Did you know his son was run over on Saturday? Jake, the oldest, a hit-and-run.'

'Oh,' Charlie said. That explained the cops. Allardyce thought he'd done it.

'How is he?'

'Hurt pretty bad,' Sue said. 'He was out jogging.' The line went dead.

The news creeped Charlie out. Forces were at work.

32

IN THE STILLNESS of those days in early February, Charlie walked. Walked and brooded.

Sometimes, halfway to Swanage, he'd cut through the dunes to Balinoe Creek and head back along it and then skirt the campground on his way to the beach, eyeing the small dome tents of schoolkids, their chip packets and Red Bull cans accumulating in the grassy verges. Sometimes he saw these kids, chaperoned by a couple of teachers, toiling self-consciously along the beach, saddled with boredom, obligation and massive backpacks. There always seemed to be a Somali kid alone at the rear.

Walking soothed him, his bafflement and formlessness. He made mental lists as he stamped along, transferring them to paper when he got home. All the names he could recall, his mother's friends and workmates, and, in the evenings, he phoned them, hoping something might have shifted, now that the world knew her body had been found.

But nothing had shifted: they were sympathetic, they knew nothing—and a crabbed kind of cynicism grew in him to learn that Bekker and McGuire hadn't bothered to reinterview most of them.

He could think of only one other avenue of investigation and one morning, back from his swim, showered, shaved, comb tracks in his hair and coffee and toast at his elbow, he sat at the kitchen table, working his phone and his laptop, tracking down the title history of his mother's old rental house, 12 Longstaff Street, Swanage.

Real-estate ownership was a matter of public record, and there it was: BM Holdings. Well, that told him nothing; it was part of EKW Nominees anyway. What was interesting was that the property had not changed hands since 1998. Charlie continued to search, conscious that current and original police investigations would have covered the same ground. They'd not found anything, presumably, so what made him think he could do better? Unless Bekker and McGuire were already following a new lead. Following a lead that traced back to his father?

The names listed under BM Holdings were Brian and Madeline Wilson—who were also linked, with one Evangeline Wilson, to EKW Nominees. Charlie's eye might have let the name Wilson slide unnoticed off the page. But Evangeline…

Memories flooded in. He remembered a shy, gentle woman on the margins of the backyard barbecues, the beach games and birthday parties when he was about thirteen. Married to a CID detective constable, a Keith or a Ken? Based at a police station near Dandenong. He hadn't registered with Charlie back then—but his wife had, the grief in her beautiful face after he was killed in a pile-up on the Monash Freeway. Charlie, still a boy, halfway a man, full of sweet yearning and drama, wanting to make things better for her.

The Wilsons had lived in a rental house in Menlo Beach back then. Must have bought the Swanage site with a view to building a permanent home. Evangeline—the words to the old song in Charlie's head now—had moved away with the kids a few months after the accident. Apparently she'd not done anything with the block on Longstaff Street. Too-hard basket, maybe.

Charlie googled her. She'd died in 2018. The kids Brian and Madeline inherited, presumably. Brian was an accountant in Geelong, Madeline a cellist with the Tasmanian Symphony.

He called Wilson Financial Planning and was put through to Brian, who was irritable.

'I've already been over this with you people, just last week.'

'Ticking boxes, Mr Wilson. Sorry to interrupt.'

'Like I said, Maddy and I thought we'd get a better price for the block if we built on it. I mean, who wants to buy an old slab? If only we'd known.'

'Your mother was never tempted to sell or develop it?'

'She just wanted to get away from the Peninsula. She never got over Dad's death.'

A reproving note: Charlie was trespassing. He said, 'You were quite young when the three of you left?'

Wilson snorted. 'Oh, well done the police. You think a three-year-old and a five-year-old and their grieving mother killed and buried two strangers first.'

'Thank you for your time,' Charlie said, but the line was dead. He curled himself into a self-castigating ball.

33

OUT OF SORTS, out of leads, no worthwhile surf anywhere on the coast but needing to do something, Charlie climbed onto his father's old bike that afternoon and bumped along the potholed clay roads behind the clifftop mansions, then down to the store and up to the road to Swanage. Pumping hard, burning away his mood. The Woodleigh school bus swept past, a kid pressing his bare bum against the rear window. What I'm reduced to, thought Charlie.

His ride took him to his mother's old street—of course. Not much of a police presence now, crime-scene tape and one forensic services van, but he U-turned before he could be spotted and freewheeled away from the street and down to the sea, and there was Mark Valente, cycling uphill towards him, scarcely puffing. His legs flexed and pistoned, and the bike, a trifling bit of metal tubing, tilted violently left and right beneath his bulky frame. When Charlie was a kid, you were careful to avoid Valente and his bike. He was apt to suggest a marathon ride somewhere, forty, fifty, sixty kilometres up hills and around blind bends.

Halting, setting one foot on the ground, the other on the pedal, Valente said, 'Charlie.'

'Mark.'

They were in the middle of the street like two local geezers on a back road. No cars in sight.

Valente leapt right in. 'Been to your mother's?'

'You got me.'

'I see her car's been found.'

'Yep.'

Silence. Charlie wanted to say, I've got a good reason to be here—what's your story? He stared at Valente with mixed feelings. In some ways, the old cop had supplied what Rhys hadn't. Dad was warm and loving, Charlie thought. Funny. But disengaged. No good at advice or guidance, or explaining things. Dad didn't show me how to surf, how to wax a board, how to fix a bike—Mark did all that. Dad had seemed baffled to have two sons; Mark had seemed to want sons he didn't have.

He watched Valente take a swig of water from the

bottle attached to the frame of his bike. He was kitted out for cycling: gloves, shoes, helmet, Lycra. And the old Valente was there in him when he scowled at Charlie's bike. 'Jesus, Charlie, look at the rust on that thing.'

'It's Dad's, been in the shed for years.'

'Get it seen to, mate.'

'Will do.'

The old pattern: Valente stating how things should be, Charlie acquiescing.

'Sea air,' Valente said. 'You need to protect against it.'

'I know.'

'Ride with me.'

Ride with me, walk with me, Charlie thought. I'm a biddable guy, overlooked and ignored, a man without agency. He rode with Valente all the way back to Menlo Beach.

At Tidepool Street, Valente leaned his bike against the driveway fence and wheeled the offending rust-bucket into the shadowed reaches of the carport while Charlie, feeling railroaded, unlocked the sliding door and leaned into the fridge. Valente wanted a light beer. Charlie found one, a Boags nestling in the door next to some out-of-date orange juice. A full-strength beer for himself; cheese, olives, crackers.

He pulled out a tray for the snacks and found it wasn't just any old tray, it was one that took him back to a day before it all went wrong, Rhys returning from

Tasmania with an extradited prisoner and a gift for his wife. A Huon pine tray. Its paleness and smoothness; its soft odour.

Get a grip. Surely he could deal with Mark Valente for an hour. The bike was probably already upended, ready to be stripped down, Valente ready to show Charlie how it was done. With the tray unwieldy in his right hand, he opened the sliding door with his left, stepped out onto the veranda and the podcast twins were there.

'Charlie,' said Ashleigh Deamer, 'we were sorry to hear about your mother.'

Why was she the talker of the two? Nadal always a step behind her with his slick face on—as if he had plenty to say. Charlie looked past them at the street. Their yellow Beetle was partly obscured by the banksias. The tray grew heavy in his hand; he set it down on the lid of the footlocker and looked up again. Deamer and Nadal stood where the lawn met a low retaining wall of redgum sleepers and so were looking down at Charlie and he hated that.

'What do you want?'

'To pay our respects,' Deamer said.

Charlie glanced at Nadal, who didn't confirm but stared back, slim and at ease in cargo pants and T-shirt. Deamer wore baggy shorts, strappy sandals and a boat-neck shirt, baring a tanned shoulder. She'd cut her hair, a tousled look, faintly post-sexual, and Charlie saw again the pair's gorgeousness.

He returned his attention to Nadal and his sleepy eyes.

'You didn't know my mother and you don't know me. Why pay respects?'

'May we have a quick word?' Deamer asked, stepping blithely down onto the veranda, tendons flexing in her legs. Nadal joined her and Charlie was trapped.

'Look, I don't know what you want, not interested in fact, and I'm entertaining a friend.'

A hunter's light in them now. They were too close, peering past his shoulder, hankering for a glimpse of Charlie's friend inside the house.

'Just a quick word,' Deamer said. She bared her dazzling teeth.

'As I said, I—'

'Hate to say this, but are they treating your father as a suspect?'

'Suspect for what?'

'Oh, come on,' scoffed Nadal.

Deamer touched her boyfriend's arm—she knew he'd subside—and turned again to Charlie, saying, 'We believe there was a lot of behind-the-scenes mopping up going on around the time your mother was murdered. Can you shed any light on that?'

'Not interested,' Charlie said, shunning them, reaching to pick up the tray.

With his back turned briefly, he didn't at first register the strange, diffuse prickling on his bare legs and arms as water droplets. Or why Deamer was shrieking, Nadal swearing.

He turned. Valente was spraying them with the garden hose, the fingers of one hand on the nozzle, the other hand resting casually in his pocket. Charlie knew that evil old grin and dodged as Valente flicked his wrist, sending another loop of water, messing with Deamer and Nadal, soaking their shirts and shorts, hosing their dignity.

He stopped firing; pretended to blow away the gun smoke.

'That counts as assault,' Deamer said, calm now.

'So report me,' Valente said. He thought he was comical as he feinted with the hose again.

'You old shit,' snarled Nadal. 'Everything's going to come out, you know.'

'Go your hardest.'

When they were gone, Valente said, 'Let's sink those beers, young Charles.'

'Mark, what's going on?'

'They're digging up dirt. Weren't you listening?'

'About?'

'About? Your mother. That old heartache.'

34

WHEN VALENTE HAD GONE home, Charlie angled the garden table umbrella so that his phone was shaded and put in a Skype call to Rhys and Fay.

Fay's face appeared, lit by the porthole. Even with the distortions of distance and technology, she looked tense, her hair limp, bags under her eyes as if she'd been fretting.

'Your Dad's just been taken to the mainland with a handful of others. To hospital.'

Charlie blinked. 'His heart?'

'They think it's the virus that's been in the news.'

To Charlie the virus was a story that he glimpsed on TV. Deaths in China, an elderly Chinese man in France. Face masks in the streets. Maybe he should start paying attention.

'A Japanese hospital,' he said, with more reassurance than he felt, 'he'll be in good hands.'

'I hope so.'

'How did he get it?'

She shrugged. 'Three thousand passengers, Charlie. From all over. And we've stopped at heaps of places, taken side trips by bus here and there...'

'Does that mean you have it, too?'

'I don't have any symptoms, but they took a sample and I have to quarantine in my cabin until the results come in.'

He saw her glance around the confined space, then return to the camera. 'As you can imagine...'

'Stir crazy.'

'And it's only been a couple of hours,' she said.

He grimaced sympathy. 'So what are Dad's symptoms?'

'Coughing, aches. It was like he had the flu. He could be in hospital for a couple of weeks.'

'But if the ship—'

'The ship's not going anywhere. We're anchored offshore for the duration.'

He made reassuring noises then said goodbye and dithered. Message Liam?

He called. 'Just letting you know Dad's been taken to

hospital. They think it's that virus in the news.'

Liam said nothing for a moment. Then: 'Okay.'

'That it?'

'Well…Is he going to die?'

'Don't be a prick. Fay's upset. I think you should call her.'

A mistake. I implied he's got ethical shortcomings; I dared to tell him what to do. Charlie visualised the granite set of his brother's shoulders.

'Or not,' Charlie said. 'Just thought you'd like to know, that's all.'

There was another silence. Then Liam said gruffly, the closest he'd get to appeasement: 'How sick is he?'

'I don't know. Enough to go to hospital.'

'They won't finish the cruise, surely?'

'The ship's in quarantine. They'll fly home as soon as Dad's allowed to travel.'

'Does Fay have it?'

'Maybe. She says she feels all right.'

'Okay, thanks,' Liam said, and was gone, leaving Charlie to wonder if he'd ever navigate the reefs and currents of a conversation with his brother.

The phone rang as soon as he placed it on the kitchen bench. Anna. He hadn't been ghosting her exactly, but he hadn't called for a couple of days.

'Hi.'

Her brightness was forced. 'Just wanted to hear your voice.'

'Thanks, good to hear yours.'

'I've missed you.'

'Missed you, too,' Charlie said.

'If you're not doing anything, come up and see me tomorrow. Mum's fussing is driving me up the wall.'

'Actually,' Charlie said, 'I've been a bit flat out. And I just had bad news, my father's in hospital, that virus.'

'Oh, Charlie,' she said, her sympathy palpable. 'Is it bad?'

'I don't know.'

'If there's anything I can do, just—What's that noise? Where are you?'

'Knock on the door,' Charlie said. 'Speak to you later,' he added, completing the call and crossing the room.

And so she didn't hear the noises that followed the knock on the door—the flurry of punches, Charlie grunting as air was driven from his lungs, Charlie stumbling back into the room, his body thumping to the floor.

35

HIS FIRST, FLEETING thought: a bunch of thugs was throwing punches at him. But it was only Inspector Allardyce with a full head of steam on, forcing him inside. Another punch to the stomach, his jaw, left cheek, the back of his neck, each blow a punctuation mark: 'You. Run. My. Son. Over?'

Then Charlie was flat on his back, on fire, and thinking he should probably roll away as Allardyce lifted his foot, ready for a piston shot at his groin. He put up his forearm: 'Don't!'

'Eh? You go for Jake?'

'Don't.'

He rolled away as the foot came down. Allardyce, in mid-stomp, stumbled forward, off balance and Charlie, behind him now, spun around on his lower spine, lifted both feet, slammed them into the man's overfed rear. He watched his old boss fall to his knees, hands outstretched, making a grab at the sofa but shoving it back against the bookcase instead, revealing dustballs and a sock. 'Huh,' grunted Charlie. He'd thought that sock was gone for good.

Testing every articulation of his limbs, he rolled again, onto his side; then, starting with one arm to prop up his torso, by degrees to his feet. He hurt all over, new pain upon old. He wanted to kick Allardyce again, the fat cunt.

But he was thoroughly a policeman. He had come in as a cadet, then clawed his way up to a halfway decent detective senior constable. There had always been officers of higher rank acting like arseholes. You didn't quibble, you didn't defy. It was 'Yes, sir' and 'Yes, ma'am' all the way. He'd shoved Allardyce over a desk—but that was an unprecedented spurt of indignation. This...This was his inspector storming in and beating the shit out of him.

The inspector was down among the dustballs now, wheezing in a way that seemed dangerously unhealthy. Charlie was torn—help him up, or plant a well-placed foot on the massive buttocks?

'Sir?'

Allardyce stirred, manoeuvring until he could sit with his back against the sofa, hair demoralised and legs outstretched, trousers rucked up to reveal huge white calves and sensible, mismatched business socks: small diamonds on one, larger on the other.

He was Charlie's inspector, and he was nothing. Charlie fetched a glass of water. Knelt to offer it. And, for a moment, thought that Allardyce wanted to slap the offending hand aside, the resentment heavy in his features.

Allardyce took the glass. Sipped, sipped again and handed it back with a muttered 'Thanks,' not looking at Charlie.

'Want me to help you up?'

Allardyce was silent but for his constricted breathing.

Charlie stood. 'I'll make tea. We'll have a picnic on the floor.'

He had the jug under the tap, skin prickling to think of Allardyce creeping in behind him, when he heard the man say, 'Got something stronger?'

Charlie settled the jug and turned. Allardyce hadn't moved. 'Sir, you're already drunk. I'm not giving you more booze.'

'Fuck you, then.'

'That's the spirit.'

The water began to boil. It was the noisiest jug in creation, conversation impossible, so Charlie returned to the sitting room, getting close but not too close to Allardyce. He got into his face and spoke clearly: 'Someone else ran over your fuckwit son.'

He knelt back on his heels; watched Allardyce.

Allardyce wouldn't look at him. His expression was the one that incited the squad to call him Dullardyce.

'Look, sir, I've been questioned,' Charlie said. 'I was here on the Peninsula all day Saturday.'

'You had it done.'

'Like Kessler had me and Anna Picard run over, you mean?' Charlie said.

Allardyce gave Charlie his mulish look and, raising his voice above the sound of the jug, said, 'Since we're speaking of alibis, my son can also show he's in the clear. He didn't run you and your tart over.'

'That's it, sir—stay classy,' Charlie said. 'Alibied by half the club, right?' He paused. 'How is he, incidentally?'

'What do you care?' Allardyce said, looking away— but something in his tone indicated weary disgust and Charlie thought: He doesn't believe his own son.

The jug switched off. 'How do you like your tea?' Charlie said, returning to the kitchen.

Hearing a grunt and a groan behind him, he chanced a quick look. Allardyce, heaving himself upright, repositioned the sofa and settled in it, his spine squashing one of the cushions. 'Black. Strong.'

Charlie poured, peppermint tea for himself, and returned to the sitting room. His knees when he sat were a metre from the inspector's, but Allardyce was a spent force. 'Sir, I didn't knock your son over and I didn't have it done.'

'Someone did. Your girlfriend.'

260

'She's in a wheelchair now, and she doesn't know those kind of people.'

'So she claims.'

Charlie froze. 'You went to see her?'

'Don't get your panties in a twist. Her parents were there.' Allardyce blew on his tea and sipped, an unhealthy heat in his face. Heart problem? Indigestion? Or just his shitty personality.

The silence deepened. Charlie had no intention of breaking it. He could smell Allardyce now: perspiration, booze, aftershave and futility. 'You okay to drive home?'

Allardyce snarled, 'You think we're finished?'

'I do, yes.'

Allardyce screwed up his face, as if weighing options. 'Maybe.'

Then, from far, far away, he muttered: 'Kessler's guilty.'

'Yes.'

'That other victim you and your girlfriend found.'

'What about her?'

'Credible.'

'Yes.'

'Two victims,' Allardyce said, 'never crossed paths with each other, raped two years apart at a club event.'

'I know that, sir.'

'He was going places, you know?'

He means Luke Kessler, Charlie thought. Not his kid.

'He had recruiters sniffing around. The Saints, the Bulldogs.'

'And that makes it okay?'

Allardyce flushed. 'Fuck you. The evidence wasn't there, last year. A classic case of he-said, she-said.'

'That's not entirely true, sir. Everyone went straight down the victim-blaming route, including you. Tunnel vision. You practically told us not to look too hard.'

'I object to that.'

'Object away.'

'Doing my job, that's all. People lie, including so-called rape victims. You would know that if you were a halfway decent police officer.'

Charlie drained his tea. 'You barged into my home. You punched me several times. I can go to a police station as soon as you leave here and file a complaint. Strip off and show them the bruises. And again tomorrow, when they should be a nice, rich colour.'

Allardyce shook his head. 'I'm an inspector, you fool. You're a fuck-up on suspension.'

'Sir, why are you here?'

When Allardyce finally lifted his face, it was full of nothing but confusion. 'I wish I knew.'

'I didn't hurt your son—but I'm damn sure he ran me and Anna Picard over, despite what his little pals swear to.'

Allardyce screwed his fleshy face up again; a man in pain. 'That club of his. They're all...'

Allardyce didn't have the words, but Charlie felt able to supply some of them. 'Woman haters,' for example. 'Rape apologists.' Not to mention criminal and lost to shame.

Charlie watched as a succession of moods passed through Allardyce. Weepiness, sulky anger, self-castigation and finger pointing. He understood that mostly the guy felt betrayed by his son and his son's friends. Felt that he'd betrayed himself, too. And that the need to deflect had sent him crashing in here to blame Charlie.

He left, finally, without apologising for his actions or his son's but with a choice parting shot: 'Don't go thinking I haven't forgotten you helped fuck up a trial and assaulted me in front of everyone.'

'Etched on my soul, boss.'

'Prick.'

Charlie watched the inspector climb into a maroon Pajero and tear away with a spurt of street gravel. He was tempted, just then, to report him. But the aggravation, for a start, let alone proving that Allardyce had even been to his house. A classic case of he-said, he-said. And he'd feel small.

It paid to be safe, though. What if Allardyce gets steamed up again? What if he's told his son's football mates where I live? Where Anna lives? Oh, Christ.

'Charlie,' she said, her voice flat.

'Look, sorry about before, I had a visitor—Inspector Allardyce. He said he went to see you.'

'This afternoon. That's partly why I called you before.'

'Sorry.'

'You're always saying that. How did he find me?'

'He's a cop,' Charlie said. Overweight, hidebound, a

263

miserable sack of guilt, but he'd have tracked her down to her parents' house in five minutes.

'I hate this,' she said.

Charlie didn't know if she meant she hated being tracked down by Allardyce or ghosted by her boyfriend. If this was their first fight, he hated it too. 'Are you all right? Was he threatening?'

'No. But it was all a bit strange,' she said, softening a little. 'Mum and Dad were hovering around, just in case, which seemed to bother him.'

'Was he drunk?'

'Yes. I could smell it on him. I think that's partly why Mum and Dad didn't want to leave me alone with him. Mainly he just seemed sad, and I finally persuaded them I'd be all right.'

'What did he want?'

'Not entirely clear. On the one hand he was sorry I got hurt, but on the other he seemed to be saying it wasn't his son, as if he thought it probably *was*. Or his son's friends, meaning Luke Kessler's friends.'

'An actual apology? More than I got.'

'More than I got too, really. It came across as regret. He talked about the culture of football clubs and how the original Kessler investigation could have been tighter.'

'Tighter,' said Charlie.

'Tighter. He also said, wait for it: "The fact remains, Miss Picard, your actions did precipitate a mistrial."'

The Allardyce we know and love, thought Charlie.

'He's good at deflecting. Did he stay long?'

'No. That was it, a kind of apology and a kind of telling-off.'

'Okay,' said Charlie eventually. 'I'd better call my sergeant, let her know what he's been up to.'

'Don't you dare hang up on me. You've not been to see me. Why is that?'

Charlie stumbled. 'You know, trying to keep a low profile, people hassling me.'

'That's not good enough, Charlie. We were going really well.'

'I know. Look, Anna it's…I just…' He swallowed. 'I don't want to involve you in all my shit.'

'I want to be involved. I love you.'

'Me too.'

What else could you say? But he felt like he was returning a favour before he was quite ready.

'Then come and see me. Talk to me. Tell me what's going on. I'm a good listener.'

The silence went on for too long. She said, 'Or not,' and cut the call.

He paced around the room, aching everywhere. Picked up the sock. Dropped it again and called her back. 'How about tomorrow?'

'I'm not going anywhere.'

'I'm black and blue all over. He got a few punches in.'

'Interesting you should forewarn me. Does that mean you expect post-breakup sex?'

Charlie gave a strangled laugh. She'd made a joke?

'See you tomorrow,' she said airily, and was gone.

He called Sue Mead.

'Are you going to report it?'

'No point, sarge,' Charlie said.

'Probably wise.' There was a pause and she added, 'Charlie, you didn't hurt his kid, did you?'

'Fuck you, sergeant,' Charlie said.

She called him back half-a-dozen times. Charlie stared at his phone, watching the notifications come up on the screen. He felt small, sulky. Dr Fiske would have a field day.

Finally he answered. They got their apologies out of the way. Scant comfort in that, though.

36

IF HE WAS going up to the city, he might as well see everyone.

Emma first. Vast carparks ringed the LaTrobe campus and most were empty this early in the university year. He slotted the Skoda under a slender gumtree near the sports centre and set off for the main library. He saw only a handful of staff and students—not that he could tell them apart, necessarily. Youngish, scruffy-chic, they ambled along, glued to their screens or sprawled on the grass, but here and there he saw family units of a self-conscious fresher clutching enrolment forms, trailed by stunned parents neat as pins and sulky younger siblings. Charlie didn't know what any of these people made of him—if anything. But he quite enjoyed striding the paths and crossing the footbridge as if he had a brain and belonged in the place.

He reached the Agora and texted his daughter: *Here*.

She replied: *Info desk*.

He entered the library and saw her break away from a cluster of kids and skip across the carpet towards him, arms as wide as the world. That gave him a buzz and, in the milliseconds before the collision, he took her in: a ribbon of movement, swinging yellow hair, lithe and brown in shorts, sandals and a green T-shirt. The Deravin look, he thought, as she wrapped herself around him.

'Daddyo.'

'Daughter of mine.'

'I've got twenty minutes,' she said, leading him to a café in the corner of the library's ground floor. Twenty minutes' break from shelving, processing and serving at the help desk, five mornings a week. That would drop to three when lectures started.

Charlie fetched coffees and pastries and was settling them on the table when she asked, 'How's Grandpa doing?'

'Not good. It's knocked him around.'

'Fay?'

'Not as bad.'

'Poor Grandpa.' She glanced past Charlie worriedly, as if looking for a link between her world and her grandfather's. 'I have Chinese friends who went home before

268

Christmas and now they might have to stay there.'

This place is usually thronging with overseas students, Charlie thought. He looked around him; out at the Agora. 'That's rough.'

She shrugged and he sensed that her observation had dimensions he hadn't fathomed. 'Anyway,' he said, 'they'll be home in a week or so, but it would really cheer them up if you'd Skype with them.'

'I will,' Emma said. She paused. 'Mum said the police will want to talk to Grandpa now.'

Charlie sighed. 'Unfortunately.'

He watched his daughter play with her coffee mug. 'Dad, what was Grandma like?'

She'd been asking this since her early teens. When she was little, Fay had, in effect, been her paternal grandmother. Then, while still acknowledging that connection, she'd become curious about the woman who had disappeared when she was a baby. The mystery touched her, the horror. And Charlie had always tried to portray the Rose Deravin who was his mother, not the Rose Deravin who was the wife of Rhys. That had seemed to satisfy Emma, but he suspected that a different need drove her now. Her grandmother had been murdered; her grandfather might have done it.

So he didn't know how to answer this time. He faltered as he began. 'She had this...she was always calm and gentle, always held something in reserve. It was a pretty rowdy crowd at the beach back then, mainly Grandpa's police friends, and she was...not standoffish, but she only took part on her terms. It seemed to bother some of the others.'

'The other wives?'

Charlie looked appreciatively at his daughter. 'You're not so dumb.'

Emma hunched over, as if weighed down by the book-crammed floors above her. 'Sometimes I wonder.'

Charlie patted her hand. 'Take it from me. Anyway, Mum was her own person. Not a snob, but she didn't need any of the others. Then I'm sorry to say that Grandpa cheated on her, and I think she was devastated.' He paused. 'I *know* she was.'

'Did he cheat with others,' said Emma, 'or only with Fay?' She flapped her hands. 'Sorry, I'm not judging her, you know how much I love her. But, you know…'

Charlie did. 'I don't think he had other affairs. I think he and Mum were drifting apart. But it still hit her hard.'

'It doesn't make sense,' Emma said, just then noticing pastry flecks on her T-shirt and swiping at them. 'Wouldn't Grandma have wanted to hurt Grandpa and not the other way around? They were getting a divorce; he was getting the other woman. Why would he want to kill her?' She paused. 'Hypothetically.'

'We need you on the defence team,' Charlie said. 'But actually you know I can't see either of them wanting to hurt the other.'

Emma was sad. 'The whole thing's really strange. Two bodies? What's that about?'

'Yeah.' Charlie squeezed her hand. 'Wish I knew.'

Just then her phone pinged, and she read the message with a strange, secret, buoyant smile. A new boyfriend, he thought. Or an established one that I'll be the last to know about. And his phone pinged, and it was Anna: *ETA?*

He texted back *12.30*, and saw that Emma was texting too, her thumbs a blur. A certain kind of togetherness, he thought: father and daughter messaging their lovers at the same time.

He kissed her goodbye, watched her skip back to work at the help desk, and walked to his car. Ten minutes to Ivanhoe, according to Google Maps, and he set out, feeling antsy: Anna had sent a follow-up message: her parents were out for the afternoon, and he should come around to the back door, which would be open. He didn't like that. She was still a target.

He said as much when he found her in the sunroom and leaned in to kiss her.

She wasn't fussed. 'Nitro will sort them out.'

Charlie cast the labrador a dubious look. 'Slobber them to death.'

'Relax. We left the door unlocked because you were coming. Otherwise it's always kept locked if I'm here alone.'

'Here alone,' said Charlie and the knots in him didn't ease.

'Honestly, relax. I see you brought lunch.'

He waggled the delicatessen bag. 'Cheese, olives, salami, bread, pâté.'

'Major food groups.'

Charlie placed a 1950s heirloom traymobile next to her hip then walked through to the kitchen and arranged everything on small plates, which he took, with a water jug and glasses, back to the sunroom. Then he sat, the traymobile between them, and he looked at Anna and she was looking at him.

'The very definition of a meaningful look,' he said.

'Yes.'

'I'm sorry I was avoiding you.'

She reached across to take his hand. 'I know.'

He'd felt inert and aimless, he told her. 'Like I'm playing a waiting game.'

Faint exasperation threaded through her. 'Yes, you're waiting, but you've also been doing things. Talking to people, gathering information, theorising…It will all help.'

'Sure,' Charlie said, but dejectedly, as if her words hadn't registered. 'I guess I'm a bit fed up with myself.'

'Yeah, well, I'm stuck here like a lump, I'm bored, my parents are driving me bonkers. But, you know, life goes on…'

A cliché; but the sentiment was sincere. Charlie shook himself. Leaned in and nuzzled her ear. 'Sorry.'

She said, 'I'm sorry, too. But I shouldn't complain.'

He held her hand now. 'I'll mention your memorial service idea when I see Liam later.'

'Good.'

'You'll come, won't you?'

She tocked her knuckles against her plaster cast. 'Funeral chic. But no, Charlie, I won't. For a start I don't want to be a hassle—a wheelchair; maybe crutches—but also it wouldn't be right, it's your show, your family, whom I haven't met.' She watched him for a moment. 'Yet. And people are going to be eyeing you like a hawk, meaning me as well, and I don't know if either of us wants that level of scrutiny.'

'Oh. Okay.'

'Take me to bed.'

Charlie opened and closed his mouth uselessly. 'Er...'

'Come on—we've got two hours before they're back. We'll manage.'

Three-thirty now, Charlie grinning to himself as he drove to Northcote, reminded irresistibly of his late adolescence, a few hours snatched with a girlfriend while her parents were out. He was an adult—an unsatisfactory one, probably—but fuck it, life could be a tonic sometimes.

Liam and Ryan showed him to a metal chair at a metal table under an umbrella tree in the backyard, then joined him with cheeses on a plate and bottles of micro-brewery beer. Typically it was Ryan who twigged. 'You look like the cat that got the cream.'

'What?' Charlie shut down his face. 'I don't know what you mean.'

'What did she think of your face? You look like you've been used as a punching bag.'

'It's nothing,' Charlie said, but he could feel Liam watching with an imperfect impression of perfect ease, waiting for him to explain himself.

He tried. 'Just a minor difference of opinion.'

Liam sniffed. Ryan touched his arm lightly. 'How's the lovely Emma? You saw her, right?'

'She's fine, sends her love.'

And they sat like that for a while. Charlie felt resentment stir in him: the leafiness of the yard, tucked away from the world; the fancy label on the beer; Liam's snootiness and Ryan's go-betweening. He struggled against it. 'A friend of mine suggested maybe a memorial service for Mum. We can still have a funeral,' he added, 'but small and private. A memorial service would be more of a celebration.'

He was watching Liam. Liam gave the merest nod. Encouraged, he turned to Ryan, who said, 'It's a great idea.' Darting a look at Liam, he added, 'We haven't spoken to Fay for a few days. Do they have a return date yet?'

'No. Dad's still in hospital.'

Ryan tipped his bottle, watching Charlie. He sipped; set the bottle down again. 'His underlying health issues.'

Not for the first time, Charlie wondered if everyone knew more than he did about everything. How would Ryan know about Rhys's health issues? 'I've been googling the virus,' he said. 'If your health's compromised, it can really knock you around. People have died. What if he does?'

'At least he's in hospital. Tokyo? They'll know what they're doing.'

Charlie nodded. 'Anyway, he'll need our support when he gets home. Not only his health—the Homicide Squad are standing by to have another go at him.'

Even seated, Liam was tall and disparaging. 'And so they should. Maybe now we'll get some answers.'

'Oh, fuck off, Liam,' Charlie said. He looked to Ryan for support: Ryan stared back, not unfriendly but with an air of judgment in reserve. Maybe he was sticking with Liam on this issue.

'He dishonoured our mother,' Liam said.

From anyone else, this would have sounded comical. Charlie heard it as a warning rattle. 'Are you going to dob him in?'

Liam looked at him with distaste. 'Dob him in?'

'Tell them you saw his car.'

'No. What do you take me for?'

Charlie could feel Ryan. He chanced a quick look and saw Ryan give a little jerk of the head.

'Sorry. Of course you wouldn't.'

Liam nodded, but his look said he thought Charlie's apology makeshift and unsatisfactory. He sipped his beer, placed the bottle on the table, reclined in an attitude of certainty. A good-looking guy. Ryan liked to say that Liam was the aesthete, he was the rough trade. Just then Liam looked to Charlie exactly like their father when they were kids: dark, suave, insultingly courteous.

So he stood; jangled his car keys. 'Thanks for the beer. I'd better go. Traffic...'

Ryan stood, stepped up and hugged him. 'Drive safely. Thanks for calling in.'

Liam stood, reaching out an arm—and Charlie's phone rang. Fumbling it from his pocket, he saw the expression on Liam's face and felt an old sensation creep in: his brother the disapprover, disapproval being essential to his sense of who he was. 'Sorry, I need to take this.'

The caller was Sue Mead. He turned his back on the two men. 'Sarge?'

'Charlie, where are you?'

'Northcote, just leaving my brother's place. Why?'

'Thought I'd better warn you. Allardyce could be on the warpath. His son went into a coma a couple of hours ago, and he went storming out of here.'

37

CHARLIE STARTED THE car, then froze. Where did he think he was going? He felt an undirected impulse to move, that's all. Who would need him? Who did he love the most? He sat there, engine running, and tried wearing Allardyce's grief as if it were an old coat. What the man was feeling, who the man would want to hurt...

Coldness threaded through him, and he called Mrs Ehrlich first; asked her to look for an unfamiliar car in his driveway or on Tidepool Street. 'In particular, a maroon Pajero.'

'I wouldn't know what that was, but there's nothing here, Charlie.'

'Call me if one does show,' he said, going on to describe Allardyce.

'I will.'

Anna sounded warm, a huskiness in her throat, an echo of their afternoon and he hated to cut across that. 'Anna, listen. Allardyce might come after you. His son just went into a coma.'

A pause. 'Oh. How awful for him.'

Charlie wanted to scream. 'I know, but please, if he turns up, don't let him in.'

'Don't worry.'

'Are your parents home yet?'

'Yes. I'll be fine, Charlie.'

'If he shows up, call triple zero.'

'That sounds unnecessary.'

'Anna.'

'Okay, all right.' Her sharpness lingered when he broke off to call Emma.

He counted the rings—ten—and then heard her voice asking him to leave a message. He stumbled through it, trying to sound unconcerned: 'Only me. Look, nothing to worry about, but to be on the safe side, could you not go home for the next few hours? Go to a friend's. Or stay at uni. Or if you're out jogging, maybe stop somewhere for a coffee? In any case, call me back.'

And he texted her, a short version, as dread elbowed in.

She's at home, he thought. Allardyce has hurt her and left her lying on the floor.

Who next? Jess.

A planner with Moreland Council, she answered distractedly. Hearing her interrupted-in-the-middle-of-something voice was sufficient to bring up his defences. 'Sorry to call you at work, but do you know where Em is?'

She was silent and he read a trace of judgment in it. Eventually: 'It's four-fifteen. She's due to start work at five, so she should still be at home. She's probably plugged in.'

'What work?'

Terse now, Jess said, 'The Hive.'

A community garden-cum-environment park on Merri Creek. Emma volunteered there for an hour a couple of times a week, generally rotating between the grocery, the plant nursery and the café; sometimes digging, weeding or watering the herb and vegetable plots.

'Okay.'

'What's going on? Something's got you worked up.'

He told her the gist, managing to sound at once agitated and offhand.

'This man blames you?'

'Yes.' Charlie amended that: 'Possibly.'

He waited for her response. Back when they were married, Jess had been on the receiving end of threats and intimidation aimed at him. Landline hang-ups in the small hours. Tyres slashed. A note on her windscreen outside netball training one evening: *Your kid looks cute in her little skirt.*

'He blames you enough to hurt Emma?'

'I don't know. But I'll order a car to go around there.'

'You haven't already?'

'Jess, I'm about to.'

'Would he hurt me?'

'Sweetheart, I don't know,' Charlie said. He wondered why he'd used that old endearment.

She carried on as if she hadn't heard him. 'I shouldn't go home yet, in other words.' Then, a wretched note in her voice: 'Charlie, not again.'

'It could be nothing,' Charlie said, but she'd cut the connection.

Now he shot away from the kerb, one hand finding Sue Mead's number.

'Charlie?'

'Can you send a car around to my ex-wife's house straight away? They'll listen to you.'

'Charlie...'

'Please, Sue, I can't get hold of my daughter.'

'Don't snap at me. If you must know, I've been calling and texting the boss and he finally got back to me. He's with his wife, so...you know, panic over. I feel shit enough, okay?'

'Did he call you back on a landline?'

'What?'

'Did he call back on his mobile or his home phone?'

The sergeant was silent. 'Oh,' she said, regret dawning.

'Like I said, I can't get hold of my daughter,' Charlie said.

'I'll try the landline and call you back.' And she was gone.

Charlie was halfway to Coburg when she called. 'You were right, he hasn't been home and his wife's beside herself.'

'Car, Sue. Please.'

'Yes: done.'

Lydiard Street was short and steep, plunging to a turning circle at the bottom, with squat wooden bollards separating it from parkland. This was a leafy green strolling-and-cycling world, a short walk from the community gardens and Merri Creek, and a short drive from Lygon Street if you wanted to eat Lebanese with hipsters, buy an amaro in a boutique bottle shop or service your $10,000 bicycle.

Knowing that parking would be a pain, Charlie left his car outside a netball court on the main road and walked. Lydiard was a mix of new townhouses, glass and concrete cubes and well-tended Californian bungalows. He was halfway down it, headed for the only townhouse with a glossy black door, when a marked police car swept past him. No siren—but not fucking around, either: good old Sue. It double-parked about halfway down. He increased his pace and was still fifty metres away when Allardyce stepped out of an alleyway between one townhouse complex and another, holding up his ID. In his suit, wreathed in smiles and neater than the last time Charlie had seen him. The uniforms got out, joined him on the footpath, Allardyce shaking hands amiably, a big guy who could turn on the charm or the malice without an intervening thought.

He's going to send them away, Charlie thought. He began to run, calling, 'Wait!' and feeling ridiculous.

Allardyce saw him first. Swept back his jacket flap and shouted, 'He's got a gun!'

Murder by cop. Charlie skidded. Almost fell, then shrank to a half-crouch in the middle of the road, grabbing at the air. 'I'm unarmed!'

The uniforms, who had also crouched, one behind the police car, the other still on the footpath, began to straighten. They stared at Charlie, one with his hand on his pistol butt, the other fiddling at his belt for the capsicum spray.

Charlie repeated it, shrill now: 'I'm unarmed.'

The older uniform stepped off the footpath and started up the slope, saying, 'On your knees, please, sir, hands laced behind your head.'

'I know the drill,' Charlie said, complying.

The road surface was sun-softened tar and small stone chips. His best jeans. 'My daughter lives in that house,' he shouted. 'That man intends to harm her.'

The younger uniform joined his partner and they both came closer, eventually blocking Charlie's view. Then they parted, one on either side of him, and he saw Allardyce hoofing it down to the park at the bottom.

'He's getting away!'

They ignored him, coming in carefully, hauling him to his feet, cuffing him neatly.

'I told you, I'm not armed. I'm here to protect my daughter.'

'A precaution, sir.'

Charlie nodded his head downhill. 'He's the one you need.'

They ignored that, the older one saying, 'Your business here, sir.'

Charlie shrugged away from them and tottered a few steps towards the house with the black door. 'My daughter.'

'Whoa. Stay where you are.'

'My daughter, moron. That man you just spoke to came here to harm her.'

Something twigged in the man's eyes: perhaps Sue Mead's strange call-out request was beginning to make sense. 'The inspector's the one?'

'Yes.'

They were uneasy now. The young one glanced downhill. 'Where's he gone?'

'He ran into the park,' Charlie said.

They made to run after him, but Charlie was handcuffed, and they dithered.

'Can we please check on my daughter?'

Another exchange of uneasy looks before the cuffs were removed, but they kept hard against him as he led the way down to Jess's house. He knocked. Nothing. The house had the blankness of death just then and his whole body fretted as he picked up and put down his feet pointlessly.

It was a corner house, an alleyway path leading to a

backyard and a side gate. 'She might be in the yard.'

Still suspicious, they accompanied him, the pathway overshadowed by the adjacent units and cooler, suddenly, out of the sun. Charlie was about to rattle the gate handle when it sprang open and Emma wheeled her bike out, helmet on, singing away, buds in each ear, and she yelped and shrank to see them, her panic hurting Charlie the most.

38

THEY THRASHED IT out, Charlie insisting that he walk Emma to The Hive, Emma insisting that she'd ride her bike, the uniforms insisting they both stay until senior police arrived.

Barely holding on, Charlie told his daughter: 'I'll walk you there, I'll wait around, I'll walk you home afterwards.'

'Sir, we need you both to stay here.'

Charlie turned. 'Are we under arrest?'

'No, but—'

'You accept that this is my daughter, and this is where she lives?'

'Yes, but—'

'You spoke to Sergeant Mead just now and she told you that Inspector Allardyce may pose a threat?'

'Sir, this is above our pay grade, frankly,' the senior uniform said. 'Please wait here for the time being.'

'No.'

Charlie grabbed Emma's bike by the handlebars and tussled with her, winning a little tug-of-war and wheeling it back into the yard. Propping it against Jess's feijoa tree, he returned to the side path, shut the gate behind him, and stood there a moment, glaring at his daughter while she glared at him. Then they both moved at the same time, Emma heading downhill towards the trees that fringed the grassland leading to the creek, Charlie catching up.

'Sir...'

Charlie flung the words over his shoulder: 'You have my mobile number. We'll both be back here at about six-fifteen.'

Father and daughter walked in silence then, across the grass, winding through to a footbridge, then up the slope towards a motley patchwork of roped-off tomato, lettuce, herb and sunflower beds, greenhouses and compost heaps stitched together by crooked paths and rickety gates in weathered post-and-rail fences. Still climbing, they passed through to a flat area, a central hub of grocery, bakery, plant nursery, classroom and café, open until six in summer.

People walking or cycling home from work would stop in for vegetables, bread, seedlings, an iced tea, leftover morning pastries.

Emma broke the silence as they neared the café. 'Sorry I snapped at you.'

'Sorry *I* snapped,' Charlie said.

'Is he really dangerous?'

'I honestly don't know. But we must assume he is—he did come to your house, after all.'

'He blames you?'

'I think he's lashing out at everyone,' Charlie said.

'You don't have to wait. Mum could fetch me when she gets home.'

'I've asked her to stay away for a few hours.'

'Bet she didn't like that.'

'She didn't,' Charlie said.

Emma, spotting a fellow volunteer, waved. 'I'd better go. Bring you something to eat or drink?'

'Iced tea.'

'It's going to be boring for you.'

'There's always social media. Get my follower count up.'

'Ha, ha,' Emma said, and she was gone.

Charlie found a bench seat at a wooden table under a shade cloth and people-watched for a while; sipped his tea; read the news feed on his phone; watched a trailer for a TV special in which a current affairs crew had embedded themselves for a week with an actor cleared of sexual misconduct charges. Apparently the guy had spent a lot of that week weeping, his wife stoic at his side. Spent a lot of it bare-chested, too.

Charlie dreamed through the hour. Watching kids and parents, the grey-hairs and the scruffs and the sharp young things, he thought that the world was split in two. On one side, sex offenders cried foul, reality-show idiots became presidents and marketing-executive prime ministers asked what God would do in their shoes. On the other side, people thought to create and work a place like The Hive: people whose salaries were cut, jobs rationalised, benefits slashed. He looked across the yard to the café; watched his daughter smilingly take and deliver orders. Her quick, subtle instincts, her good heart, would be imponderable to a politician. His self-interest imponderable to her.

My crosspatch soul, Charlie thought, getting up to return his used glass. He found himself standing in a short queue. Ahead of him was a helmeted cyclist wearing suit pants and, ahead of the cyclist, a thin twitchy woman holding out a blue ice-cream container to Emma. She had a toddler hanging off one leg, a girl of about eight on her other side, restlessly humming and pirouetting on the spot.

Emma took the container and flashed a smile as the woman thanked her, touched the toddler, the girl, as if for reassurance, and waited. Emma returned with a little tray: two chocolate drinks, soup sloshing in the ice-cream container.

'Thank you so much,' the woman said again, and

Charlie realised that she'd been begging. She was hungry; the kids were hungry. The three of them headed for a table in the shade and tucked in with plastic spoons that the woman fished from a Coles shopping bag.

It all complicated his sadness. He felt breathless suddenly, close to panic, and returned to his table. He watched the woman. Wolfing it down. The kids filled up quickly and went off to play a game of hidey at an unattended table. The toddler got filthy; his sister went to Emma and returned with paper towels to wipe his knees and palms. A kid forced to grow up quickly, he thought. Obliged to be a parent when her mother's parenting fell short.

Feeling large and inept, he crossed the yard. Didn't want to stand too close, a subtle intruder, but gave the woman privacy as he leaned in a little and murmured, 'This might help.'

Thirty dollars. All he had in his wallet.

She went very still, and an unwashed odour rose from her, and the money disappeared. At a chilly remove she said, loudly, 'Thank you so much,' once more and bent to her spoon again. Charlie returned to his table, wondering if what he'd just done was sound or wise or praiseworthy, or anything at all.

He tried to explain all of this to himself as he explained it to Emma when she finished work and they were walking back.

She shrugged. He realised she wasn't surprised. 'Sure we feed her.'

'Where does she live?'

'I don't know. Walking distance.'

'Is she homeless?'

'They live in her car, I think. Couch-surfing when they can get it.'

Sensing his frustration, she took him by the wrist, squeezed it to buck him up. 'If I've learnt anything here, it's don't sweat it. You must have done that in the police?'

Must he? Had he? He wasn't sure. He was sure he had a shallow, fabricated sense of himself. He was sure his daughter was wise.

She tugged him again. 'Let's take the long way home.'

Down to the creek and along it, passing under electricity pylons to another footbridge and up to a path that ran along the edge of the park, and there was Allardyce in his maroon Pajero. Charlie grabbed Emma, jerking her back. 'Wait.'

'What?'

He pointed. 'There.' He fumbled out his phone. 'We should probably go somewhere safe and wait.'

She dithered. 'You sure we can't just talk to him? He's upset, Dad.'

Yeah, well, working at The Hive might make you a good person but it didn't necessarily foster a self-protective instinct. And Charlie wanted something to hold on to, at this fag end of his career: don't be a hero, let the real heroes deal with it.

He informed Sue Mead, then tugged at his daughter

and she stumbled along with him, looking back. Then her face cleared, and she came willingly. 'I just saw his head move.'

Not sitting there dead, in other words. Charlie had been fearing that, too.

39

'JUST SITTING THERE in his car,' Charlie said, a few days later.

Dr Fiske continued to regard him calmly, as incurious and outwardly neutral as she'd been about his other catch-up stories: his mother and Billy Saul, Fay and his father, the Homicide Squad, the hit-and-run. Seated primly on her plain chair, as if reluctant to take up space. As if to give him all the room he needed.

If she moved, it was to ask a question. 'What will happen to him?'

Charlie shrugged. 'Stress leave?'

He considered his own situation. His suspension would be a permanent note in his record and follow him through the years. Senior officers would continue to bully and lie, and junior officers to close ranks and come snapping at his heels. He'd already been found guilty, was already being punished, even before any formal judgment had been passed.

Giving Fiske a crooked grin, he said, 'Maybe they'll send him to you.'

A minute relaxation of her face. Either she was amused or had expected that joke. 'We'll see.'

Feeling aimless and uneasy, Charlie glanced around her office. The same carpet separating them, the same furnishings and layout, but the photographs were new. With a glance to ask for permission, he crossed the room and peered at the rectangle of wall beside the door. Firefighters: shell-shocked, grimy, deeply fatigued. A burnt-out farmhouse. A kangaroo lying on its side, smoking, bloated—you could almost smell scorched death.

'You took these?'

'Yes.'

Charlie returned to his chair. 'Powerful.'

The nod she gave him was reasonable, wise, assured—but not forthcoming, as he veered into personal territory.

Charlie persevered. 'Your Mallacoota holiday?'

Her voice was flat. 'You might say it turned out to be a working holiday. Quite a few people in need of counselling.'

Charlie felt useless suddenly, his concerns paltry in

comparison, and began to tell her so and out of nowhere tears spurted and his words tumbled, all the hurts and the sense of lack that drove him. Painful hiccups interrupted the flow. He hunched in misery, grinding the heels of his hands against his eyes, and, when he recovered, she was standing in front of him with a box of tissues.

'Sorry,' he gasped.

'Don't be,' she said. 'Take your time.'

'Never happened before.'

'Never?'

He thought about that. 'Yeah.'

Well, never a full-blown bawling session before. A handful of tight, angry tears back when Jess walked out, but he wasn't counting them. They'd been easily erased, a brisk wipe of his eyes. Now he was exhausted.

He looked at Fiske. 'You've been waiting for that, right? As a sign of a successful consultation?'

'That's not worthy of you, Charlie.'

His eyes were still damp. He blinked a few times and tried a smile. 'Not worthy. Doc, I'm shocked. Are you allowed to express judgments?'

She returned the smile faintly. 'The occasional kick up the bum can do the world of good.'

'It's what I need,' Charlie admitted sadly.

Fiske shifted in her seat. The reserve between them was evaporating. 'Quite a few things surfaced just then, Charlie. Why don't we unpick them one at a time.'

'Unpick,' said Charlie flatly.

She held up a hand. 'I know, horrible word. Should be banned, along with "cohort". But you know what I mean.'

Charlie gestured at the photographs. 'After what those people have been through…'

'It's not a competition. You're hurting—to use another horrible expression.' She waited. Then: 'Why don't you start with your parents?'

Charlie stumbled through it, the whole sad mess. 'The hidden hatreds of married life, right?' he concluded.

'Theirs—or yours?'

'Yeah, yeah, yeah.' Pause. 'Both, I guess.'

'You said it felt like stepping back into old habits, an old dialogue, when you warned your ex-wife about Inspector Allardyce.'

Charlie rolled his shoulders, avoiding the point. Then: 'Yes.'

'When she left you five years ago, what did you feel?'

He answered at once: 'A vacuum.'

'What do you suppose she felt?'

'Hey, doc—this is all about me, remember?'

Her smile was tired. 'What did she feel?'

'You mean, what do I suppose she felt?' Charlie took a deep breath and said, 'That she'd found a breathing space.'

And he'd found a vacuum.

Fiske gave him a tiny nod and he realised what she was doing. This *was* about him: him in relation to others. He glanced at one of the photographs again, a fireman with gaunt, ash-grimy cheeks, and visualised Fiske counselling him. She'd be personable but not personal, involved but not invasive, firm but not bossy, sympathetic but not sentimental.

He returned his gaze to her, close to tears again. 'I don't think I'll be coming back to see you.'

'You don't think you will, or you don't need to, or you don't see the benefit?'

'All of the above.'

'But you are here now, Charlie. Make the most of it.'

He nodded. 'And I'm going to quit the police.'

If he'd announced that to anyone else, they'd have said, 'No. Why?' or 'Think about it for a while,' but Fiske said, 'What will that be like for you?'

Charlie laughed, recalling a retirement function he'd attended years back, for an inspector who had always kept to herself, didn't sleep around and had never attended a booze-up. A superintendent who didn't know her read from her service record and presented her with a plaque, two colleagues struggled through a handful of embarrassingly tame stories, and barely anyone went to the pub afterwards.

None of that for him. 'A relief,' he said.

'Retiring from the police will be a relief?'

'I don't want to be like my father,' Charlie said.

Where had that come from?

'What would that entail, being like your father?'

'When he retired he seemed to shrink,' Charlie said. 'Mentally and physically. For years he'd worn a dark blue or grey suit and carried a badge, and without those he was nothing. Exposed, laid wide open. Floundering. My stepmother's lovely, they've been together for years, and he's probably got heaps of superannuation, so he won't struggle financially, but in other respects he's defenceless. He feels…irrelevant.'

'You don't want to be like your father, who you say feels irrelevant.'

Charlie flared a little. 'You keep quoting me back to me.'

She was unmoved. 'Tell me more about your father.'

'Right now, he's ill. Underlying health issues and he caught that Chinese virus. And now that my mother's been found, the Homicide Squad will go in hard.'

'Charlie,' Fiske was sublimely attentive. 'Do you think he's guilty?'

It was as if the air in the room had become charged with unheard testimony. 'Do you think so?' he asked. 'Does it point to that?'

Then he caught himself. She didn't know. How could she? It was a tactic; she was teasing out his thoughts.

'I wish I knew,' he said. 'I wish someone would tell me what to think.'

A kind smile. 'Maybe you're not finished with me after all.'

'Maybe,' Charlie said, gloomily contemplating the floor.

He looked up. 'Do I challenge him about it?'

'Challenge. Interesting word.'

'Fuck off, doc. Do I accuse him?'

'Would it help?'

Charlie winced. 'He can be a slippery sod.'

'Slippery.'

'I mean, he never gives much away.'

'Go back twenty years. Your mother's disappearance. Tell me about relations between you, your brother and your father in the aftermath.'

Charlie shook his head in a kind of wonderment. 'Nothing was said. Ever.'

'About...?'

'About what might have happened to her. Liam had nothing to do with Dad by then anyway, and we weren't living in the same house anymore. As for what might have happened to Mum, I thought her lodger knew something about it, and Liam thought Dad did it—he still does—but it was never talked about between us. It was up to me to do all the agonising and investigating over the years.' He cocked his head. 'I'm exaggerating, but you know what I mean.'

'I do. But is it possible your dad and your brother were agonising and investigating too?'

'I don't know. We didn't talk about it.'

'But you, at least, continued to think about it over the years? You speculated, investigated?'

Obsessively, according to Jess. To the detriment of their marriage. 'Yes.'

'What will you do if your father is tried and found guilty?'

'Appeal. Keep digging.'

'You're torn between his guilt and his innocence, aren't you?' Fiske said, head tilted back a little as if she had no stake in it. Which she didn't.

Charlie stared at her mulishly, wanting to snarl; knowing it would be unreasonable, reining himself in.

Fiske read it in his eyes. 'Let it out, Charlie.'

'This is unlike any therapy session I've ever been to.'

'You've only ever been to one, as far as I know.'

'You know what I mean,' Charlie said. He slouched, arms folded, legs outstretched and crossed at the ankles. 'Is this what typically happens? Therapist and client read each other and develop an intimacy?'

'The smart ones read me—although there are those I'd rather not have crawling about in my mind. And there are those I wish I *couldn't* read,' Fiske said. She paused. 'Ever thought of doing a counselling course? Police Veterans are crying out for volunteer support officers.'

'Me?'

'Think about it.'

'Become someone's buddy,' Charlie muttered, thinking of Allardyce and his meltdown.

'Worse things to be.'

But Charlie was looking at Dr Fiske without seeing her, an image of Fay in his mind. Had she started steeling herself, expecting to return from the supermarket one day

299

to find Rhys hanging from a beam in the garage?

Was his father depressed? Why hadn't he asked?

What about Mark Valente and Noel Saltash and all the other old-timer cops? Were they anxious, depressed, controlling, violent, suicidal? Did they need a buddy?

'Charlie?' Fiske said.

He blinked. 'Yep?'

'Have you been working up to leaving the police, or has it only just this minute occurred to you?'

'Does it matter?'

Her shrug could have meant anything.

No point second-guessing. He said, 'I think I've been considering it for a while now.'

She nodded. 'Give some thought to what I said. Do a course. You're empathetic—sorry, another buzzword. Help people.'

'I can barely help myself.'

'Well now, that simply isn't true,' Dr Fiske said, and Charlie heard that little bit of bucking-up, soaked it in, and felt his incapacity shrink a little.

40

'HE'S DOING WELL,' Fay said, the second week of February.
'Out in a few days.'

Her face, still haggard, filled the tiny screen. 'Meanwhile I'm going crazy here.' She looked about her at the walls closing in. 'They bring me things to read—magazines and sex-and-shopping novels mostly—and the food's good, but I miss the sun and the air and the company.'

Charlie was sitting at the kitchen table with his laptop. Curiously, he'd been googling the virus when she'd logged on. 'But you don't feel ill?'

'I feel fine. It's funny we both had it and it hardly affected me at all, yet it put your poor dad in hospital.'

'Can you Skype with him?'

'We tried a couple of times. It's easier to talk on the phone.'

'What does he look like? Is it taking a toll?'

'Let's just say he's aged a little,' Fay said. She hesitated. 'How are you doing? Is the counselling helping—can I ask that?'

'It's helping.'

'You can't talk about it, I understand.'

'I've only had two sessions.'

She smiled; it eased the strain in her. 'Oh well, either she's busy or she's no help or you don't need much curing.'

'The curing part remains to be seen. The urge to shove authority figures arse over tit hasn't entirely left me.'

She shook her head. 'You're more like your father than you think.'

Was he? Charlie peered back down the years, looking for his father. His varying and variable father. An amiable—mostly amiable—ratbag when it was just the four of them at home. A man who could make you laugh, a grabber and tickler. But whenever he was around Valente and his other police mates, Charlie realised, he was different. The smiles more forced; the eyes watchful. In time the rat-baggery faded altogether and he met another woman and the family split apart and his wife disappeared...

It struck Charlie for the first time that you could draw

a causal link between those events, and that's what everyone had done. He gave a mental shake of his head: Only taken me twenty years. He eyed Fay, who was frowning at him, concerned. He had no doubt that she and his father made each other happy. He'd seen them laugh together plenty of times. But it wasn't the kind of laughter—cheeky, irreverent—that he remembered from his childhood.

Suddenly his mother's voice was in his head, making that same observation: You're so like your father.

'I'm better looking than him,' he told Fay now, 'and I can use Skype.'

She rolled her eyes. 'Don't get me started.'

After a pause, Charlie said, 'Fay, they're going to come after him.'

'He knows that. He doesn't seem as bothered as he ought to be.'

'He needs a lawyer.'

'Do you know any?'

'Yes. Her name's Jenna Baird.'

'Is she good?'

'Very.' Charlie had already lined her up, in fact. He'd contacted three defence lawyers he'd encountered in court whose style he liked—not relying on humiliation, denigration or wearing down of victims—and who had an eye to justice, not the big bucks. Baird was the best; she was available. 'She'll meet with Dad when you get home.'

'Charlie, thank you.'

'Another thing: can you run past Dad the idea of a memorial service for Mum? Maybe a few days after you get back. It could be weeks, months, before we can have a funeral.'

'Leave it to me.'

'You won't have to do anything. Liam and Ryan are all over it.'

After that, Charlie waited through the mid-February days, walking, pottering, surfing. Good surf was sometimes predicted at Point Leo, but usually he found himself waiting patiently, just one of the hopeful regulars—tradies on their way to work, retired guys Mark Valente's age, a couple of maternity-ward nurses from Mornington, kids who should have been at school. They variously sat, chatted, lay prone, paddled further out, attempted with little heart but no disappointment to catch the wave that would surely break. Charlie had read enough surf writing to know what a wank it could be, but if you pinned him down he might confess to feeling cleansed when the sea rose and rolled. You went with it, not against it. If you went against it you weren't a surfer. You shouldn't be within a thousand kilometres of the sea.

But it was as if he didn't know what he was waiting for—only that he wanted something that would open up the world somehow, not cramp it. Then one afternoon, on their semi-regular Skype, Fay said, 'We've been cleared to come home.'

Charlie peered at the screen. 'You in a different part of the ship?'

She laughed. 'No, thank god. Tokyo. An actual hotel.'

'Good to get out?'

'You have no idea.'

'When you know your flight details, let me know, I'll pick you up at the airport.'

'Oh, no, Charlie, we can get an Uber or a taxi.'

'I'm picking you up,' Charlie said.

Fay seemed to accept that. Next day she texted him: *Arriving Cathay Pacific 6.30 am Feb 19.*

41

CHARLIE LEFT HOME at 5 a.m. and was waiting in arrivals by 6.20. He found it curiously distracting—a little sad, a little heartwarming—to see the hugs, kisses and handshakes enacted all around him. These people had social and familial contexts.

Did he? Who would welcome him home from Japan, or anywhere else?

Emma didn't have a car, and didn't, as she often told him, do mornings. Anna? He hoped so, but it was new between them, and at the moment still fragile. He would not presume. Anyway, right now her leg was in plaster…

He found himself looking for travellers who had no friend, family member or lover waiting. They strode head-high through the crowd as if to disdain ordinary human connection. A mask for regret or dejection? Probably. At least that's what he'd feel in their shoes.

Lost in these thoughts, a little sorry for himself, he didn't immediately realise that the crowd had thinned, time had passed, and Rhys and Fay were the last to totter out from behind the screen.

He barely recognised them. It wasn't that Fay had altered by much, it was that she was steering a wonky trolley heaped with luggage, accompanied by a woman in uniform pushing a wheelchair in which was his father. He had altered.

Fay saw Charlie first. She gave him a spirited wave but he could see the deep fatigue in her drawn features. And then Rhys was being deposited at Charlie's feet, they were hugging, and the wheelchair was being whisked away, Fay calling, 'Thank you!' forlornly to the airline woman's oblivious spine.

Clasping his father, feeling the bones move beneath his hands, Charlie said, 'They finally let you into the country.'

Fay gestured negligently. 'They were very blasé. We could have been riddled with the virus.'

'Took us a while to get through customs,' Rhys said. 'I had a bit of a dizzy spell. How are you, son?'

'Fine, but you don't look too good.'

The old Rhys would have had a comeback. This one's eyes lost focus. He looked around with a peevish expression that eased when his eyes came to rest on Fay.

'I'm in the short-term carpark,' Charlie said, grabbing the trolley handle. 'You both okay to walk it? Should I get another wheelchair?'

'Forget it.' Rhys was sharp again. 'More hassle than it's worth.'

'But let's make it an amble, not a mad dash,' said Fay.

'I can do ambling,' Charlie said as they made off. He grabbed to save a small bag as he manoeuvred the trolley onto the roadway. Rhys, behind him, said, 'Was that his duty-free Roku gin I heard breaking?'

'Behave yourself,' Fay said.

Across the lanes of traffic and into the parking structure. Charlie pushed the lift button and, as they waited, he took closer note of the diminution in his father. Thinner. Pale, sweaty, short of breath. He kept touching the flat of his hand to his chest and coughing weakly, with tight, dry little exhalations.

And he'd zoned out again. He was facing the lift doors, uncertain of his bearings. Charlie, shooting Fay a look, saw her mouth the words, 'Brain fog.'

'Straight home and straight to bed, Dad,' Charlie said. 'Take a load off your feet.'

'Taking a load off is all well and good,' the old Rhys said. 'The problem is, as soon as I get up again I have a dizzy spell.'

'He had a fall, in fact,' Fay said. 'During our stopover in Sydney.'

'Felt like a bloody idiot,' Rhys said, as the lift doors opened, and they shuffled aboard.

It was new to Charlie, his father being vulnerable and acknowledging it. This was a man who always liked to say he didn't have time to be ill. Who had told his sons, laid up with a cold or the flu, 'It'll pass.'

'The virus really knocked you around,' Charlie said.

'You could say that.'

Charlie glanced at Fay. 'Rafferty's Rules, it didn't affect you much at all.'

'That's about the size of it.'

The lift rose two floors and they filed out again, shuffling through dim concrete halls to the Skoda.

They struck morning traffic on the ring roads, and Charlie sensed a nervy agitation in his father, who sat slumped against the door, his chin dipping and tilting as he seemed to alternate between napping and monitoring Charlie's route. A notorious backseat driver, the old man. Charlie, intent on circumventing that, said, 'What's Japanese hospital food like?'

Rhys snorted. 'Couldn't taste it, couldn't smell it. It was fuel, that's the best you could say for it.'

Fay leaned into the gap between the seats. 'Lovely food on the ship, though.'

A conversation bound to stall sooner rather than later.

Charlie was hunting around for another topic when Rhys said, 'Homicide'll want to talk to me.'

'Yes.'

Rhys didn't follow up. Charlie glanced at him. Asleep?

From the back seat, Fay said tiredly, 'Don't worry, he does that. He'll wake soon.'

'I am worried. He's cured of the virus, right?'

She reached a hand past Charlie's headrest. Patted the side of his neck. 'We both are, dear. But he's finding the after-effects hard.'

'You're not?'

'I didn't really have any to begin with.'

Charlie caught her gaze in the rear-view mirror and asked, 'What did the doctors say?'

He saw her look into her lap. 'I've got it written down.'

He waited while she rummaged in her handbag.

'Here it is. One of the doctors had very good English. "Nonspecific multisystem post-viral symptoms," that's what he said.'

'Sounds...well, unspecific.'

'It's supposed to be short term, but I don't know, I wonder if his heart's been compromised.'

'His heart?'

'We didn't want to worry you—*he* didn't want to worry you—but in the past year he's had a couple of little episodes, and since coming out of hospital he's been complaining of chest pains. Can't breathe in properly, irregular heartbeat, that kind of thing. He gets sweaty, one arm feels strange, he said, and he's simply exhausted.'

Charlie checked the mirror. 'Jesus, Fay.'

'I know, I know. Let's just get him home and I'll ask the doctor to call in this afternoon.'

'Shouldn't we take him straight to hospital?'

She was gazing out of her window. 'Try telling him that. Anyway, he's not getting any worse.'

'Second opinion.'

'Like I said,' Fay snapped in her worry and fatigue, 'try telling him that.'

Rhys in the seat next to Charlie said, 'Settle down, you two.'

'Dad, it couldn't hurt to get a second opinion.'

'How about this, son—like Fay said, we'll get the doctor to pop in.'

'Didn't know they did house calls anymore,' Charlie muttered.

'This one does.'

Charlie drove; Rhys gazed out at the unrolling suburbs; Fay's eyes were closed, her head tilted back.

A sheet of newsprint slapped against the windscreen and was gone. 'Hot wind. Nasty wind,' Rhys said.

Charlie glanced at the dashboard, reading off the outside temperature. Thirty-four degrees. He could see gum trees bending, scrappy leaves and packets flying, an old man's straw hat bowling along. A real grit-in-the-eyes day, scented by inland dust and smoke. Far-off bushfire smoke.

As if he'd read Charlie's mind, Rhys said, 'We watched a lot of CNN on the ship. The bushfires. Unimaginable.'

'You worried about your place?' Charlie said. Hot northerlies racing up the Warrandyte gullies, wrapping around the eucalypts.

It was as if Rhys hadn't heard him. 'Koalas with their paws all burnt up. Heartbreaking.'

'I know. It's been the main news topic for weeks, here. We're all obsessed with it.'

Again eerie dense skies were in Charlie's head. Evacuees crowding the state's south-eastern towns and beaches—dazed, huddling, clasping pets and bewildered children. Stuffed suitcases; crammed trailers; cars stalled bumper to bumper; the sooty firefighters and the false-faced, lip-service politicians.

'You ever think,' Rhys said, 'the world's running down?'

Exactly what Anna had said. 'Constantly,' Charlie replied.

Rhys grunted and they rode in silence and came to the tight corkscrewing roads dense with waiting houses, oily trees waiting in the tossing wind.

42

MID-MORNING NOW, RHYS in bed, the doctor due late afternoon. Fay was imploring Charlie to stay for a while longer.

'Wouldn't you like to put your head down, too?' he
asked. 'Unpack, at least?'

'Charlie, I'm dying for a good chat. Is that all right?'

She was at the kitchen sink, chin aimed at him stubbornly, her northern-hemisphere layers swapped for shorts
and a T-shirt. A thin woman who had aged in the past
weeks. Pale, pleased to be home but, Charlie realised, in
dread of the next stages of life.

'Just for half an hour or so.'

'Of course,' he said, settling into a kitchen chair. Watching her prepare the coffee, he understood that she'd spent the last weeks in suspension, nothing secure, cabin walls closing in. The love of her life ill, fretful and then beyond her reach in a Tokyo hospital. She'd been strong for him. No one had been strong for her.

Charlie got to his feet, crossed the room and stood beside her at the sink, his arm around her, hoping that if he possessed any fortitude, a little of it would flow into her.

It seemed to. Everything that was tight in her began to ease and then, strangely, he felt her warmth flow into him, and he thought unaccountably of his mother.

But Fay has been my mother all these years, he thought. Will continue to be, in her reserved way.

They returned to the table wordlessly, but presently she said what was on her mind. 'What do the police intend, exactly?'

'They want to talk to him, for a start. Everything's changed, now there's a body. Bodies.'

'Will they arrest him?'

'I honestly don't know. Depends on what new evidence they have, I guess.'

'It would have to be evidence tied directly to the bodies, surely? All the rest, his movements on the day and whatnot, that was all checked off twenty years ago.'

Charlie looked past Fay's head to the window and

the trees fretting in the wind and recalled Fran Bekker's dismissal of the original investigation. 'New evidence, new witnesses; I have no idea.'

'And you're sure about the lawyer?'

He nodded. 'She'll do right by him.'

Glancing towards the door to the corridor, as if Rhys stood there listening, Fay lowered her voice. 'I shouldn't let him talk to the police unless she's with him, right?'

'Ideally.'

'But what if they just turn up out of the blue? He could get cranky—you know what he's like—and say the wrong thing or rub them up the wrong way.'

'I'll coach him.'

'Will you? He's…He's vague sometimes. He could say anything.'

Charlie went very still. 'Fay, what's he said?'

The coffeepot was burbling. She turned her head to it, wanting a lifeline, a distraction, a detour sign, so Charlie asked again: 'What's he told you?'

She got to her feet, poured the coffee into two mugs, sat again. Rotated her mug, gathering her thoughts. 'He told me he was at your mum's house the day she went missing.'

Since Liam first told him that, Charlie hadn't known what to do with it. It didn't signify guilt, but it looked suspicious—the fact, and the failure to disclose it—and the police would seize upon it. Unless they already knew.

'I know,' he said. 'Liam saw him.'

'At her house?'

Charlie shook his head. 'Near there. On the road.'

'Will he tell the police?'

'I don't know. He says not.'

Fay touched her throat. It indicated doubt, and they sat with their thoughts.

She said, 'Liam and I did a couple of Skype sessions. I think he's stopped despising me.'

'Hope so.'

'Of course, Ryan probably put him up to it. Ryan's good for him, don't you think?'

'I do.'

'But that doesn't alter the fact that Liam still thinks Rhys killed your mum. That's always going to be the elephant in the room.'

Charlie nodded. There was nothing to add.

'Is there a reason *you* think he's innocent and Liam doesn't?'

'Old sibling dynamics.'

'Oh, rubbish.'

Charlie felt ungracious. 'Okay, Liam took against Dad for two reasons: he thinks he hurt Mum, and he thinks Dad and his mates were old-school gay bashers. His words.'

'I don't believe it. They hit him?'

'No. But they weren't very kind to him, and he thinks Dad took their side, not his.'

'Your dad's no homophobe, and he'd never put anyone

ahead of you boys. He loves you both. He's proud of you.'

'I know.'

'There must be more to it.'

She was probably right. Liam was older, he'd seen more; he'd have understood more back then. 'Maybe.'

She changed tack. 'I asked Rhys why he went to your mother's place that day. He said there was a stack of table linen he thought she should have, so he took it around and left it on her veranda.'

Charlie recalled Senior Constable McGuire's reaction when he'd asked if his mother's remains had been wrapped in anything. That glint in her eyes.

He focused on Fay again. She was watching him, her head cocked. 'But how do you verify intent?'

They were silent, contemplating imponderables. Eventually Charlie told her what he'd been up to: Lambert, the Wagoners, Quigley, Billy Saul's mother.

'Long shots, really.' He shook his head. 'I was so sure Lambert was somehow involved.'

'I know what you mean. Creepy. I met him once.'

Charlie was astonished. 'You did? Where? How?'

She wriggled uncomfortably. 'It was early on. Your mum was at work, and I went down to tell your dad it wasn't right to go on seeing each other if he wasn't properly separated or divorced, and Lambert was just leaving their place as I arrived. Something about security—installing lights and better door locks.'

'Huh.'

Into another silence Fay said, 'Did I ever tell you about my husband?'

Charlie blinked. 'She said, changing the subject.'

Fay grinned. 'Bear with me.'

'You've mentioned him a couple of times. He died?'

'His name was Andy and he died of a heart attack. He was only forty-six. It ran in his family.'

'Sorry.'

She shrugged. 'Years ago now. He was a good sort. It hit me hard. What I'm trying to say is, your dad saved my life.'

'Okay.'

'Not till a few years later, mind you. Along with all the other shitty aspects of widowhood, I was awfully shy and obliging. A little mouse. After Andy died I just drifted, not really looking for anyone, but somehow or other I found myself engaged to a man I worked with at the time. Looking back, I think I was trying to get away from my mother and my sisters as much as anything.'

She grinned. Charlie returned it, grateful for the nugget.

'Anyway, this man was ten years older, and he idolised me,' Fay said. Her hands went to her head. 'He'd brush my hair. Do my ironing. Tea in bed every morning. And I had these complicated lace-up boots that he insisted on doing up or taking off.'

'So you felt what?' Charlie said. 'Smothered?'

She closed her eyes briefly. 'It seemed like everyone

around me had energy and opinions and ideas, while I was wearing a set of clothes made for someone else. I was just living…adequately. Blamelessly. That's about all you could say. I wasn't stupid, I knew people didn't really like Michael, but at the same time they didn't *dis*like him. One day I told him I didn't love him, and he said, "Don't be silly, of course you do."'

She snorted—as much a yelp of dismay as laughter— and looked crookedly at Charlie. 'We hardly ever had sex. I wasn't that interested, but the thing is it didn't seem to bother him. He'd give me this little smile that was so understanding it made me want to scream and run for the hills.'

The upcoming wedding must have seemed like an ending to her life, Charlie thought—with nothing beyond it. 'Takes all kinds,' he said weakly, as the wind rattled the window above the sink.

'It took your father, that's what it took,' Fay said emphatically. 'He saved me.'

Charlie reached across and took her hand. 'I'm glad. You're family, you know.'

Her hand, inert for a moment, twitched like a creature in his as she removed it. She gave him a pat. Settled both hands in her lap. She wasn't finished.

'Thank you for saying that; it means a lot. But it wasn't smooth sailing. I told Rhys that I needed to be able to hold my head up. We didn't have anything to do with each other for six months. I told him he had to sort himself out first.'

319

And clearly he'd done that, Charlie thought. Now the pair of them are indissoluble. He thought back five years, to when Jess had walked out. If he was honest with himself, he'd been a sketchy husband. Distracted, undemonstrative, his footsteps upon the earth jarring, not harmonious. Consumed with finding out what had happened to his mother, not nurturing his own family. He had been unmoored for a time; five years without love.

Then Anna. It didn't matter that she coincided with his career going down the gurgler, he felt more supple now, felt some grace and power within. That's what love did.

'I'm glad it worked out for you both,' he said.

'Me too. But your mother's disappearance changed him, you know. I noticed a difference in him. He stopped being such a larrikin, for a start. Became...I don't know, harder to reach. And he wanted to put it all behind him— his marriage and his old life at the beach.'

'Does he ever talk about it?'

She shook her head and Charlie knew there was more, but before he could ask, she was patting his wrist absently. 'Charlie, we'd love to come to the memorial service, but if you have any doubts...'

Next Monday, Balinoe Hall, Mrs Ehrlich to give the main eulogy. 'Come,' Charlie said.

The doorbell rang and he exchanged a glance with Fay. She looked frightened, diminished. She mouthed the word 'Police?' at him—as if, throughout the whole conversation, she'd been waiting.

43

'THE DYNAMIC DUO,' Charlie said, getting in first.

Bekker was there on the doorstep, McGuire glowering behind her. 'A courtesy call. May we come in?'

'You can't be serious. He's only just got home.'

Bekker raised a forestalling hand. 'I promise we'll be quick.'

'Quick courtesy call,' scoffed Charlie, propping his forearm against the edge of the open door. 'I'm police, remember?'

'Yeah.' McGuire smirked. 'Memories, eh?'

Bekker made a semblance of shushing her. 'We do need to talk to him. Things to clear up.'

McGuire beamed at Charlie. 'He may have a lawyer present.'

The hot wind continued to thrash the hills and trees. Heat was entering the house, so Charlie stepped out onto the veranda, shutting the door behind him. 'When?'

'You want to do this out here?' said McGuire.

'When?' repeated Charlie.

'Ideally, in the next few days,' Bekker said.

'He's not well. He caught that virus when he was away.'

Bekker and McGuire stiffened—a kind of polite recoil, as if Charlie was a virus carrier. Full of smiling malice, he advanced on them. One step, another. 'He was hospitalised, in fact. He's still shaky.'

Bekker gathered herself. 'Is he still infectious?'

'No. He was cleared to come home. But he's suffering after-effects. Plus jetlag. He's not up to being grilled by you lot.'

'Grilled...A talk,' Bekker said.

'Yeah. Sure. Under caution.'

'When will be a good time?'

'When his doctor gives the all-clear.'

'Next week?'

'Not my call,' Charlie said. He knew they would keep at him and eventually wear him down. Wear Rhys and Fay down. So he said, 'We're having a memorial service on Monday. Maybe you can talk to him later in the week.'

Bekker gave an abbreviated nod. Then she cocked her head at him. 'Meanwhile, Charlie, what did I tell you about sticking your nose in?'

He waited.

'I said to quit doing it, if I recall.'

McGuire muscled in. 'You've been representing yourself as a police officer on active duty rather than as a fuck-up on suspension.'

'Paid suspension,' Charlie said.

'That makes a difference? People are complaining.'

'What people?'

Bekker said, 'Just knock it off, Detective Senior Constable Deravin.'

'All I've been doing is gathering information,' Charlie said.

'Obstructing...'

'*Helping*,' Charlie said. He pasted on a smile calculated to inflame. 'You've heard the expression "lawfully audacious"?'

McGuire flared up; Bekker grew weary. 'Come,' she said, and ushered her sidekick down the path to their unmarked car.

Charlie returned to the kitchen, mists of foreboding closing around him. Rhys was at the table, a fresh cup of tea steaming between his stringy hands. He looked pinched—but decisive and wry. 'That who I think it was?'

'Homicide. I did warn you.'

Rhys chanced a sour grin at Fay, who was standing with her rear propped against the bench under the window. She looked drawn, troubled. She was at odds with him, thought Charlie.

'What did they want?'

Charlie sat opposite his father. 'Quote: "quick courtesy call."'

Saw his old man's nostrils flare. 'Now? Barely home five minutes?'

'I told them to piss off. But they want a formal interview sometime next week, depending on how you feel.'

Fay came to sit, her unblinking silence put to one side. 'I think we should meet with the lawyer as soon as possible.'

Rhys opened his mouth to protest; subsided when Fay touched his forearm. In a show of contrition he said, 'Happy to talk to her.'

'More than talk, Dad,' Charlie said. 'Make sure you don't speak to the police unless and until she's in the room with you.'

'I'll be fine.'

Fay said, 'Anyone would think you hadn't been a policeman all your life. And all I've heard from you for twenty years is how the justice system works and fails to work. *Listen to your son.*'

Rhys scowled. Charlie leaned in. 'This is serious, Dad. If I'm not mistaken, they intend to question you under caution. You need representation—and not from some Association hack. Have a sit-down with Jenna as soon as possible, get her up to speed. She'll try and find out what they're basing their case on—if they have one—and maybe she can delay the committal hearing—if that's where they're headed.'

'A lot of "ifs" in that sentence, son.'

'Grow up. Mum's no longer a person who disappeared in suspicious circumstances twenty years ago. She was murdered. During divorce proceedings. Also, they think the original investigation was scrappy, and, reading between the lines, I think they've turned up new evidence. Probably applied some of the forensic techniques not invented back then.'

There was a pause until Rhys said, slowly: 'Obviously they'll find my traces in her car. We both drove it.'

Charlie went a little cold, wondering why his father would focus on the car and not on an alibi that might clear his name once and for all. 'Dad, put your thinking cap on.'

Fay asked a question that must have been simmering inside her. Carefully not looking at Rhys, she said, 'Why would they have searched the house again? What could they hope to find after all this time?'

There was a snap in her husband's voice: 'Not you, too.'

'Oh for god's sake,' she flared back at him. 'Did I say I thought they'd find something? This is serious, Rhys. I have lived with you for twenty years. I love you. I trust you. But this is serious. This is our life. I need to know. *You* need to know.'

'Know if I killed Rose?'

'That's not what I meant.'

'Isn't it? You sure you haven't been harbouring a suspicion all this time?'

'Stop it.' Charlie thumped the table with a little rattle of crockery. 'Fay, to answer your question, they have to cover bases, it's a murder investigation now.'

'Looking for a huge pool of blood that seeped into the floorboards and got carpeted over,' she said disparagingly—if ill-advisedly, considering her husband's mood.

But Rhys scooted his chair across and wrapped an arm around her and made her look at him. 'Sweetheart.'

She softened a little against him, but her voice was toneless: 'What?'

'I didn't hurt her. Never laid a finger on her in all our years together.'

She said, a few seconds later, 'I know.'

'Let alone killed her.'

He needn't have said that. She tensed under his arm: 'I know.'

He moved his arm away, throwing Charlie a rueful look, and it seemed to release a switch in Charlie. He stared at his father as if at a stranger. The Hawaiian shirt—he'd had it for years—was both familiar and unfamiliar. It belonged to the old Rhys but hung now from the thin shoulders of an old man. The V at his throat revealed sparse grey hairs and a pale, scrawny neck. This wasn't Rhys Deravin the beach-lover, the out-thinker. That man had vanished in the past few weeks—or years—and Charlie had been too self-involved to notice.

Not looking at Fay, he said, 'Dad, there is one thing they might ask you. Your car was seen near Mum's place the day she went missing.'

Rhys widened his eyes. 'Let me unpick that,' he said, some of the old craftiness emerging again. 'Liam saw me, right? He challenged me; did you know that? He's probably already told the police. Anyway, I've made no secret of the fact I was there.'

'Yes you have. I didn't know till the other day.'

'He told me,' Fay murmured.

Charlie hated this. He said, 'So, what were you doing there?'

'I went to drop off sheets and towels.'

Fay touched the back of his wrist. 'You said table linen.'

He gestured impatiently. 'Whatever. Fabrics. Material. Stuff that was hers that I didn't want or need that she probably *did* want or need. I didn't want to run into her. I didn't want an argument.'

'Tablecloths versus sheets and towels,' Charlie said. 'You need to get it right. The prosecution could take a mistake like that and run with it. You need to get it right on the day.'

'On the day...In court, is that what you're saying?'

'Dad, I'm serious.'

Rhys lost interest, in that instantaneous way of his. He pushed away from the table, saying, 'Not to worry.'

He swayed and closed his eyes, and Fay was swiftly at his side. 'You need to go back to bed.'

Rhys seemed surprised that he was at home; that his son was there. Bafflement in his eyes as he blinked, pushing against the tide of it. He dropped back into his seat. 'Just need a moment.'

Charlie watched him. His old man seemed to shrink further. Then he opened clear eyes and smiled tiredly at Charlie. 'Sorry, son. It comes and goes.'

'Another thing we need to talk about: Shane Lambert.'

'Who?'

'You know perfectly well who. Mum's lodger.'

Rhys Deravin twitched his mouth left and right, frowning in concentration, and an intuitive conviction lodged in Charlie: He's going to lie.

'I have a vague memory. We're talking a long while ago.'

'He went to the house to advise on security.'

'Did he?'

'He disappeared for years and now he's back. The police have reinterviewed him.'

And learnt nothing, according to Bekker, but Charlie wanted to gauge his father's reaction.

'Well, I don't know what he has to do with anything,' Rhys said, standing again, slowly this time, no rush of blood, eyes clear. 'Thanks for collecting us and bringing us home, son. See you on Monday.'

44

MONDAY, THE FOYER of the Balinoe Hall. Charlie was ferrying stackable chairs to the main function room when Susan Mead arrived. Deeply touched, he gave her a quick hug. 'Thank you, sarge, means a lot.'

She shrugged, embarrassed. 'Sorry I'm early, I misjudged the time.'

Just then Liam came through from the storeroom, carrying a stack of chairs, trailed by Emma. Charlie felt tentative and disadvantaged suddenly, stumbling through the introductions. He wanted them all to like each other and felt that this was the beginning of the day's many fraught moments.

But Emma, with her effortless grace, shook his old boss's hand. 'It's good to meet you at last.'

Charlie saw relief flow. 'Good to meet you. Your dad used to brag about you all the time.'

Liam was more circumspect. Shook hands briskly and at an elegant remove, then turned to Charlie. 'People will be arriving soon.'

Good old Liam. Summoning some careworn strength, Charlie said, 'Be right with you.'

Liam nodded, reclaimed his stack of chairs and toted them through to the main hall. Casting Charlie and Mead a crooked grin, Emma followed.

'He likes to micromanage,' Charlie said.

'Well, someone like that can be useful. I'll leave you to it,' Mead said, looking around for somewhere to park herself.

'How are you at food preparation?'

She looked at him, eyes alert as a cat's. 'I've been known to chop a carrot.'

So Charlie took her through to an annexe, where Ryan and Jess were flicking around a long table, setting out jugs of water, paper plates, napkins and sandwiches under cling wrap. But then a little of his confidence left him, the day drew clumsily around him again, and he leaned to murmur in her ear: 'The ex-wife. My brother's partner.'

'I'll cope.'

He made the introductions. Ryan reacted with a warm fuss; Jess, as Charlie expected, was cooler, preoccupied.

Charlie had pressed for a small service, Liam a large, triumphal send-off—an up-yours to Dad, Charlie thought sourly. And so his morning continued to fracture. Cameras and microphones gathered outside the hall, dozens of random mourners inside, bright and avid. Charlie had the sense of them looking at the Deravin boys, in front-row seats on either side of the centre aisle and spinning a hundred stories out of nothing. What are they feeling? Where's their father? Why aren't they sitting together?

Wait till Dad gets here, he thought, casting his eyes around. All the aspects of grieving: delicate, hesitant, tiresome, dishonest, self-denying. Then his expression tightened: why the fuck were Bekker and McGuire here? Hoping Rhys might break down and confess in front of everyone? And, Jesus Christ, the podcast twins. Charlie wanted to throw the lot of them out, these cynics and frauds.

There was further warping of the air around him. Noel Saltash and Mark Valente slipped in but did not sit together. Then a couple of cop widows arrived, and Charlie wondered how many of the original crowd were left. The women caught his eye; nodded. They didn't come down to offer their condolences but sat unmoving, helping to fill the hall with a hard old history.

Susan Mead, a few rows behind him, gave him a little

smile. The minutes dragged and then a queer kind of half-silence fell. A hiss. A mutter. Charlie knew, but craned his neck to see: Rhys and Fay had walked in. He'd wanted them in the front row, but Liam had scotched that idea. So had Rhys: 'Quiet seat up the back, son.'

Charlie stood. Heads swung and eyes lit up. Facing them down, he stepped past Emma's knees and into the aisle. She followed him and that was the cure he needed. One after the other, they strode to the rear of the hall, where Rhys and Fay waited with constricted smiles.

They hugged and kissed, Emma whispering, 'Grandpa' and 'Fay'. Rhys was pale, damp, beaten down, his right hand tucked into Fay's elbow. She seemed to stand tall and strong, not defiant but not consenting to be the embarrassed wife of a killer, either.

Chairs had been reserved for them. Watching Fay guide Rhys, watching Rhys grip her elbow until the last moment, as if afraid of falling, Charlie thought: What if he dies before I can clear him?

Liam spoke first. 'Let this be a celebration of Rose Deravin's life, not a reminder of the way she died.' But he did remind them of her death. He embraced his grudges, his voice carrying to the ceiling, the back wall. Charlie had elected not to speak: even if he didn't muff it, anything he said would remind the world that this was brother pitched against brother. Then Emma read unguardedly from Emily Dickinson, a concentration of light on the little stage at the front of the room, and Charlie felt the old crack in his heart again: the hard fact that his daughter had only the faintest of memories of her grandmother.

Mrs Ehrlich saved them. Gathered them in and steered them away from the shoals.

'I want to mark a day forty years ago, when I was in my sitting room, vacuuming—I could tell you stories about Rose Deravin with a vacuum cleaner in her hand—and saw a Holden station wagon pull in next door, flat to the springs with boxes and cases, luggage skew-whiff on the roof rack. Do any of you remember that car? It was always breaking down, Rhys or Rose knocking on my door, asking my late husband for a jump start.

'Funny how the past repeats itself. When I was widowed, rogues and scallywags would come knocking on my door, selling things too good to be true or offering to mow my lawn or repair my gutters, and Rhys would give them what for. Then only a few weeks ago his son Charlie'—the smile she gave him lit up the room, full of substance and warmth—'sent another ratbag on his way with a swift kick up the bum.' She paused. 'Literally.'

Laughter. Something eased in the hall.

'And there was Rose, dear Rose,' Mrs Ehrlich said. 'Thirty years separated us, but we became firm friends. We did the things that neighbours do—had each other over for a cuppa, exchanged recipes and gardening tips—and she was a rock when Tom died. But what I remember most is her self-deprecatory, teasing manner. She didn't take the world seriously and yet she took it very seriously. She didn't doubt herself and yet never big-noted herself. Whenever the world around her became too altered, she brought it back on track. But the world was altered when she disappeared—and it continues to alter as awful truths are revealed. It's our job to mend it for her.'

Charlie blinked. Felt a nudge: Emma was offering him a tissue.

Noon now, Liam announcing that mourners were invited to join the family in the supper room—which was the last thing Charlie wanted. He didn't stir as the hall emptied.

Sue Mead came in on his flank, placed her hand on his shoulder, squeezed. 'Sorry, Charlie, I have to go.'

He placed his hand briefly on hers. 'But the stale sandwiches. The bricklayers' tea.'

'I know, a real wrench, but I have a stack of interviews to collate.'

A pat and she was gone. Still Charlie sat. He felt numb; wished Anna was with him.

Then Fay was there, her face strained and depleted. 'Charlie, your dad's not well. I'm taking him home.'

He stood. 'Does he need a doctor?'

'He's just tired.'

'Stay at my place tonight.'

She shook her head. 'His own bed,' she said. Then, gesturing at the main door, she added: 'Plus we wouldn't want the hyenas to follow us to your front lawn.'

Charlie nodded. The appetites and assimilations of the media. 'I'll help you get him into the car.'

Out into a surge of young cameramen and sound techs wearing boardshorts and T-shirts, middle-aged print reporters with beer bellies and notebooks, young TV talent in summer dresses—all with the light of pursuit in their eyes...

'Did you kill your wife, Mr Deravin?'

'Why did Billy Saul have to die?'

'What did you think when the bodies were found?'

Charlie bulldozed his father through the mob, Fay in his wake, and realised a moment later that Mark Valente was helping, looking vivid and energised. An old head-banging cop, Charlie thought, the kind you didn't find anymore.

They reached Rhys and Fay's Peugeot but found themselves trapped, Charlie pinned against his father, his father against the passenger door. Then a microphone was thrust at Rhys and the cute little face behind it was speaking: 'Some might consider it bad form that you dared to attend your late wife's memorial service, Mr Deravin.'

Charlie struggled to elbow her away, struggled with the door. Where was Valente? Where was Fay, for that matter? He looked across the roof of the car. She was still several metres away, running a smaller gauntlet. A reporter, a photographer—and the podcast twins. As he watched, she said something to them. Deamer nodded; Nadal helped her reach the car.

He returned his attention to the reporter. 'Please move so I can open the door.'

'Who are you?' she asked. 'One of the sons?'

Her eyes gleamed as she thrust the microphone at him. Then he saw her gape, a wild light of agony in her eyes as she doubled over. And Valente was there beside her, his elbows flying, a dropped shoulder tackling. 'Clear a way for the lady,' he shouted, 'she's about to be sick.'

The throng fell back. The pressure eased and Charlie opened the passenger door and bundled his father into the car. 'See you soon.'

By now Fay was opening her door. He called over the roof, 'See you soon.'

She nodded climbed in, buckled up. Started the car, eased it out onto Frankston–Flinders Road in a series of little spurts.

Then Valente joined him, brushing his palms together. 'Most fun I've had in years.'

'You punched her in the stomach,' Charlie said.

Valente shrugged. Cast a look at the reporter, who was still doubled over, hanging onto a friend. 'And his name was death, and hell followed after him.'

'Yeah, I think we could do with a bit less of that,' Charlie said.

He counted: twenty-eight mourners had stayed for sandwiches, cupcakes and tea, and, as he flicked among them dutifully, still dazed, his brother stood back looking awkward.

Shyness? Disapproval? You didn't always know with Liam.

From Mrs Ehrlich to Alby the aircon mechanic to Noel Saltash to a long-lost aunt, to Alan Wagoner and Pat the dog-woman. Hands pressed his warmly, his cheek was kissed, arms were flung around his shoulders. Meanwhile Valente was also working the room. He knew everyone. He was affectionate with Emma, Jess, Ryan. Ignored Saltash. Was reserved with Mrs Ehrlich—as if they knew too much about each other.

No sign of Bekker, but McGuire sidled in.

'You still here?'

'Manners, Mr Deravin.'

'Where's your boss?'

'Fetching the car.'

'I thought that would be your job.'

McGuire smiled. Stood close alongside Charlie and, with him, surveyed the room.

'This is private,' Charlie said. 'Fuck off, okay?'

'One of the reporters made a good point,' McGuire said. 'It was bad form for your father to turn up here.'

'Fuck off, I said.'

'I mean,' McGuire said, 'the sheer nerve of it.'

Charlie walked away from her, and she called, 'One o'clock tomorrow.'

He walked back. 'What?'

'It's been arranged with your dad and his lawyer. One tomorrow.'

Charlie walked off again and found a quiet corner

from which to watch the crowd dwindle. Saw all the little dramas play out. Valente turning a cold shoulder when the podcast twins wandered in, for example. His normal swagger and bluster curiously dialled down.

45

CHARLIE DIDN'T SO much wake as realise that he'd been awake for some time. And as he lay there, washed in the light of a full moon, the memorial service that had hijacked his dreams last night—hectic, confused—began to fade, replaced by memories of the actual service. The actual service was hardly an improvement, though. Two awful hours of his life, over which hovered the media scrum, Mark Valente's hungry gaze, the hissing whispers of strangers. He shifted under the bedsheet. For twenty years he'd dared not grieve for his mother. He'd not known what to grieve for, apart from her absence. Now all he wanted was simple mourning, and the bastards weren't letting him have it.

He checked the bedside clock: 4 a.m. He'd gone through this enough times to know that sleep wouldn't come now. And he felt rested anyway, after a fashion; to lie there gazing at moon shadows would achieve nothing.

He slipped out of bed, pulled on shorts and a T-shirt, and padded through to the kitchen. Tea and toast. The armchair beside the sitting-room floor lamp. Em's bird book in his lap.

Instead of reading he found himself scrolling through the news feed on his phone. He was doing that too often, not good for him, not wise, but still he continued to do it—several times a day, headlong down rabbit holes of stupidity. How the world economies were controlled by Jewish bankers, the British royals were lizard people and China had unleashed the virus upon the world. And, closer to home, how your average fuckwit can fuck up—like last night, a junkie, impatient to make a buy, had interrupted undercover Drug Squad officers who were grilling her dealer.

But mainly he chased down virus stories, a deepening obsession ever since Rhys's hospitalisation. The first deaths in Europe; growing anxiety in Italy; fifteen cases in Australia. The susceptibility of cruise-ship passengers and crew—days spent mingling at close quarters, onboard and on mini-bus daytrips. The bushfires, the virus: as one source of dread eased, another stepped in neatly to replace it.

At 6.30 he walked down to the beach carrying his long-board, his right arm tense and ropy. Reached the sand and turned left, around to where low waves rolled slowly in. Half-a-dozen heads were in the water, including a couple of heroes on wide-nosed, chunky-tailed shortboards. He paddled out to wait. Bobbed there a while, idly waiting, positioning himself, keeping ready, casting one eye back over his shoulder for breaks that never came. How often had he done this, starting when he was a kid, out on the water with Rhys and Mark? Lifted, lowered; the rolling sea beneath him false, late and benign. He nodded to the other surfers. He knew most of them. 'Dickhead,' they all said when a newcomer came through on a swell that almost but not quite paid off, shouting that Charlie was a useless old man who should fuck off out of the way.

He was wading onto Balinoe Beach when he saw Mark Valente in bathers, a towel over one shoulder, talking to Noel Saltash in his shire ranger's beach buggy. The odd couple, he thought. They turned to face him as he drew near, and he had that old sense of them: a predatory under-current in Valente and Saltash faintly aggrieved and put upon.

'Morning, gents.'

'Charlie,' they nodded, the greeting hobbled by the

events of the previous day. Soon one of them was going to say, 'Beautiful morning'.

Charlie cut across that: 'Thanks for coming yesterday.'

Relieved, Saltash said, 'Least we could do.'

'She'd been a part of our lives, Charlie,' Valente said.

'Anyway, it was appreciated.'

That was the signal for awkward handshakes before Saltash trundled on down the beach in his buggy and Valente dropped his towel onto the sand and kicked off his footwear. Charlie gave a little half-wave goodbye and was a few metres along the beach when Valente called, 'Would you like to come for lunch? About twelve-thirty?'

Charlie stopped. 'Sorry, can't,' he said. 'I'm picking up Dad around then.'

'Oh? For what? The doctor?'

Charlie walked back to where Valente stood with his big feet planted in the lapping sea. 'Homicide want to interview him. Formally. He could be charged.'

'Shit. Sorry. Tell him good luck.'

'I will,' Charlie said and found himself looking help-lessly at Valente, whose return glance was so full of open curiosity that he was tempted to dive back into the water, cleave through it and abrade himself against the rocks.

By 12.45 he'd collected Rhys and Fay and driven them to police headquarters.

Jenna Baird met them outside the building. She was older than Charlie, dressed in a white shirt hoicked halfway out of the waistband of her wrinkled linen trousers, dead-straight black hair more or less kept off her face by struggling alligator clips. The untidiness was deceptive. Baird always looked distracted, as if she'd overslept and thrown herself together before rushing out the door. And if she had a concealed self, if something dramatic lurked in her, Charlie had never seen it. She got the job done, though. A lawyer of the sharp, skewering kind.

The handshakes were brief, almost perfunctory. 'Thanks, Charlie,' Baird said, 'I'll text you when we're done.'

Fay was agitated. 'I thought I could sit in. He's not well.'

Baird shook her head. 'Not possible. You might be called as a witness.'

What she didn't say was: *In fact, you might be on the list of suspects.*

Like me, Charlie thought. 'If you need more information,' he said, 'just shoot us a text.'

'That won't be necessary. I've had two long consultations with your father, and I have some knowledge of the police case against him.' She didn't say how she'd got it. 'Now: I need you both to prepare for the fact that they might arrest him today. In which case I will ask that he be bailed. But that will mean that one hour stretches to five or six hours.'

'We understand,' Charlie said, not confident that Fay did.

Then Rhys was taking Fay aside. A kiss, a hug, reassurance; Baird waiting nearby with the kind of patience that is impatient.

'Ready?' she said.

She took Rhys away.

Fay joined Charlie and he could see the tension thrumming in her. When he put his arm around her she leaned into him.

He took her to a shaded outside table at a Southbank café. Tense, out of sorts, they sat and watched the sun glittering on the water and the glass towers on the north bank, playing with iced tea and cake they didn't want, and why was the place teeming with people on a workday?

Fay picked up and set down her glass. 'When we moved to Warrandyte I couldn't wait for our new life to begin. Instead, your dad got sick and it stopped in its tracks. Does that sound ungrateful?'

Love and its expectations, Charlie thought. He touched the back of her hand. 'No. I wish you'd told me how sick he was, though.'

She shook her head, but whether that meant she didn't know why she'd said nothing or didn't want to be challenged, Charlie couldn't tell.

Presently she said, 'It was just chronic at first. He was fine, we could do most of the things we liked doing, he just had to be careful not to put strain on his system. But he did get worse last year. The cruise was meant to be a treat before he, before he…' She shook that off and looked directly at him, her face raw, her voice rising and spreading: 'Tell me the truth. Is he going to jail?'

'You can't think like that, I—'

'Don't patronise me.'

'Sorry,' Charlie said. He cast about for the words: 'It seems they think they have a case, so it's possible he'll be arrested, but there's a big difference between that and going to jail, and Jenna's good at her job.'

She nodded gloomily. 'She drove out to see him on the weekend, which was good of her—'

'Wait till you get the bill,' Charlie said.

A strangled smile. 'And they had a long talk on the phone last night.'

'Did he tell you what they talked about?'

'She took him through the sorts of things he might be asked. How to answer, what to look out for, how to let her step in.'

'Good,' said Charlie. Although Rhys Deravin was a wily old coot who knew all the tricks of interrogation and evasion, this was different. He was ill. He was the target. And given that his fuse could be short, there was no guarantee he wouldn't blurt out the wrong thing.

Clearly Fay had thought about that, too. 'What if he gets confused, or incriminates himself without knowing it?'

'Jenna will take care of him.'

Fay wet her finger and collected a crumb.

Charlie said, 'Her knowledge of the police case: did she talk to Dad about any of the specifics?'

Fay looked up at him, hooking a perspiration-damp tendril behind her ear as she weighed her words. 'Not much. She said she wanted to see how it went today before she worked out what her defence strategy would be. I mean, they might not even have him in their sights—might just be after information.'

Charlie could see waves of emotion in his stepmother, but before he could say anything, she added: 'But one thing she did say, there's something wrong with his alibi.'

Liam, Charlie thought.

'And something about him hiring a carpet-cleaning machine from the Coles supermarket in Hastings.'

'Everyone cleans their carpets,' Charlie said. 'Doesn't prove anything.'

Yeah, you hold on to that thought, Charlie. He picked morosely at his own crumbs.

Then his phone pinged. He picked it up, saying, 'Let's hope we can take him home.'

A text from Jenna Baird. *Come right now.*

46

AS THEY FOLLOWED the ambulance, it occurred to Charlie that he was fed up with hospitals.

Cabrini this time. Half an hour frittered away dropping Fay at the main entrance, finding a park, heading inside to locate her again. She was in a waiting room, kneading a handkerchief. 'They've taken him for tests.'

He pulled his chair closer. 'Heart attack?'

She nodded. 'Possibly not major, but still...'

And they sat side by side with that knowledge. They barely spoke. And then Fay was touching her fingertips to his jiggling leg. 'No need for you to hang around, Charlie. If you have things to do...'

Demand information and answers, that's what he had to do.

Two hours later, responding to her text, he was back, standing in the doorway of a room where Rhys—hooked to machines—looked frightened. Not even Fay could dispel that and seemed to know it, too, seated beside his bed, holding his hand. When Charlie stepped into the room she said, with an air of precarious good humour, 'Look what he's gone and done this time.'

Charlie struggled to go along with it. 'Dodging his responsibilities again,' he said, hearing the words crash leadenly around him.

Rhys stirred. 'Son.'

Fay patted the side of the bed. 'Sit.'

They're both glad of the intrusion, Charlie thought. 'How are you, Dad?'

'A little heart scare, that's all.'

Little, Charlie thought. He was about to remonstrate but Rhys's face had gone slack; eyes half-closed, chest rising and falling sluggishly.

'It's okay, he'll wake up again,' Fay said, seeing Charlie's expression.

'Had me scared for a moment.'

Fay's phone pinged for an incoming text. Charlie watched her read it and clear the screen and a moment later reach out and squeeze his forearm. 'What have you been up to?'

Charlie shook his head: how to express the gradual erosion of his intentions? He'd driven back to the Homicide Squad, where he was given the brush-off by Bekker and McGuire, and then he'd had a sit-down with Jenna Baird in her Richmond office.

'I had a word with the lawyer,' he said.

'What did she say?'

'She apologised; she hadn't known how wound up Dad was. They went at him hard apparently, even showed him photos of Mum's remains. Then halfway through their arrest spiel, he grabbed at his chest and fell to the floor. She made them call an ambulance.'

Fay looked at her husband again. 'Poor old boy.'

A curious endearment. In this room thick with electronics, disinfectants and a hopelessness kept barely in check, did she see Rhys as old? Barely three years older. And did she see him as a boy? Boyish when she'd first met him, probably, but that had dwindled in the aftermath of Mum's disappearance. 'Poor old boy'—curious, but full of love and pain.

'They haven't posted a guard,' Fay said, with a note of bitter humour. 'Presumably they don't think he'll do a runner.'

Charlie nodded. 'I think Jenna put the wind up them. She told me there's a Magistrates Court committal hearing slated for next month; she says she can delay it. I mean for a start, is Dad in any condition to contribute to his own defence? And…look, she couldn't tell me much, but when the physical evidence was tested again recently, she said they found another DNA trace. Male. Not in the system.'

Fay glanced uneasily at Rhys. 'Yes, he told me. He said they asked him who his accomplice was.'

'They would ask that. But Jenna's confident she can spin it another way. Reasonable doubt.'

Charlie recalled clearly what Baird had said. She'd argued before him, as if before a magistrate: 'In light of the fact that DNA from another, unidentified male person was present at the crime scene, it appears to me that the Crown should regroup with a view to deciding if their case against your father is prosecutable.'

'Let's hope she's right,' Fay said.

Another thing Jenna Baird had said: if the virus worsened there might be limitations placed on public gatherings—in which case trials and hearings were likely to be delayed anyway.

A nurse whisked in and about, throwing them a distracted smile, checking the machines, the chart at the foot of the bed, Rhys's position on the pillow. Waiting until she'd gone, Charlie said, 'Did Dad say much else about the interview?'

'No. He's been fading in and out. And strictly speaking he's not supposed to talk about it to anyone, in case they get called as a witness.'

They both sat there and watched Rhys, his shallow breathing.

Charlie said, 'Fay, I never asked, but you were questioned back then?'

'Of course.' She touched the back of his hand. 'I had nothing to tell them, though. I'd been at a conference in Sydney.'

'How about since then? The cold-case unit looked at it a couple of times.'

'The same. Nothing I could add to what I originally told them.'

Charlie wriggled his shoulders, embarrassed. 'Sorry.'

Fay said, 'But I expect behind the scenes they looked at me pretty hard. Unusual bank transactions. Who I hung out with.'

'It's what they do,' Charlie said. It's what I used to do.

Their little burst of conversation lapsed again until Fay, glancing at her watch, said, 'I'm just going for a walk. I've been sitting around all day. Do you mind?'

'Of course not.'

'Call me if anything changes.'

She grabbed her bag and left and a minute later Rhys said, 'Is she gone?'

Slippery old bugger. 'You're not at death's door, then?' Charlie said.

'Feels like it,' Rhys said. He attempted to boost himself in the bed but flopped again, stretched to his limit. 'Things I need to tell you.'

Deathbed confession? Charlie swallowed. 'Okay.'

Struggling for air, Rhys said, 'They laid it all out for

me. I had a strong motive to kill Rose—I didn't want to sell the house or pay her anything. I took up with Fay almost immediately and didn't show the requisite grief. I couldn't even be bothered to attend the inquest. I got my mates to lie for me. And my alibi was weak.'

He trailed away. Charlie waited, then said, 'All circumstantial.'

That triggered another burst from Rhys. 'Compelling though, with a good prosecutor. Plus, they have my mobile phone records for that day, which show two calls of interest, from their point of view. One to your mother—their argument is, I called her to find out where she was so I could go there and kill her.'

'Did you call her?'

'Yes. There's no big mystery. Like I told you the other day, I wanted to drop off some tablecloths but didn't want to run into her, it would be awkward for both of us. The thing is, it was a five-second call—her answering machine.'

'What was the other call?'

Rhys shifted uncomfortably. 'The school, to check that your mum was at work.'

Charlie knew that could be spun a couple of ways. 'You think someone at the school has remembered?'

Rhys looked at him bleakly. 'The receptionist put me through to the staffroom and I found myself on the line with Karen Wagoner, remember her? The last person I wanted to talk to. Anyway, she said Rose had just slipped home to collect something but would be back after lunch, so I just filled in time for a couple of hours before I dropped off the tablecloths.'

'Shit. You didn't see anything at the house? Mum's car?'

'No.'

'Dad, if Liam saw you in the area maybe others did, too.'

'I know. Actually, Bekker and McGuire know I was there, but not through Liam.'

'Karen Wagoner.'

'Probably. I must've let slip I was leaving the tablecloths and they went back over the original photos and saw the carton on the veranda.'

'That could sink you.'

'I know. But what's interesting, I was also asked about vehicles that *I* might have seen. Specifically a motorbike—one was reported haring through the crossing outside the primary school—or a white van—one was seen near where Rose's car was found.'

Bekker keeping an open mind? 'At least they're looking at other possibilities,' Charlie said.

Rhys snorted. 'They're looking at my so-called accomplice, but your Ms Baird really knows her stuff. She got Bekker to admit that the original investigators were told this at the time but never followed it up.'

'Dad, Shane Lambert had a motorbike.'

Rhys looked baffled, an old man. 'Did he?'

'You know he did. He would have driven it to your

place when he came to give that security advice.'

Out of the reaches of time and space, Rhys said, 'You could be right, come to think of it.'

Then he shifted up on the pillow again, suddenly sharp as a tack. 'Anyway, Bekker said Lambert was in the lockup that day.'

'Yeah.' They both chewed on that. Charlie checked his watch: Fay might return, or Rhys might fade or shut up again. Time seemed urgent suddenly. 'Jenna told me they found a second DNA trace, male, not in the database.'

Rhys nodded. His gauntness seemed more acute. 'She was arguing it weakened their case; they were running the accomplice line.'

'I forgot to ask what kind,' Charlie said. He paused and added awkwardly: 'Semen?'

Rhys shook his head, a weak flop left and right on the pillow. 'They retested the blood on her keys. Found a male sample with it.'

Those keys…A big bunch, keys for everything. Charlie thought irrelevantly: Dad must've sold her car with the spare key. 'How well did you know Lambert?'

'Hardly at all.'

'His friends?'

'Charlie, I barely knew him. Let's just say he had his uses. God, I'm tired.'

He's being evasive, Charlie thought. 'What about the carpet cleaner you hired?'

'Oh, for god's sake, I threw wine over your mother the

354

day she walked out and made a bad job of getting it out of the carpet, all right?'

Protesteth too much. And Charlie hated to visualise that spurt of anger. 'Did you ever hit her?'

Rhys Deravin was shocked. 'Never. I don't like where you're going with this. Throwing wine over someone isn't the same thing as hitting them.'

Not far off though, Charlie thought. He regarded his father gloomily. Even at this extreme, his heart failing him, barely holding on, he was capable of wriggling out of a mess.

'Can I ask why you didn't stay on in the house?'

He thought Rhys would say, 'Because I wanted to live with Fay.' Instead, all of his father's reserves seemed to drain out of him. Shrinking in the bed, he said, 'Look what they did to your mother. I couldn't stay.'

'What? What do you mean?'

Rhys's chest rose and fell, barely disturbing the bedclothes, and his eyes were closed, his mouth slack, an old man sleeping. Charlie checked the time: Fay had been gone for half an hour. He texted her and took the lift down to the ground floor. Out on the street, he winced: the afternoon sun struck his eyes, struck against windscreens and even the chrome on an old MG burbling along the street. His sunglasses were in the Skoda, and he was halfway to fetching them when he paused, stepped into the concealing shadows of a signboard and watched Fay cross Wattletree Road from a yellow VW and hurry into the hospital.

355

47

AS THEY SPOTTED Charlie steaming towards them, the podcast twins climbed out of their car and leaned against it, their arms not folded but their postures suggestive of that. He wanted to slap the smugness from their faces.

'What are you doing? Leave us alone. You're not wanted.'

Nadal, turning up the wattage on his smirk, stepped away from the car, spoiling for a tussle. 'Keep your shirt on.'

'First you turn up at my mother's service,' Charlie said,

''and now this? Fay's got enough on her plate.'

Deamer fronted up to him. 'If you must know, she contacted us.'

Charlie went still. Giving himself time to regroup, he said, 'What do you mean?'

Holding up both hands, warding him off, Deamer said, 'Let's not do this out here. Too hot, for a start. Hop in.'

'And go where? You must be crazy.'

'Pub,' she said. 'There's a pub round the corner.'

Charlie expected a hipster joint, pretentious cocktails and a themed décor, but they drove him to an old corner pub with a vast, dimly-lit, high-ceilinged lounge and islands of club chairs on a floral carpet. The kiddies had lemon, lime and soda, Charlie a beer—which seemed to confirm something for Nadal.

They had driven in silence and ordered in monosyllables. Now it was time to talk.

'What do you mean, Fay contacted you?'

'She's concerned to know the truth,' Deamer said. 'Same as me and Will.'

Charlie brushed that aside. 'The truth about what?'

Ashleigh Deamer scooted her chair around until it was elbow-to-elbow with her boyfriend's and took his hand in hers. 'You don't know who I am, do you?'

'Enlighten me.'

'You went to see Karen Wagoner a while back?'

'So?'

'She's my grandmother.'

Things started to slot into place. 'Oh. And?'

'She and Mum don't get along.'

Charlie stared at Deamer without seeing her. What he saw were lines of familial affection and disaffection. 'And you don't get along with your mother either, but you're close to your grandmother.'

Deamer shrugged. 'She looked after me a lot when I was little. And Mum's bi-curiosity...' She gave a little grimace that suggested contempt and bitter amusement amidst the usual fallout of family breakup.

Bi-curiosity. Grandmother and granddaughter, collaborators in disapproval, thought Charlie. He recalled his conversation with Wagoner and could have kicked himself. She'd mentioned, with pride, a granddaughter, Ash. In television.

'Okay, so Granny told you things, is that what you're saying?'

Deamer jerked Nadal's hand up and down emphatically as if unaware she still clutched it. 'In particular, about her Menlo Beach friends.'

Charlie watched a woman at a nearby cluster of club chairs get to her feet unsteadily, cross the thick carpet, rest one hand on the jukebox, sway her bum, ponder her selection. John Denver leaked into the room. I'm in a time warp, Charlie thought—in more ways than one.

'What about them?'

'Bent cops,' Nadal said in his sleepy way.

Deamer hushed him, sending Charlie an apologetic look. 'We don't know for sure and we're trying to find out.'

'What do you mean, bent?'

'An armed holdup, the Medicare branch in Rosebud. Half an hour before opening, the security system was breached, and two men came in through the back door.'

'How does that involve police corruption?'

'The police did the robbery, the same police investigated.'

Charlie's first mouthful of beer had been hugely welcome, a balm to his soul. He'd have sighed in pleasure if he hadn't been with the podcast twins. Now the taste was flat, tepid and he pushed his glass away. 'Is that right.'

Deamer said, with a pretty twist to her mouth, 'Your dad was investigating it.'

'Is that a fact.'

'We think the other man was Mark Valente,' Nadal said.

'Really.'

'Yes, really.'

Deamer cut in. 'Let's go back a bit. Nanna says it was a bit of a wild time. Heavy drinking, gambling, sleeping around.'

She watched Charlie tensely. He remained expressionless, thinking: She suspects her grandmother was a willing player.

'So?'

'A particular kind of culture,' Deamer said. 'Old school. Very blokey.'

Nadal leaned in. 'We found two women who were junior constables when Valente was at Rosebud. They said the sexual harassment and abuse was ongoing.'

'Well, it wouldn't have involved my father,' snarled Charlie, 'he was based in the city when Valente was at Rosebud.'

'We're not saying your father was into that kind of thing,' Deamer said. 'We're trying to paint a general picture. Macho culture: rules don't apply.'

If Karen Wagoner had been a player, Charlie thought, she might have tried to hook up with my old man, or Valente, and been rejected. She's stewed on it for years, and now she's after revenge. 'Twenty years ago the whole damn culture was macho. It doesn't add up to armed holdups.'

'I haven't finished. It was more than drinking and gambling and whatnot. We think they did things that were actually corrupt. Including evidence tampering.'

'You think, or you know?'

'They were friends with a man called Shane Lambert. Your mother's lodger, right? He knew how to break into places, bypass alarm systems.'

Charlie tingled. 'Your grandmother told you this?'

'He was arrested a couple of times and let go.'

'I repeat, your grandmother told you this?'

'Nanna said sometimes there'd be a bit of money floating around and a kind of nudge, nudge, wink, wink about where it came from. Then suddenly a lot of money. Enough for your dad to pay off the mortgage and Mark Valente to buy a house in Noosa. A win at the horses, they said.'

'You just said they were gamblers. Maybe they did have a big win. Did you even check?'

'Nanna said it happened the same time as the Medicare robbery.'

'A Medicare branch carrying enough cash to buy a house or pay off a mortgage? Come on.'

'Maybe enough for a down payment,' Deamer said. 'The thing is, they were friends with a guy who knew how to bypass security systems and one day they were all rolling in money.'

Nadal showed his disdainful teeth. 'And it happened on Valente's turf. And your father was assigned to investigate.'

Investigate, thought Charlie, or 'investigate'? When Mum disappeared, he'd been investigating a security van holdup. Useful cover then, too?

Swallowing, he said, 'I'm not convinced, and no one listening to your pissy little podcast will be either.'

'Don't be a prick,' Nadal said. He looked down his nose. 'Ash has a Master's in media studies.'

Deamer touched his forearm; turned to Charlie again. 'Sometimes context can be compelling. Nanna had a feeling things weren't right. Suddenly with all that money floating around there was tension, maybe a falling out. Then your mother disappeared, and she got frightened and left. She's been thinking about it ever since, putting two and two together.'

'And coming up with five. Context isn't enough, all you have is vague conjecture. And isn't it a basic rule of reporting that you double-check your sources? Have you asked yourselves why your grandmother wants you to dig into it? For the greater good? Or so she can settle some scores?'

Deamer flushed. 'Context does matter. Part of that is skillset—your father belonged to a specialist squad, he was trained by Mark Valente, and they were friends with Shane Lambert.'

Nadal leaned in. 'We're not the enemy, Charlie.'

'You're someone's enemy. My father, for a start.'

'Maybe he was influenced or duped,' Deamer said. 'It would be useful to talk to him.'

'Is that what Fay promised?' Charlie said, feeling disloyal.

A shake of the head. 'Actually, she just wanted to pick our brains. She said to leave your father alone and concentrate on others in that circle.'

'Good on her. My father's ill, and he won't talk to you anyway.'

'We'd just like his side of the story.'

That old chestnut, thought Charlie. 'And what was Mark Valente's side of the story when you rocked up and said, "Hey, Mr Valente, did you rob a Medicare office twenty years ago?"'

Charlie, watching their faces, saw that's exactly what

they'd done. And been told to fuck off. But then he recalled Valente's edginess yesterday. Maybe they'd buttonholed him again; maybe this time they'd struck a nerve.

'Ashleigh,' he said, 'what exactly did your grandmother say? How were you going to find out anything?'

'She said Shane Lambert was the weak link. Find him and we'd be up and running.'

Charlie started to tell them where Lambert was but thought better of it. 'You've been hitting brick walls, right? His cousin? A guy he used to work with?'

Deamer was startled. 'How do you know?' Her face cleared. 'Never mind. Anyway, he was going to be our way into the story.'

They hoped Shane Lambert, locksmithing and security expert, would betray Rhys Deravin and Mark Valente? Charlie wondered why he was even talking to them. Because he'd begun to suspect there was something to their theory? Because his father was evasive?

He said, with more feeling than he intended, 'Forget the Medicare robbery for the moment: does anything you've heard or discovered have anything to do with my mother's murder? Billy Saul's murder?'

Deamer shook her head and looked about ten years old as she picked up her glass with both hands and drank. Placing it on the coaster again, she reclasped Nadal's hand. 'Our prime focus is on police involvement in the Medicare robbery. We think Lambert bypassed the security system so the others could get in. We don't know

363

how he relates to your mother or that little boy.'

Nadal leaned in. 'She's not our way into this story,' he stressed.

'Nor is my father,' Charlie said. 'Leave him out of it.'

'Maybe we can't do that,' Deamer said.

'You'd go after a sick man?' Charlie asked, and watched her wince. Guilt? Embarrassment? She's the principled one, he thought, snatching a look at Nadal, who still seemed merely smug.

'He's not going to talk to you,' he went on, 'and neither is Mark Valente. One thing you learn in the police, play your cards close to your chest. You need hard evidence.'

'Like this?' Deamer said, releasing Nadal's hand and working her phone.

She set it down, nudged it across the table. Charlie peered at a photograph; a two-storey house on a waterway. Palm trees, a dock, a motor cruiser. 'Mark Valente's little Noosaville shack.'

'Currently valued at two point four million,' Nadal added.

Charlie slid the phone back across the table. 'But maybe valued at a lot less twenty years ago. Or maybe he still owes two million.'

'Owns it outright.'

'Proves nothing. A win at the horses, a purchase when the market was on a downturn...'

But Charlie was troubled suddenly. Rhys and Fay had never seemed rich—but never poor, either. The Warrandyte house wouldn't have come cheap. Two incomes—or a string of armed holdups? He recalled the scene outside the Balinoe Hall, the apparent contact between Fay and the twins. Had she been starting to wonder where the money came from?

'Show me that photo again.'

Deamer handed him her phone wordlessly, thinking she'd convinced him, but he cleared the screen and went directly to messages. 'You texted Fay this afternoon.'

'Give it back!'

Charlie shook his head; read through the message history. 'How did she know your number?'

Deamer's hand floated in the air, waiting for her phone. 'We first made contact last November—had she heard any rumours, that kind of thing, but she told us to get lost.'

'Good for her,' Charlie said, returning the phone.

'Yeah, well, she must've held on to our business card,' said Nadal in his lazy way. 'She contacted us on Sunday.'

'Except we were at a family thing,' Deamer said, 'which is why we tried to talk to her yesterday.'

'At my mother's memorial service,' Charlie said. 'Tactful.'

Deamer flushed. But she was defiant. 'Like I said, she approached us, Charlie.'

To be young and stupid, Charlie thought, feeling old—or somewhat old, somewhat wise. 'Okay, what did she want?'

'Like I said, to pick our brains. She seemed a bit lost, like she'd heard things. She asked what we'd meant last year when we asked if she'd heard any rumours.'

Maybe Rhys—suddenly infirm, aware of his mortality—had wanted to unburden himself?

'We told her what we just told you,' Nadal said. 'She didn't really want to hear it and said we should be looking at others.'

Charlie shivered a little in the air-conditioning. The pub lounge less like a dim, non-threatening cavern, more like an icy cell, the walls closing in. His mind raced: the possibility that Valente and his father had pulled an armed robbery—or many robberies. The possibility that his mother had found out—and had to be eliminated. But would Rhys have hurt a kid? Would Valente? And why was Billy Saul there, anyway?

'The fact remains,' he said, staring at Nadal, 'no one's going to talk. You need evidence.'

Then he heard himself: he was helping these idiots now?

Deamer was looking at him musingly. 'Charlie, we're at cross-purposes. You want to know who killed your mother, we want to know if there was, you know, criminal behaviour by your father and others back when she was killed. Maybe the two are linked, I don't know. But it seems to me that Shane Lambert might have information that helps both of us. I mean, why did he vanish? Is he dead? Did someone shut him up, and if so, who?'

Charlie had no intention of putting her straight. He had hard questions for Lambert, though, and one thing Deamer had said began to resonate with him: the rumoured existence of a police culture capable of turning a blind eye, tainting evidence and arresting people only to release them later. He needed to delve into the records again.

Oh, right: he was suspended.

48

'MY SYMPATHIES AREN'T boundless,' Susan Mead said.

'I know.'

'Pretty much used up,' she added, but not unkindly.

'I know, thanks, sarge,' Charlie said.

They were nursing glasses of lemon, lime and soda in a Docklands bar. Four o'clock, and homeward-bound workers were beginning to stop in for a drink. Charlie's old Sexual Offences and Child Abuse Investigation Team was headquartered nearby, and there was a chance one of his SOCIT workmates might stroll past, but, as the sergeant had just informed him, they were less likely to toss him into the sea now. Much of the stink had faded, with Luke Kessler pleading guilty that morning, and Allardyce off on sick leave.

'I expect you feel vindicated?' she said.

'I'm magnanimous,' Charlie said. 'No intention of rubbing it in your face.'

'Big of you.'

'I hardly covered myself in glory, sarge.'

'Running background checks using the LEAP database? Shoving the boss over his desk? You could say that.'

Charlie saw that she was waiting for him to get to the point. In the dim lighting she was expressionless, her hair escaping pins and clips at the end of a long workday, but when she aimed that expressionless face on anyone—subordinate, victim, culprit—she generally got the truth out of them.

'I'm thinking of quitting,' he said.

She nodded, unsurprised. 'Your life's become somewhat full of distractions.'

Charlie wanted to say, That's not the reason, but she went on: 'You'll go out on a high. We got Kessler.'

'A lot of that was down to Anna Picard. She did something we should have done from the start.'

'Like what?'

'She found another victim.'

'So?'

'Kessler's teammates and family friends and even his

old girlfriend were character witnesses, right? We accepted that, it's par for the course in he-said, she-said cases. Meaning we had to depend on Gina Lascelles, who was pulled apart on the stand.'

'Charlie, there was more to the investigation than Gina's story. We looked pretty hard for a self-clustering rape culture in that club.'

'I know, I did some of the digging. But everyone clammed up, we couldn't find anything. Anna, on the other hand, did something that paid off. She found *enemies* of the ex-girlfriend.'

Including one who had also partied with the team and was prepared to testify to her own rape. Her story differed from Gina Lascelles' but was no less horrific: she'd awoken at a party to find herself naked, Kessler's penis in her mouth, his hands choking her, calling her 'bitch' and 'slut', his mates watching, cheering on. And Charlie would have bet his best surfboard that one of the onlookers had been Jake Allardyce.

The bar had become noisy. Running his fingers up and down his glass abstractedly, soothed by the condensation, he watched Mead absorb what he'd said. Maybe she'd start making it customary to approach the enemies of the main players in future rape investigations.

Then she was fishing an iPad from her bag. 'This favour you ask for,' she said abruptly.

Charlie gave her the details: Shane Lambert, arrested for public drunkenness in Rosebud, Victoria, on 4 February

2000, and held overnight in the station lockup. 'If you could dig out all the circumstances,' he added, 'including contemporaneous notes if they exist—anything that might not appear on an ordinary arrest record.'

'Who is he?' she asked, her fingers flying on the screen.

'He was my mother's lodger for a while.'

Mead stopped; looked up at him. 'I'm sex crimes, Charlie. How do I cover myself if there's any follow-up?'

Charlie had expected that. 'The Peninsula paedophile ring we've been tracking?'

She put her head on one side and paused. 'So I tell professional standards I was wondering if Lambert might have snatched the boy who was buried with your mother?'

'Yeah.'

'Might fly,' she muttered, her gaze returning to the iPad.

He watched her peer at the screen, scroll down, scroll up again. 'Well, like you say, he was arrested and locked up overnight. But if you knew that, why are you looking at him?'

'Just double-checking.'

She stared at him for a while. 'Uh huh. I'd have thought homicide would have already done that.'

Charlie indicated the iPad again. 'Any other details? Take your time.'

A mistake. She pushed the iPad away. 'No, Charlie, I won't take my time. I do have a life.'

'Sorry,' Charlie said. Maybe sorry was his default state.

Eventually she sighed; looked at the screen again. 'There's nothing much on him. A couple of early arrests, a short prison term when he was young, and his DNA's in the system, that's about all.'

'But the actual day of the arrest...'

She shook her head, weary of him, and scrolled up and down the screen. 'He was arrested for being drunk and disorderly—he even took a swing at a uniform but wasn't charged for that.'

'Who arrested him?'

She looked again. 'A local.'

Charlie tensed. 'Mark Valente?'

'No. A Constable Riggs.' She scrolled down. 'Picked him up in the front bar of the Rosebud Hotel, and...Yeah, brought him in at four in the afternoon.'

Charlie began to rock; he didn't know he was doing it. Why hadn't that been noticed before? Why hadn't *he* noticed it?

'Earth to Charlie: what's wrong?'

'He was cleared of suspicion and never looked at again because he was in the lockup—about the most watertight alibi you can get. But the thing is, the murders happened well before four o'clock.'

49

PRIOR TO THAT news, Charlie might have wandered back to the hospital. Instead he was stuck in peak-hour traffic on the Monash Freeway. He'd cleared it with Fay: Rhys was in good spirits, in good hands. He should go on home, come back tomorrow.

He touched the accelerator, rolled four metres, stopped again, the world reduced to close-ups of brake lights, and called Bekker.

This time she didn't give him the brush-off. 'You on speaker?'

'I'm in the car,' Charlie confirmed.

'Look, Charlie, we're really sorry about your father. We pushed too hard today; we should have waited a few days.'

'You can say that again. McGuire shoved photos of my mother's body under his nose.'

Charlie had visualised it, not only the eye sockets, the dirt and rotted fabric clinging to the bones, but also the cold, satisfied gleam in McGuire. And Bekker had allowed it. He was beginning to see how they worked.

'As I said, we're sorry. How's he doing?'

'Is he under arrest?'

'We didn't actually complete the process. How's he doing?'

'Well, you put him back in hospital.'

'Obviously, we have no intention of troubling him while he's unwell. But the investigation continues, and when he's up to it we do need to speak to him again.'

'Oh, so you're not going to arrest him after all?'

She lashed back at him. 'You called me, remember? Is it to give me a hard time or is there something else?'

Charlie rolled a few more metres, braked, rolled again. It was unlikely there'd been an accident; it was just the Monash. 'The reason I called,' he said, 'is I think Shane Lambert needs to be looked at again.'

'We've been over this. He was cleared at the time—about the only thing the original investigation did right—and we've cleared him again this time around. He didn't leave his DNA on anything, and he couldn't have done it anyway, he was locked up.'

'Yes, he was locked up, but did you check the arrest report?'

'Bev McGuire did. She confirmed everything.'

'Yeah, well, she did a shitty job,' Charlie said. 'Lambert was roaming around free until four in the afternoon. He has no alibi for earlier in the day. The murders probably happened between one and two-thirty. It fits with finding Billy Saul's stuff on the beach mid-afternoon, around the same time my mother's car was reported.'

There was a silence, Charlie imagining Bekker's mind at work. Eventually she said, 'I won't ask you how you obtained that information.'

'That would be best.'

'Rest assured, I will look into this, Charlie.'

Charlie shook his head; eased the Skoda the length of a cricket pitch with semi-trailers on either side, blocking out the sun. 'Rest assured': like 'Don't worry' and 'I'll get right on it', a phrase to sap your confidence.

'Can I rest assured that you'll give McGuire a bollocking?'

Bekker said coldly, 'Lambert was jailed for drunkenness, don't forget. He'd been drinking for hours, presumably, to get to a state where the police locked him up for his own good. So explain to me how he was able to murder and bury two people, plus lay down a bit of misdirection?'

He faked the drunkenness, Charlie thought, or binged

375

for an hour on spirits. He might look like a beaten-down old alcoholic now, but he'd been around. He was banking on the psychology working for him: if the police record showed he was arrested and jailed, why dig deeper?

'Okay,' said Charlie, completing the call. Maybe Bekker would double-check now. Maybe she wouldn't. Or maybe she'd check, and the wheels of justice would turn just as slowly as they always did. As for Charlie, he had more thinking to do—the shunting, stalling and sandwiching of the traffic a kind of wholesale representation of his conclusions and counter-conclusions.

50

A FREEWAY HOUR passed.

Assume Lambert had nothing to do with the murders. He simply went on a bender and got locked up for public drunkenness.

That left Rhys, or Valente, or both, and Charlie couldn't see either of them as killers.

Not really. Not yet.

But reluctantly—assuming the podcast twins were correct—he could see them pulling an armed robbery. Robberies.

What if none of them was responsible—it was a stranger or strangers? But this didn't feel like that kind of crime. Strangers wouldn't go to the trouble of a burial and two sets of misdirection. They wouldn't need to.

Or Lambert had been involved in the murders. Knowing he'd be a suspect, he'd staged being drunk and disorderly so he'd be locked up—an alibi gamble that had paid off for twenty years. But could he have done it all by himself? He'd have needed help from someone capable of creating a smokescreen, capable of misdirecting. That mystery DNA sample.

Yet Charlie kept returning to one simple conviction: neither Valente nor his father would murder anyone. He could almost hear Valente's voice: 'Me break bread with the godless? Bend to the wills and ways of evil?'

On the other hand, he was certain Valente was responsible for the Jake Allardyce hit-and-run. Valente was a man who took care of his flock. Had he needed to protect his flock against Rose Deravin, too? Maybe Fay's appearance on the scene and the resulting separation had let loose a vengeful streak in Rose or liberated her sense of justice. Maybe she was threatening to talk; and Lambert was monitoring her, placed there by Valente. And then Liam and I came along and turfed him out.

But why would Lambert and Valente go to her house in the middle of the day?

Charlie could think of one reason: to collect the cash from the security-van holdup—or some other robbery or series of robberies. Plenty of good hiding places in that old house. They go back for the money—and Rose comes home unexpectedly, Billy Saul wanders past unexpectedly. And the slab house is a convenient burial site because Valente knows who owns it; knows they won't be coming back.

Or Lambert went there alone, everything went wrong, and he put in a panicky call to Valente.

If Valente was involved, then the unknown DNA sample was his. He'd have been careful handling Billy Saul's possessions, and he'd have gloved up in Rose's car—but somehow he'd been careless with her keys. Had he stowed his bike in the boot and ridden back? No—too slow. Lambert had followed on his Ducati, then given him a lift back to Rosebud and the next stage of the story.

Or none of the above. Maybe Lambert, or Valente, had tried it on with Rose Deravin and been rebuffed.

Or it was all bullshit, all false, Karen Wagoner sowing mischief because of hurt feelings all those years ago.

This was Charlie thinking like a cop, as the traffic eased on Eastlink, bunched again on Peninsula Link and dwindled to a handful of cars on Balinoe Road. But old habits of love, loyalty and fealty to the past die hard. He'd been partly forged by Mark Valente. A source of both intimidation and encouragement for a young kid. The special thrill of being egged on and singled out: you felt loved, wanted, recognised. Us against them. A big man, a big presence.

Charlie recalled summer evenings when he should have been in bed but sat unnoticed in the garden shadows as the barbecue cooled and bottle tops somersaulted: Mark Valente telling a string of Irish jokes or leading the song when there was a birthday. Or—Charlie's favourite—telling his thirty-minute duck-shooting story, except that in his version it was 'dulfuck shoolfooting with his trulfusty gulfun dolfog Rolfover'. Charlie almost grinned now; he was almost a kid giggling in the corner again.

A kind of love. A kind of fear—but respectful fear, of a man who looked out for you.

The king of Menlo Beach. Clever, graceful, arrogant, wealthy.

Help you if you got into strife. Save you. Avenge you. You felt loved, wanted, recognised. Us against them.

Until you dropped a catch, cried when you'd been hit on the hand, gave up and curled into a ball. Was it Valente's voice shouting, *Jesus, what a mummy's boy. Go home to Mummy, you great sook. I'll give you something to cry about*? Or was it Dad, or one of the other men? Liam had borne the brunt of it, but Charlie had walked on eggshells too. For entire summers. Year after year.

Rhys had said, 'Look what they did to your mother.'

Meaning they'd shut her up. And Rhys heard the warning. He'd left the Peninsula and never returned.

Please god he hadn't been forced to witness it; hadn't been told—by Valente, Lambert?—'This is how we deal with weak links.'

That unidentified DNA. DNA is used to prove, and it's used to eliminate. All Charlie needed was a couple of evidence bags—brown paper bags would do—and access to Valente's garbage and recycle bins.

He was drawing into Menlo Beach by 6.20. The sun was low above the water but a couple of hours short of smearing the horizon. He parked in his driveway, unlocked the house and paced for a while, thinking. Take Valente's DNA to a private lab, he thought. Present Bekker with the results and kick up a fuss if she doesn't test the profile against the unknown sample found on Rose's car keys.

As the gums, shrubs and tea-trees lost definition, he changed into dark hiking pants, runners and a long-sleeved shirt—the colours of twilight—and folded a few brown paper bags into his pocket. Then he stepped out onto Tide-pool Street and the evening absorbed him.

He turned left, away from the beach, then left and right until he reached the entrance to Sargasso Lane. He paused there among a cluster of nature strip hakeas and banksias, eyeing Valente's house, a big Cape Cod on a corner block. The position was good: he could see along the front and left-hand-side walls. Two lights were on, one towards the rear, the other upstairs. Kitchen and bedroom, he thought.

He crossed the intersection and stepped into denser shadows, tea-trees and a flowering gum in Valente's front yard. Then he ran lightly to the side wall and along it to the rear of the property. Poked his head around the corner, trying to spot Valente's bins, but they weren't against the wall and a motion-detector light came on.

Heart thumping, he scurried back to his corner observation post. A dog barked next door, someone was playing Norah Jones, someone else was watching evening TV. Smells wafted: sausages on a barbecue. The sensory impressions of summer and Charlie was rooted to the past, he had no future.

He was about to move again and saw, at the house across the road, a pair of bins at the kerb. It was bin night. He'd been intent on Valente's side wall and backyard, not the leafy stretch of kerb at the front of his house.

He ran across the road again, keeping low, waiting for a voice to challenge him. No one walked by, no one opened a door to look out, as he reached the footpath, then the driveway entrance. The rubbish bin first. Opening a paper bag with a rustling fit to wake the dead, he flipped back the lid and slid his hand into the messes there, torn garbage bags that spilled eggshells, cellophane, cling wrap, chicken bones. And a tissue. He bagged the tissue.

Then the recycle bin. A mineral-water bottle this time, a takeaway coffee cup marked Tulum Store and a Fanta can.

All of it into separate paper bags. Enough DNA to sink a killer. Then he jumped: his phone had buzzed in his pocket.

He took it out, heart hammering. Murmured, 'Sarge?'

'You owe me a drink or two,' Susan Mead said. 'I tracked down Riggs for you. He remembers the Lambert business because an outside cop made the actual arrest. An off-duty sergeant named Noel Saltash, now retired.'

51

RELIEF WASHED OVER Charlie. As he replaced Mark Valente's trash and checked that he had sufficient paper bags for a dive into Saltash's bins, he began to substitute the latter's name in the narrative he'd woven around Valente.

Saltash had been an arms instructor at the police academy, so he'd had access to handguns. And the job would have enabled free movement about the place: no partner to monitor his whereabouts; several periods during the day when he wasn't required in the classroom. Plenty of opportunities to pull armed holdups.

With Rhys? Valente? Charlie didn't want to think so. It was more likely he worked with Lambert, a guy who could get him past security systems and who would hide the proceeds for divvying up later—until one day they lost ready access to it and their way around the problem had resulted in murder—followed by a clever cop's cover-up.

Lambert had vanished a few days later. Charlie was betting that Saltash had paid him to stay away, thinking he was unreliable. Except he'd come back. With his hand out for more money? To blackmail the old cop?

Charlie closed the lid on Valente's recycle bin and wiped his hands on his pants. But it wasn't easy reconciling Saltash the killer with the Saltash of his childhood and of the past couple of months. The glum, drab man he'd known as a kid had morphed, barely altered, into a glum, drab shire ranger.

He'd barely registered with Charlie back then, barely registered now. A man always on the fringes of ordinary life—as if he were a fumbler, as if he disapproved. Never married; a man who hovered, irresolute, in a passageway or a corner of a garden with a glass in his hand from which he barely sipped. Cautious and uninspiring compared to wry charmers like Rhys Deravin and Mark Valente. If you addressed him, he flinched. His opinions—if sought—never sounded deeply felt or hard won and were expressed with all the verve of a corpse. Even Charlie's mother—tolerant, forgiving—had said damningly of Saltash: 'He's quite a nice man.'

Ha. What he'd been all along was a sly killer driven by panic and greed.

Charlie turned to leave but paused, realising he felt unnerved by the stillness of Valente's house. The stillness of someone watching him from a darkened window, the stillness of empty rooms, the stillness of some shit about to come down.

And so he was listening intently and heard a thud. Glass shattered, followed by silence. Then a stutter of desperate thumps, as of someone drumming their heels on a floor.

First he darted a look through each of the ground-floor windows. The unlit rooms were full of shadows that moved bulkily if he watched them for too long, but the kitchen, starkly lit, told a suggestive if banal story: Valente had been interrupted at dinner. A centimetre of wine in one glass, water in another; a fork paused mid-scoop in an omelette; a napkin tossed aside; his chair at an angle.

Someone had knocked on his door, thought Charlie, or his landline rang, or he needed to change the CD. No, not a CD: flickery colours washed the room; he'd been watching a little kitchen-bench TV as he ate his evening meal. A lonely life interrupted.

Charlie waited: one minute, another, but when Valente didn't return to the table, he went right around the house again, still hearing the thumping sound, less frantic now. Softer; helpless.

The back door was unlocked. Charlie opened it and

stepped soundlessly into the house, finding himself in a mudroom hung with coats, the laundry door on one side, the kitchen on the other, Shane Lambert stretched out on the floor. He'd been shot in the back, the blood dark on his Levi's jacket. Charlie knelt, felt for a pulse, didn't find one.

Jittery now—registering, in air still warm from the day's blinding sun, an old, familiar, police firing-range odour—he eased through the kitchen and into the hallway. Valente was halfway down, slumped against the wall, one hand cupped around his stomach, the other clasping a mobile phone. His lap was full of blood. He'd kicked over a slender antique hallstand, toppling a glass vase, now in shards on the floor.

'Saw you out there,' Valente whispered, barely a thread of life in his voice.

Charlie glanced at the front door. Glass. And beyond it the front yard, the spindly shrubs and kerbside bins illuminated by a distant streetlight. 'I was after your DNA.'

'Thought so.'

'Should be going after Noel's.'

'Yes and no,' Valente whispered.

Charlie crouched, reached out a hand. 'Let me look.'

And he encountered weak resistance, Valente saying, 'Gut shot—twice. Can't do anything about it.'

'Bullshit, Mark. I'll call triple zero.'

'Done that,' Valente said, lifting his hand, letting his phone thud to the floorboards.

Charlie looked back the way he'd come. Looked at the

staircase, the hint of a light burning dimly above. 'It was Noel? He's still here?'

'No.'

'I'd better check.'

'He's been and gone. Stay with me, son. Till the ambulance gets here.'

Charlie crouched. 'What's he armed with?'

'Target pistol. Silenced.'

'I found Lambert by the back door.'

'Dead? He was making a run for it.'

Charlie stood. 'I'll get you a towel, help stop the bleeding.'

Valente grabbed him weakly. 'Stay. Just stay. Please?'

Charlie crouched again, feeling useless. 'Mark, I've been hearing things, you and Dad robbing a Medicare office. Was there a whole gang of you? Is that what this is about?'

Out of a long silence and shallow, panting breaths, Valente said, 'I broke bread with the godless.'

'Knock it off, Mark. Just tell me.'

Valente lifted his bloodied hand as if the seeping wounds were all the information or evidence that Charlie needed. 'Requiem for a fool.'

'I said knock it off.'

Valente struggled and said, 'Noel killed your mother and I helped him get away with it.'

'Why didn't you stop him?'

Valente shook his head. 'I wasn't there. They called me in a panic.'

'Noel and Lambert?'

'Yes.'

'Not Dad?'

'Your dad had nothing to do with it,' Valente said, and he coughed. Recovered and said, 'Noel all the way. Not a nice guy.'

Movement outside. Charlie tensed: then was astonished to see an old woman dump garbage in Valente's bin.

'That's Mrs Oliphant,' Valente murmured. 'Her bin's got a broken wheel.'

The pulse of side-street life, thought Charlie. 'Mum walked in on them, right? Retrieving the money from the security-van hijack?'

Valente scoffed weakly. 'Us? Rob a security van? Hardly. Brothel in Cranbourne that time. Seventy thousand.'

The effort of speaking cost him; he slumped onto Charlie. Charlie straightened him again. 'Was Dad in on the robberies?'

Valente nodded. He coughed. His wet hand flopped to the floor, and he looked at it as if to make it levitate back onto the slickness of his mid-section.

'I'll get a towel.'

'No,' Valente croaked. 'Stay here.'

Fetching a towel would have helped Charlie to avoid the pictures in his head. The moment it all went wrong for his mother.

She enters Longstaff Street, pulls up at the kerb, recognises Lambert's Ducati, maybe recognises Saltash's car, and barges into the house demanding to know what they're doing there.

'Where was the money?'

'Don't know,' Valente whispered.

Liam and I had simply gathered Lambert's gear, Charlie thought; we hadn't looked for hiding places. In the ceiling? Under a floorboard? Behind the bathtub panel? In the tool shed?

'Why was Billy Saul there?'

Valente winced—from his own pain or from what he went on to say, Charlie couldn't tell. 'Wrong place, wrong time. Noel said they chased your mum into the street and there he was.'

Billy Saul, fleeing from bullies—or, more likely by that stage, trudging along feeling miserable and thirsty—and Rose Deravin streaking out of her house in fear. Charlie visualised both attacks and swayed, one hand going to the crown of his head unconsciously.

'They panicked and called you.'

'Yes.'

'It was your idea to bury them, stage the drowning, et cetera?'

'Yes,' Valente said.

He struggled to elaborate, thought better of it, his head slumping—then rallied weakly. 'Couldn't just leave two bodies lying around, and Lambert would be the first person the police would look at.'

My fault, thought Charlie. Mine and Liam's. If we

hadn't kicked Lambert out, he wouldn't have needed to go back for the money. Dr Fiske would say, 'Not your fault, Charlie, you didn't kill anyone.' Or she'd say, 'If your mother had her suspicions, they'd have found another way to kill her. Not your fault.'

Yeah, Doc, you go on telling me that.

'Why the slab house?'

Valente rallied weakly, and in his dying state was derisive. 'How do you think Ken Wilson could afford to buy a vacant block in Swanage? He was in it too. Then he got killed and his family cleared out and…the foundations had already been dug. Better than hauling a couple of bodies out into the bush.' Pause. 'Didn't occur to me they'd extend the slab.'

A long speech for a dying cop. He swayed again. Charlie sat him up. 'Did you tell Dad any of this?'

'None of it.'

'He said something to me earlier: "Look what they did to your mother". Why would he say that?'

Valente looked away and there was shame in him. 'We let him think it was a warning.'

Charlie saw the scope of it: Valente's stranglehold on all of them. 'Did you arrange for Lambert to rent a room in Mum's place?'

Valente nodded.

None of this lets my father off the hook, Charlie thought. I have seen his feet of clay—as Mark Valente might have put it.

'That ambulance is taking a while,' he muttered.

No reply—and Charlie felt uneasy then. He picked up Valente's phone and checked the call history. None to triple zero; only two calls in the past half-day. One from Cabrini Hospital, the other from Noel Saltash.

'You didn't call the ambulance.'

Valente's eyes were damp, his skin loose, everything in him dwindling. 'Charlie, he's got a gun, he's running, and I'm a goner.'

Charlie didn't listen. He switched to the keypad to call triple zero. Three bars of reception. But he'd barely pressed the first '0' when the phone was swiped from his hands and smashed against the bulky base of the shattered vase.

'Leave it.'

'Mark, you need an ambulance.'

'I'm dying, son,' Valente whispered. 'Stay with me, that's all I ask, there's no one else.'

I'll stay until he dies, thought Charlie with a cold clarity that he'd lost along the way. 'Okay.'

'I've always looked out for you,' Valente said.

This isn't quid pro quo, Charlie thought. 'You telling me you ran over Jake Allardyce?'

'I did. I have led a worthless life but not always have I bent it to the wills and ways of evil.'

Charlie wondered what kind of upbringing the old cop had had. Evening light was drawing in outside, blurring the little streets and the mansions and the shacks and Noel Saltash, running.

Charlie's phone buzzed but he ignored it, realising that his hands were sticky. He wiped them on his pants, and that, more than anything, curdled his soul. 'Tell me what happened tonight.'

Valente gave a little headshake. 'Your dad…two and two together…things said in his interrogation. He knew that DNA wasn't mine. Had a case together where our DNA was taken for elimination.'

'He rang Noel?'

'Noel brought Shane here for…powwow, but things went south, and…punches thrown…he started shooting. In a panic or he might have stuck around to finish me off.'

'I feel panicky myself,' Charlie said, scrambling to his feet. 'He's not heading for the hospital is he? I need to warn—'

Valente grabbed his arm. 'He's running.'

Charlie resettled reluctantly. 'He drove Mum's car to where it was dumped?'

'Yes.'

He injured himself when he hurt my mother, Charlie thought. Their blood mingled and he transferred it to the car keys. 'Lambert followed on his bike?'

'Yes.'

Charlie was itching to go. He needed a phone. But Valente seemed to sense it, and fingers manacled his wrist. 'Stay.'

'What did you tell the podcast people?'

'Nothing.'

'Did you know Karen Wagoner's the girl's grandmother?'

Valente slipped neatly onto his left side and his pants broke free of the blood with a little slurp.

Charlie scrabbled around until he was on his hands and knees. He slapped Valente's cheek.

'Mark!'

'She had a thing for us,' Valente slurred. He coughed blood. 'A thing for bad boys.'

'Including Lambert?'

'He bought her a Rolex…the moron.'

And you threw a scare into her, thought Charlie, which simmered for twenty years. He sat, checked the time, wondered if Valente had a landline.

'Mark?' he said, but the word amounted to nothing.

52

THE STREETLIGHTS HAD come on, but the sky was still spread with the last traces of the day's sun as Charlie grabbed Valente's bike and pedalled madly down the slope to Tidepool Street. Skidding into his driveway, he dumped the bike on the lawn and ran in to grab his car keys and call 000.

Then dithered for a couple of seconds. If he turned up in the Skoda it would alert Saltash. And did he need to call an ambulance? Valente was dead.

Did he need to call the police? Probably. Sometime. If

he was a good citizen. Right now that coat didn't fit.

The phone was in his hand. His agitation had awoken the screen. Four missed calls from Fay, and a text. He read, *Charlie dear things have changed and the doctor says it's a matter of time so you might like to—*

Charlie didn't read on. Instead, he pocketed the phone and raced out of the house and mounted the bike again and pelted along the potholed streets behind the clifftop mansions and down into Balinoe Beach.

Noel Saltash lived in the head ranger's cottage at the edge of a campground, a few metres from the creek and across the road from the store. Charlie tore into a clearing where children had built tepees from sticks and bark and plastic bags and other scraps of modern life, and dumped the bike. Evening shadows protected him now, as he stepped deeper into the trees and shrubbery that divided campsite from campsite, and campsite from ablution block. No one was camping this late in the season: he was relieved; hadn't wanted to go knocking on tents, asking people to evacuate.

He began to close in on the hedge surrounding the ranger's residence, yard and maintenance shed. Stood concealed by tea-trees and took stock: a high-end Mercedes sat in the carport, a twin-cab ute with shire markings and the beach patrol buggy nearby. Lights on in the house.

As he'd done at Valente's, Charlie slipped through shadows to the side wall and went from window to window, peering in, and saw, on a forlorn double bed, heaped clothing and two suitcases with their lids open. Reaching the rear corner, he edged around to the kitchen window and Saltash stepped out of the cottage and shot him.

Armed engagement training says to take a body-mass shot, not a leg or a head shot, and that's what Saltash did—except that Charlie ducked and turned as he registered the flicker of a shadow at the back door, and the bullet tore some of his ear away. He fell onto his hip. Rolled away from the spill of light, seeking the moon shadows, their play of tricks and false targets.

But he was making a racket in the undergrowth and Saltash came after him, and the pistol spat again; and the pain was in Charlie, and blood streamed down his neck and under his shirt, thick, warm and wet. He scooted further into the trap he'd made for himself, whipped by twigs and leaves, then stopped to listen. Nothing. He wasn't fooled: Saltash was listening, too.

Saltash's labrador began a low, weary barking and Charlie fished for his phone. It was no longer in his pocket. Christ, his ear hurt. Try a run to one of the nearby houses, pound on someone's door? Putting innocent lives in danger...

He had no plan in mind, only jangled thoughts and nonsense; and then a small motor coughed into life. He shrank instinctively and peered through the foliage: Saltash, in his beach buggy, was trundling out of the maintenance yard and across the road to the beach.

Then he was gone, and Charlie stumbled onto a path that took him back to the clearing and Valente's bike. A low-speed chase, he thought—except that wasn't very funny and he was sore, sodden, dazed and unarmed. He pedalled to the access track, dismounted to wheel the bike over the churned sand, and broke through the fringe of tea-trees to the edge of the water. If the past few minutes had been crazy hectic, the beach didn't know about it. A benign stillness; the sleepy pinks and greys of evening; a handful of people, lover murmuring to lover, grandmother to granddaughter, father to son, letting peace settle around them.

He wheeled the bike down to firmer sand and prepared to mount it again. Looked left through the indistinct light. Three figures, one walking slowly towards Swanage, the others shoulder-to-shoulder on a low ridge of sand, eating fish and chips. Looked right: five people, a clump of three and, further along, an adult and a toddler. A hundred metres ahead of them, Saltash. The buggy headlights dimly probing, the motor sounding a clear protest in the still air. The tide was out so he'd have a clear run beyond Point Leo if that's what he wanted. And a beach escape made a certain kind of sense. A way of skirting around police roadblocks.

Charlie started slowly, wobbled, gained pace, but kept clapping one hand to his ear for comfort. So much blood. It hurt like buggery. And however would he be restored to his whole self with a part of him shredded? Mad thoughts like that.

Pumping his legs now, he gained on the ridiculous

figure in his ridiculous vehicle. He passed on hissing tyres the people strolling along the beach, bumped over the sand heaped against the breakwater, then sped around the point that opened onto the half-moon stretch of sand leading to Menlo Beach. Moon shimmers on a glassy sea, and the air, still warm from the day, wrapped around him. Saltash was not far ahead now, the buggy motor still screaming—and he was bearing down on a man with a spaniel, chatting to Pat and her trio of clapped-out dogs.

Saltash jerked on the steering wheel, veering left to pass between them and the edge of the sea, then straightened for a run along the open sand ahead—only for Pat to step into his path, waving her arms and shouting, loud enough for Charlie to hear, 'Slow down, you maniac!'

Brake lights. Saltash stopped. He climbed out.

Charlie felt panic surge in him. He raced along the sand. And Pat wasn't finished. 'I'm allowed to walk my dogs at this time of the day. No need to come over all heavy with me.'

A moment later Saltash was advancing on her, waving the gun and she was backing away from him, both hands raised, saying, 'Whoa, that's really not necess—'

Charlie charged at them. 'Pat, get away!' he shouted. 'Noel, come on. No one has to get hurt.'

Saltash turned, snapped off a shot at Charlie; turned back to threaten Pat again and climbed into the buggy. A cough of dirty exhaust, then slow acceleration towards the other dog walker, who scrambled away, up onto the foredune at the base of the cliffs, leaving a bewildered spaniel.

The dog ran at the buggy. Saltash slowed and shot it.

It dropped, kicking, and the man wailed and Pat screamed.

Charlie hadn't decided what he'd do when he caught up to Saltash—draw alongside and leap onto a moving vehicle driven by a man with a gun? All he could do was keep chasing—and was saved from making a better decision by Pat, who ran up on Saltash's blind side and smacked a plastic bag full of dog shit into his face. It burst.

Saltash decelerated, clawing at his eyes. The buggy rolled into the water, spluttered, died, and they had him.

Out of his seat and onto his belly on the sand as the owner of the dead dog shouted, 'I'm calling the police,' and a wait began. It seemed long to Charlie. He was no longer bleeding but felt dazed with pain and grateful for Pat, who sat on Saltash's legs, looking stunned.

'I'm not talking,' Saltash said at one point, spitting sand from his mouth.

'Good,' said Charlie, dropping his knees into Saltash's back.

Their exchange seemed to animate Pat; her shock ebbed. She spat out a string of fluent accusations: Saltash was a tinpot dictator, a bully, a loser who would shoot a harmless animal. Gathering her dogs beside her, she just kept going—the government, holiday-makers, shire regulations—delivered with an air of having suffered on behalf of others and knowing she'd never be thanked for it.

Charlie tuned her out. She paused long enough to ask him about all the blood on his neck and shoulder, but he shook his head and thought about his father, dying in a hospital bed. Looked at the moon ripples between the shoreline and Phillip Island. His old beat. The way things will be now, he thought. You make an accommodation with each new bit of knowledge that comes your way, or you die. And you always die a little.

A moon gleam caught his eye: the target pistol. He reached out, grabbed the barrel and almost tossed it into the sea, badly wanting to see it break the surface of the water, fracture the moon, but stopped himself.

Time slowed. He sighed, shoved the pistol into his waistband.

'Are we supposed to just wait?' Pat said. 'God he stinks.'

Charlie cut across that. 'Can I use your phone?'

He was hopeless at remembering numbers, but Anna's was there in his head. It began with 0406. Same as his.